THE OXFORD MYSTERY

THE OXFORD MYSTERY

COLIN WADE

The Book Guild

First published in Great Britain in 2025 by
The Book Guild Ltd
Unit E2 Airfield Business Park
Harrison Road, Market Harborough
Leicestershire, LE16 7UL
Tel: 0116 2792299
www.bookguild.co.uk
Email: info@bookguild.co.uk

Web: www.colinwade.com
X: @CPWADE1
Facebook: @colinwadeauthor
Instagram: @colinwadeauthor

Also by Colin Wade: *The Lost Years*
Also by Colin Wade: *Plutus*
Also by Colin Wade: *Deadly Connection*
Also by Colin Wade: *The Sins of the Father*
Also by Colin Wade: *The Devil's Code*
Also by Colin Wade: *Murder at the Manor*

Typeset in 11pt Minion Pro

Printed and bound in Great Britain by 4edge Limited

ISBN 978 1835743 041

British Library Cataloguing in Publication Data.
A catalogue record for this book is available from the British Library.

To all the baristas that made me so many cups of coffee whilst writing this book

FOREWORD

The characters in the story follow a mystery trail around the centre of Oxford in England. This is a real mystery trail that you can do yourself if you are ever in Oxford. The locations and the answers to the clues are all well established landmarks in the centre of Oxford and should all still be standing long beyond the life of this book.

It took the people that tested the trail around an hour, to an hour and a half, to complete.

If you would like to access the online resource that will guide you around the trail and give you each clue in turn, please go to www.colinwade.com or scan the QR code below for further information.

If you get stuck, the answers are contained within the book!

Good luck,

Colin

1

WALTER

It started as a quiet sound, somewhere unthreatening and distant. The kind of sound you hear in any built-up area at night. The kind of sound that stirs you but soon becomes a distant memory as you drift off back to sleep.

But this noise wasn't going away. It was getting louder. More urgent. A horrible scraping noise, like metal against wood. Walter bolted awake. His eyes couldn't penetrate the darkness as fear gripped him. Where was he? He wasn't in his flat in Jericho. The noise wasn't a typical noise that he would hear outside his flat at night. It was inside, somewhere close.

He threw the bed covers off and crept to the window, pulling aside the heavy curtains. Moonlight immediately flooded the space, and he was able to make out the shape of the room.

The bed he'd been in was a large four-poster with old-fashioned, almost medieval, drapes around the top and sides of the wooden structure. An ottoman was placed at the end of the bed. A wooden wardrobe dominated the far corner, and a standalone bathtub was on the opposite side of the room. It was like he'd been transported back in time to the royal court of some king or queen.

As his mind tried to rationalise what he was seeing, the noise started again. Long scraping sounds, like someone was dragging something metal across the wooden floor. His gut tightened as he moved towards the door of the bedroom. The noise grew louder. He held his breath. Louder still. Outside his door? He leant against it, hoping that if something, or someone, tried to come through it, his weight would stop them. The noise stopped. Walter craned his neck to listen. Could he hear someone breathing? His mind was playing tricks on him. The fear making him imagine all sorts of things.

As he stood motionless, his weight still against the door, he tried to work out how he'd got here. He was drinking heavily in his local, the Jericho Tavern. There was the usual banter from the locals and then… nothing. He couldn't remember much of anything. He put his face in his hands, trying to rub away the malaise, his dry mouth and thumping headache at least confirming the small bit of the evening he remembered.

His shoulder started to hurt with the pressure he was placing against the door. He eased off, hoping this wasn't the cue for someone to crash through the door. Nothing happened. Everything was silent.

Walter looked around. What should he do? He had to get out of this place, wherever this place was. His clothes were neatly folded on a chair, and he realised he was wearing a pair of pyjamas that weren't his. He stopped in the centre of the room and listened. There was no noise outside his room.

He stripped off the pyjamas and quickly put his clothes on. He patted the pockets of his trousers. His phone was gone. He scanned the room in the dim light, trying to work out whether his phone had been left somewhere else. The search proved fruitless.

He edged back towards the door, all the while trying to hear any sound that might explain what was going on and where he was. He stopped and listened. Was there still someone behind the door, waiting patiently to attack the moment he opened it? He stood there for over a minute. Silence. No sound, no breathing, no metal scraping against wood.

Walter started to get angry. Whatever this was, he wasn't about to stand around waiting for something to happen. It was time for action. He noticed a metal poker by the fireplace. He grabbed it and went back to the door. He grasped the handle with one hand, the poker in the other ready to strike. He flung the door open. Nobody was there.

He edged his way out. In both directions was a long corridor, which was lit by some sort of dim running lights in the floor. He could make out several doors dotted along both sides of the corridor, which he assumed were other bedrooms. As he scanned some more, he suddenly noticed marks in the wooden floor outside his room and to the right. His bravery waned and he contemplated going back into his room and barricading the door.

As he wrestled with his options, his whole body convulsed as the scraping sound started up again. It was coming from the end of the corridor to his left. He'd dropped the poker in terror, the noisy clang of the metal hitting the wood intensified in the gloom. It was fight or flight time. The noise was moving away from him. He chose fight.

Walter started to move left towards the noise. He recovered the poker, ready to strike whatever demon was making the awful din. As he walked past several doors, he realised that no one had come out of any of the rooms. Dropping the poker should have woken everyone in the vicinity, but nobody else seemed to be around.

His heart was pounding in his chest, the noise getting quieter by the second. As he gingerly stepped round the corner at the end of the corridor, he came to a wide carpeted staircase, which he started to descend. Again, the light was limited, but there was enough to make out that he was going down into the main entrance hall. More importantly, as he got to the bottom, he realised he was facing a large external door. He bolted for it. Freedom at his fingertips. He turned the large metal handle and pulled inwards. It was locked.

He manically scanned the area looking for a key, or something that he could use to force the door open. There was nothing. There was a faint sound in the distance, like someone was banging on the floor. He gripped the poker a bit tighter and went back into the main part of the house. The noise was coming from his right. He moved slowly and quietly towards it. On the left was the entrance to the library and a little bit further up on the right seemed to be a large dining room. The banging was now more distinct, coming from further up the hallway.

As he reached the end of the corridor, it opened up into a massive room, which was fully lit. Large sofas and coffee tables were dotted around the room. A grand piano in the corner. A cocktail cabinet dominated the wall on the left, adorned with a range of wines and spirits in decanters.

But Walter wasn't looking at any of this. At the back of the room, sitting on a wing chair by the grand fireplace, was a woman holding what looked like a long spear, banging it repetitively. As he edged his way further into the room, she stopped banging. "Hello, Walter, remember me?"

Walter stood frozen to the spot. "I… I… don't understand. I thought you were dead."

2

JOHN

John winced at the sunlight as he emerged from the casino in the centre of Reading. He had pulled an all-nighter, thrown out as the place closed down at 6am. He wasn't sure how much of this month's pay he'd lost but he knew it was enough to make the rest of the month a struggle.

He desperately needed some sleep but was miles from his riverside flat in the centre of Oxford. The next best option was to eat, to soak up some of the excess alcohol he'd consumed as he gambled the night away. He spotted a café. He navigated across the road, avoiding the odd car populated by early commuters. He ordered a coffee and bacon sandwich from the surly woman at the counter, using the last ten-pound note he had on him. He sat at a table in the corner.

He rubbed his face and shook his head. He had to stop. The gambling was out of control. His three credit cards were nearly maxed out and his bank was not going to extend his overdraft again. The sound of police sirens made his stomach lurch. It was lucky he was on a four-days-on, four-days-off shift at the moment. He couldn't have worked in the state he was in. His guv'nor had already spoken to him about his sickness record, a symptom of too many mornings like this. At least today, he still had a couple of days off to sort himself out. As a neighbourhood police officer, he knew his actions would get the attention of the Professional Standards team, if anyone ever saw him. It's why he gambled in Reading, away from his patch. Regardless, he knew he was playing with fire.

He was twenty-six, joining the police straight from university. Brought up in Leeds, he decided to move down south to get away from his parents, people he could barely tolerate since they had betrayed him in the worst possible way. The freedom had been great to start with, but he'd allowed himself to get involved with the wrong people. Too much drinking, not enough sleep and, over the past eighteen months, a dark tumble into the world of gambling. A habit that started with a group of so-called friends but which rapidly became a solo activity as they all drifted away.

The woman threw the bacon sandwich in front of him, with a sneer that suggested she didn't do customer service. He took a bite, trying to force the memories back where they came from. The loneliness hadn't helped his addiction. He'd become numb to it. Wallowing in self-pity.

He finished the sandwich and drained the last of the coffee. As he glanced at Ms Customer Service behind the counter, he decided against asking for a free refill.

John walked out and headed for the station, desperately hoping that one of his credit cards would allow him to buy a train ticket. The second one worked. He grabbed a double seat in the far carriage and closed his eyes, the rhythmic sound of the train soon sending him off to sleep.

Dreams invaded his slumbers. The bad memories came back as pictures of them all sat in the casino; laughing and drinking reminded him of how it all started. The images were quickly replaced by women and children, laughter and excitable screams filling the air. The local fete. His job. Looking after the community, keeping them safe. He jolted awake.

He sighed and leant his head back against the seat. What was he doing? He was a police officer for God's sake. People were relying on him, but at this point he could hardly protect himself, let alone members of his community.

John got his phone out and clicked on Google. His fingers hovered over the screen. He had to do it. He typed in *Gamblers Anonymous.* For the rest of the journey, he read through the website. Everything he read resonated. He wasn't alone. He found his local support group. There was a meeting at noon. He was going to attend. Something had to give before his whole life collapsed around him.

After a short nap, he showered and got himself ready for the meeting. It was in a community hall in Osney, a ten-minute walk from his flat. He was welcomed in and, for the first time in a while, felt that someone was in his corner. They allowed him to listen to others' stories before inviting him to speak. He stuttered and spluttered but eventually his story came out, apart from the fact that he was a police officer.

He got home and a sense of relief washed over him. He had taken the first step. The problem was he had another day and a half before he was due back for work. The downtime was normally a trigger for him to find somewhere to gamble. He opened his phone and started to talk himself down. There must be something else he could do.

John glanced at the small pile of post he'd picked off the mat when he got home. It was now strewn on the coffee table. He frowned when he realised the top letter was his credit card bill. He picked the pile up and threw the bill across the room. Next was a pizza menu, followed by a piece of junk mail from some charity or other. The final envelope was handwritten. He turned it over and over in his hand, curious as to what it could be. He tore open the top of the envelope and pulled out a leaflet, reading the large print in the middle of the document.

DO YOU WANT TO WIN £50,000? PLAY THE OXFORD MYSTERY TRAIL AND WIN THIS AMAZING PRIZE.

Below it in scrawly handwriting was a message.

Could this get you out of your current hole, John?

John read it a couple of times, perplexed at the personalised note. Who would have done that?

Suddenly, his phone rang. His heart sank when he saw who was calling. He had no choice but to answer it.

"Guv," he said, "what can I do for you?"

"I need you in, John. We've got a major problem. Seems as though some numpty has launched a mystery trail game, promising fifty thousand pounds as a prize. There are huge crowds around Carfax and down St Aldates. They're stopping buses getting through and causing chaos in the surrounding area. Get there as soon as you can and report to Sergeant Dawson. We need to get some crowd control in place."

John ended the call and glanced back at the leaflet. "How odd," he muttered to himself.

He was dog-tired but he had to do this, otherwise he was at risk of being found out. He put on his uniform and headed out. At least it would stop him gambling.

3

RACHEL

Rachel sat on her sofa idly scrolling through the news on her phone. It was her first day off in over a week. The theatre nurse job she did at the John Radcliffe Hospital was taking up more of her time than she really wanted, but she needed the money. Rent in Oxford was ridiculously expensive, but her small one-bedroom flat in Headington meant she could walk to work and just about afford to run a small car for times when public transport just didn't cut it.

The morning had been lovely. Lying in until 9.30am, followed by a leisurely breakfast. She opened Facebook, reading news from her friends, covering everything from pictures of their children in various settings to someone's beautiful summer hanging basket. Rachel loved spring and summer. The good weather, sometimes. The better moods that everyone seemed to be in. The chance to eat and drink al fresco in the hundreds of great bars and restaurants across the beautiful centre of Oxford.

It annoyed Rachel that people who lived in Oxford often didn't appreciate the architecture and incredible history on their doorsteps, which was etched into every building, from the colleges of the University of Oxford to the Radcliffe Camera and the Bodleian Library. Too many people walked with their heads down, looking at their phones, not taking time to look up at these iconic buildings.

The thought galvanised her. She drained the last of her coffee and stood up. She was going to spend the day walking around the centre of Oxford. The weather was perfect. Sunny, around twenty-four degrees with a light breeze. She would take in the history, have some lunch, do some shopping. Perfect.

She had a quick shower and got herself ready to go out. A floral summer dress complemented by a straw hat was just the ticket for the day she was going to have. She got on the bus, and as it began to move along the London Road towards town, Rachel grimaced at the groups of tourists that were stood outside the house with the shark in the roof, a local landmark fascinating to tourists but just another part of the landscape to Headington residents.

The bus made slow progress as it navigated the gridlocked roads leading into the centre of Oxford. By the time she got to the top of the high street, it was a little after midday and her stomach was rumbling. She decided to go to the top floor of the Westgate and have some lunch in one of the restaurants that had outside seating, looking out across the Oxford skyline.

The meal was good, a chicken Caesar salad with a side of chunky chips, topped off with a glass or two of decent red wine. As the sun beat down on her face, the urge to close her eyes and take a nap almost overwhelmed her, but she thought better of it. She would be mortified if she was spark out, snoring away in blissful slumber as people walked by, pointing and sniggering.

She sat up straighter and got out her phone. As she did, the familiar ping of a message on Facebook greeted her. It was from her friend and fellow nurse, Leila. The message contained a link, complemented by an emoji-filled message from Leila and the words, *have you seen this!!*

Her finger hovered over the post. You were always told not to click on random links, especially ones that said...

CAN YOU SOLVE THE OXFORD MYSTERY? THE WINNER WILL GET £50,000. CLICK HERE FOR YOUR FIRST CLUE.

She was sure most people would think it was a scam. Most of these things were. Clicking on the link would launch some virus or expose you to identity theft. She closed the message.

Rachel tried to distract herself by flicking between the other apps on her phone, people-watching and gazing out over the rooftops of Oxford. None of it was working.

She opened the message again and clicked on the link. A message came up.

Welcome to the Oxford Mystery trail. If you solve a series of clues around the centre of Oxford, you may be on your way to fame and fortune. Fifty thousand pounds awaits the person who can solve the mystery. To progress through the game, you will need to enter a series of answers in the app, which is available to download in all the usual places. Are you ready to play?

This time, Rachel didn't give it a second thought. She clicked on the link below the message.

Clue 1: being in Oxford can make you smart, where four streets converge is where you must start. Look up at the tower and you will see, two items that are struck when the clock strikes three. This lovely event happens all through the day, so enter the name of the item to continue to play.

She looked at the riddle. *Where four streets converge.* The solution was pretty easy. It was Carfax. If the game was focused on the centre of Oxford, it was the only logical conclusion.

She grabbed her stuff and went down the escalator to get to the main level of the Westgate centre, turning quickly towards the exit on Queen Street. She tried to ignore the beautiful window displays promising her everything from nice clothes to sexy underwear and too many tempting food options.

As she emerged from the main entrance to the Westgate, the noise hit her. She began to walk towards Carfax, the noise increasing with every step. As she got nearer, she couldn't believe what she was seeing. Carfax was crowded with thousands of people. The crowd was so dense that buses were queued on Queen Street, unable to get through. Some stressed police officers were trying to control the crowd but didn't seem to be making any progress in sorting it out. The noise coming from the crowd was insane, a mixture of unbridled excitement coupled with a few aggressive shouts as people jostled for position.

Rachel was gobsmacked. Had this mystery game caused all this.

4

John could barely put one foot in front of the other, but he had to get through this shift. He'd made it to an artificial perimeter that had been set up by the sergeant he'd been told to report to. It was across the road outside the town hall on St Aldates, stopping people and traffic moving any further down the road.

The stressed sergeant explained that a similar perimeter had been set up at the top of the high street. Their objective was to try and disperse the large crowd that was gathered in Carfax and was spilling down the road they were on. Traffic in every direction was at a standstill and, although private vehicles were not allowed through these parts of Oxford, the volume of buses and taxis had caused a horrific jam.

Just as John was about to be deployed to work with a group of other officers, trying to install barriers that would clear the roads, a large truck appeared containing the mounted section. Officers on horseback were quickly deployed and soon began to carve a gap in the crowd. John and the other officers began to force the crowds onto the pavements, installing barriers on the edge of the roadside.

Their combined efforts managed to push the crowds on St Aldates back towards Carfax, garnering some screams as people began to get crushed. John could hear a new voice over the radio, who identified herself as one of the local superintendents. This thing had clearly escalated, and the poor stressed sergeant now had someone of rank to steer them through it. Her voice was shouting instructions, telling John and the team to be careful as their actions were like squeezing a balloon, everything bulging at the top.

It took about twenty minutes but eventually the combined forces of the mounted police and local officers had cleared the road, the barriers stopping any pedestrians from entering the roadway. The risk of crush injuries was still very real. Although the actions of the police had forced the crowd to reduce, many realising they had to protect their personal safety, the number of people behind the barriers was still so large that people could barely move along the paths.

The superintendent deployed officers on all four streets that led into Carfax, attempting to manage the crowds and keep the roads clear. It took a couple of hours before the crowds died down, but John was still amazed at how many people kept turning up, staring at their phones, looking around at all the landmarks in the centre of Oxford before furiously tapping away. He was intrigued by the mixture of reactions, from fist pumps to screwed-up, confused facial expressions.

John was running on adrenalin, as he entered his twenty-sixth hour without sleep. Mercifully, the sergeant called him over soon after, standing him down as he handed over to the next shift. John began to walk back to his flat, grabbing a coffee from a shop well away from where all the drama had unfolded.

He got home and slumped in his chair, every muscle and limb feeling like it couldn't move another inch. Sleep was not far away, but in the midst of the melee that had been the last few hours, he couldn't help but be distracted by the chatter he'd heard amongst the crowd. They were all talking about winning fifty thousand pounds. The leaflet with the handwritten note lay on the coffee table.

Given his current financial predicament, he couldn't leave it alone and turned on the local news, intrigued to see if they were covering what had been going on and whether this promise of money was real. He grabbed his remote control and turned on the television. Sure enough, it was the headline story.

The local police were tested to their limit today as an Oxford Mystery trail was launched across social media, causing huge crowds around Carfax and down St Aldates. The message started appearing across most social media sites around 1pm, promising a prize of fifty thousand pounds to the person that could solve the mystery trail. Within an hour, thousands of people had turned up at Carfax, which appeared to be the location of the first clue. There were so many people gathered that crowds spilled onto the surrounding roads, particularly on St Aldates. This stopped buses and taxis from getting through the centre of town, causing chaos to users of those services. It took the police nearly two hours to restore order, and although the crowds began to disperse around 4pm, it has been reported that people are still turning up at Carfax. The local superintendent in charge of today's police operation condemned the organiser of the mystery trail, stating that it caused very real public safety risks as crowds grew and people were in danger of being crushed behind the barriers that the police had set up to control the crowds. She said they would be attempting to identify the organiser and requested the public's help. We would be interested in your experience of today's events, so please contact us on our social media channels.

John desperately wanted to sleep but the game intrigued him. As well as the strange handwritten leaflet, a couple of his mates had sent him the link about the mystery trail. Everyone was going mad over the promise of great riches.

He navigated to the launch page. He read the first clue and everything about the day's events began to make sense.

As he drifted off to sleep, the thought of all that money relaxed him. Maybe there was a way out of all his troubles.

5

Rachel stood a little way back from the main crowd, next to a small group of onlookers. As she tried to decide whether to turn around and come back when the hysteria passed, the mood of the crowd turned sourer. Police officers on horseback were forcing the crowds back, trying to clear the roads. People were being pushed into smaller spaces as police on foot tried to install barriers. Rachel's nursing instincts kicked in and she ran towards where the officers were clearing a path, shouting at them to stop. People were going to get crushed to death. Her pleas were lost as the shouts and screams intensified. Rachel was hit from the side by a man as the crowd burst through the barriers, the sheer volume of people making it impossible for the police to contain them.

She took a few steps back to move away from the volatile situation. As she continued to watch the horror unfold, she was aware that someone was staring at her.

"Gosh, this is so frightening. What do you think is going on?" the woman said.

Rachel glanced at the woman. She was gorgeous. Long, blonde hair was complemented by a pretty face and a body that Rachel had long since given up trying to attain. The girl was chewing her lip in concentration, which Rachel thought was the most adorable thing she'd seen in ages. She was wearing a white summer dress with a small daisy pattern along the sleeves and neckline. As Rachel's brain was trying to process it all, she realised the girl was still staring at her expectantly.

"Oh Christ, sorry, miles away. Yes, this is really scary. Did you not see the social media post about this mystery game? I assume that's what has caused all this."

The girl frowned. "Er, no. What social media post?"

Rachel opened her phone and scrolled to the message that her friend had sent. The girl's expression turned from a frown to a wide-eyed look of shock.

"Blimey, fifty thousand pounds. I'm not surprised it's got everyone going."

Rachel shrugged. "It seems like the most logical conclusion."

The girl looked at Rachel, an excited look on her face. "Were you going to do it?"

Rachel huffed. "Well, yeah, I thought I'd give it a go, but it seems rather pointless at the moment with all this going on. I don't feel safe hanging around here."

The girl put her hand out. "Hi, I'm Abigail."

"Oh, hi, I'm Rachel."

Abigail smiled back at her, before flicking her attention back to the crowd.

Rachel frowned. "I'm sorry. I don't mean to be weird, but I feel like we've met before."

Abigail looked back at Rachel. "Hmm, how odd, I don't think so. I think I'd remember someone as gorgeous as you."

Rachel was taken aback at the comment. She had to admit it had been a while and she was out of practice with how all this worked, but still, it seemed so odd. Her hesitation was met with a frown by Abigail.

"Oh shit," Rachel said, "I guess I'm just not used to people saying nice things about me."

Abigail reached out and touched Rachel on the shoulder. "Well, all I know is take the compliments when you can get them. Most people are just knobheads, so it's nice when you meet someone you instantly connect with."

Just as Rachel was trying to process what the hell was going on, Abigail made her excuses and began to walk away, leaving a *hope to run into you again* comment trailing in the wind.

Rachel watched as Abigail's outline began to fade into the distance.

6

Rachel sat in a coffee shop on the lower ground floor of the Westgate shopping centre, slowly sipping a chai latte. She couldn't shake the memories of her brief encounter with Abigail. Rachel got out her compact and peered in the little mirror. She wasn't that pleased with what was staring back at her. Despite the light make-up she applied that morning, her drawn face and the dark rings under her eyes did not shout out as the kind of person that Abigail had complimented.

She watched as people passed by where she was sat, not a single person taking any notice of her. Which is what Rachel had come to expect. She was thirty-two, but after several failed relationships, she felt like she was on the proverbial shelf, gathering dust as no one wanted her. She tried to shake off the encounter with Abigail as one of life's weirder moments and picked up her phone. The first clue was still staring back at her. She glanced at her watch. It was just gone five and she wondered whether the nightmare at Carfax had died down.

As she walked back towards the centre of town, the noise coming out of the Westgate did not hit her this time. Each step along Queen Street wasn't met with a deafening roar or an expletive-laden crowd of people.

When she arrived, she could see groups of people staring into their phones, looking up at Carfax tower and frantically typing away, which she guessed meant they were doing the mystery trail. Mercifully, the numbers of people had significantly died down, which allowed Rachel to stand without fear of being crushed. She reread the clue. The tower had a pretty, ornate clock embedded about two thirds of the way up the structure.

Two items are struck when the clock strikes three. She glanced at her watch. It was 5.23pm. Despite the time, she realised the answer was obvious. By the clock face were two figurines that had some sort of hammer in their hands that was almost certainly going to strike the item that the clue referred to. The bells.

She navigated to the app and entered the word *bell.* It worked. The second clue appeared.

Clue 2: look in one direction and try to find, an inscription on a wall, to tax your mind. Down low, some dates are shown indeed, giving the name of the tavern that we surely need. Enter the answer to continue the game, the rewards of which will bring you fame.

Rachel began to look down each street as the clue suggested. As she looked towards St Aldates, she smiled to herself. Although the crowds had died down, there were still enough people doing the game, so a small crowd of people gathered together in one place was an indicator of where the answer was. They were looking at the bottom of a wall on the corner of St Aldates and Queen Street.

She walked over, waiting her turn to view what they were looking at. An inscription in the wall referred to this being the site of the *Swindlestock Tavern from 1270 to 1509.* She entered the name of the tavern in the app. A message congratulated her on the correct answer, rewarding her with another clue.

Annoyingly, the warmth of the day and the beautiful summer sunshine had given way to a sudden onset of dark clouds, and she cursed as she felt the first drops of a summer downpour.

She read the next clue.

Clue 3: now walk down the street where you'll find the town hall, to continue the game and win it all. Next you must find a Blue Boar, and once you are there, then find a door. Engraved above it is a place to read, enter this word and you will succeed.

The town hall was in St Aldates and Rachel quickened her pace as the rain began to fall. Again, the solution to the clue was pretty obvious to anyone with a basic knowledge of Oxford. She walked to Blue Boar Street, which was a little way down the road, just before the town hall. She stopped at the corner of the street, next to the back door of the Museum of Oxford. She glanced back at the clue, the mention of the door being the key theme. She glanced up at what was engraved above the door, typing in *Library.* It worked.

The rain was getting heavier, and she was a bit perturbed that, as her dress got wetter, it was beginning to cling to her skin and all her curves. She didn't have an umbrella so navigated carefully but quickly across the road to a pub. She tried to make herself look a bit less like a drowned rat as she went up to the bar and ordered herself a gin and tonic. She noticed the barman sneaking a peak at her damp cleavage, like he was indulging in some wet T-shirt fantasy. Rachel tried to ignore it, taking her drink over to a corner table.

In all the weather drama, she hadn't looked at the next message on the Oxford Mystery app. She opened her phone. The message on the screen flashed up.

CONGRATULATIONS FOR SOLVING THE FIRST THREE CLUES OF THE OXFORD MYSTERY AND FOR COMPLETING DAY ONE. COME BACK TOMORROW FOR MORE CLUES.

But more intriguing was the last part of the message.

#whereswalter

7

She sat in her favourite wing chair in the large sitting room of the grand manor house, as the last of the evening light faded from the sky. It was just her left, lonely and bereft of love. Potentially inheriting the family pile, at this stage of her life, was not the plan she had for the rest of her existence. Her whole family, gone, way before their time. It was the anniversary of her father's death, another cancer statistic, but she felt nothing for a man she barely knew.

Her father made a fortune trading in antiques and her mother was from a titled family, with a rich heritage and cash to match. The manor house was a legacy of her mother's family, who had lived here for more than three hundred years. The weight of the family history bore down on her, but at that moment, it meant nothing. She caught herself in a sob, rage and frustration bubbling to the surface.

She eyed the spear that was leant against the arm of the chair. She remembered her father telling her all about it when he returned from one of his many trips abroad. The spear was made of ash, with a steel head, sharpened for maximum damage. She grabbed it and gently placed the tip of her forefinger on the sharpest bit, pushing down lightly. It broke the skin, and a small droplet of blood formed. She put the finger in her mouth and sucked it till it stopped bleeding.

She turned the spear upside down and placed the point on the wooden floor, scraping it from left to right. The noise of metal on wood made her smile. She had enjoyed shitting that bastard up, scraping the spear along the corridor outside his room. Watching the CCTV she had recorded in his bedroom was hysterical, as he tried to work out where he was and what the hell was going on.

The guy was a total waste of space. Even worse than she had first thought. Getting him back to the manor house had been a piece of cake. If he wasn't actually an alcoholic, he sure as hell acted like one. Pretty much every night he would be drinking in his local pub until it closed. Staggering home each night, sometimes barely able to put one foot in front of another. On the night in question, she simply waited for him to leave. As he zigzagged his way along the path towards his flat, she grabbed him and bundled him into her car. He barely acknowledged her, happy to be sat down in the comfy car. The other end was much the same. The walk from the front door of the manor house to his room was met with limited objections. She baulked at having to help him get undressed, his stinking breath far too close for comfort, bringing back bad memories. She couldn't remember how many times she had gone through this ritual with… she stopped herself from saying the name in her head. It was too upsetting.

She idly banged the tip of the spear against the floor, a repetitive clanking of metal against wood, which for some reason soothed her soul. She had dealt with that lowlife and now she had to be patient. They were playing her game.

She sighed. The anger burning inside her wasn't going away. The people who had left her in this position would have to pay. Revenge was all she could think about. She wanted them to experience even one ounce of the pain she was suffering, every waking hour.

She looked around at the grandness of the room. Chandeliers hanging from the ceiling and lavish curtains framing the windows that probably cost more than her car, together with Georgian furniture and antiques from around the world, collected by her father on his many travels. It was so him, her mother too, but not what she wanted.

Once this was all over, she would go and live in some hot country in a beachside fun pad, waited on by beautiful people in skimpy swimwear. She allowed herself a brief smile at the thought.

Patience. She would get there, but first she needed to finish this thing. She had dealt with the first one. The rest would come to her, all excited at the prospect of winning that money.

She stood up, holding the spear like some warrior. She was ready for them.

8

John suddenly came to, his whole body convulsing at the shock of waking up. The room was dark, bar the light dancing from the images on the TV screen. He had a moment of panic. Was he supposed to be somewhere? Work? He rubbed his eyes and opened the welcome screen on his phone. It read 12.03am.

It took him a minute to reorientate himself. He'd been asleep for nearly six hours, the exhaustion of the previous day finally catching up with him. The memories of the gambling binge made his stomach lurch, no idea how much money he'd lost this time. The local news was on the TV, once again running the story of the mystery trail game that had stretched his physical and mental resources to the limit. He sighed, pretty sure he'd got away with it, the nightmare of trying to control that crowd keeping him alert and focused.

He grabbed the remote control and turned the sound up. Many of the same pictures he'd seen earlier were being replayed but there was an additional part to the story. It seemed as though the final message from the mystery trail app was accompanied by a hashtag – *#whereswalter*, which had gone viral across Oxfordshire with people speculating what it meant. The reporter was encouraging people to contact them if they knew anyone called Walter that had disappeared. John screwed his face up, perplexed at how crazy people got over something that was obviously a scam.

He checked his shifts, relieved that he wasn't due in until the next day. As he flicked between the screens on his phone the mystery trail app popped up. He remembered reading the first clue before he must have dropped off. His brain started to race. It was a scam. That's what he'd told himself. People were being stupid believing in such things. Weren't they? He didn't want to do it, but he navigated to his banking app, his heart sinking as he looked at the balance. By his best estimates he'd blown nearly five hundred quid in his last gambling binge. He clicked back on the mystery trail app. Could he really win fifty thousand pounds?

He reread the first clue, now clear that the answer was at Carfax, but he didn't know what the final part referred to. He opened up Facebook and, sure enough, the answers to the first three clues had been posted numerous times. He smiled to himself. At least he wouldn't have to pace around Oxford like all those other idiots. He entered the answers to the first three clues and was presented with the message that the news had been referring to with the hashtag. He made a mental note to check the incident logs to see if the police were doing anything about this apparent disappearance of dear old Walter.

He winced at the niggling pains that seem to be ever present in different parts of his body. He was sure he shouldn't feel this decrepit at twenty-six years of age but knew his lifestyle wasn't helping. He turned off the TV and closed his phone.

He got ready for bed, the demons never far away. Another day off was not a good thing. It was usually a trigger to gamble some more. He saw the card of his new Gamblers Anonymous sponsor that he'd left on his bedside cabinet, which just made him feel more guilty. He'd taken the first step but the prospect of having to talk to a complete stranger every time he had the urge to gamble filled him with dread. John was a Yorkshireman. Therapy was for wimps. You just got on with life. At least that's what he could hear his father saying to him every time he moaned about something.

He got into bed and closed his eyes. One day at a time.

9

Rachel sat in the staffroom, wolfing down a chicken salad for lunch. The morning had been manic. Two operations back to back, hardly giving her a second to think, but as she watched the local news she couldn't believe what she was seeing.

Local police have once again been out in force as the next clue in the Oxford Mystery game was launched a little after 11am. Crowds quickly gathered around the University Church on the high street, which onlookers reported was the location of the answer to the fourth clue in this bizarre game that has captivated the Oxfordshire public. Traffic down the high street was disrupted as the sheer numbers in the crowd forced people out onto the road. The local police commander once again condemned the organiser of the game for ignoring public safety issues and made a plea for them to stop the game. The other curious development in the game, the #whereswalter, has set off a social media frenzy as people try to work out who the hashtag is referring to. So far, there does not seem to be any answer to this mystery.

Rachel opened the Oxford Mystery app and read the fourth clue.

Clue 4: if you want to worship, go on High, the year on the board will get you by.

The clue was brief and to the point. A church on the high street was the obvious answer and it seemed as though people had worked out that it was the University Church, which she recalled was about halfway down the street.

She glanced at her watch. She still had another four hours of her shift to go. In all the drama of the previous day, she'd forgotten to get some dinners in, so after work she decided to get straight on a bus into town, solve the clue and grab something to eat.

She arrived in town a little before six and walked straight down the high street towards the church. She was glad the crowds had dispersed, but there were still plenty of people hovering around a noticeboard outside the church, their expressions changing from deep concentration to delight as the game seemingly rewarded them with a positive response.

Rachel waited her turn, eventually finding a gap in the crowd to read the board. It referred to the year 1200, which she entered on the app. The answer was correct.

She clicked on the NEXT button, which congratulated her on completing the clue and promised more excitement in the coming days. The message was once again accompanied by the *#whereswalter*.

After a stressful day, she was up for some fast food. She looked around, trying to decide which food option to pursue. She began to walk back up to Carfax, sure that one of the many food outlets would tempt her in. As she walked, she had a strange sensation. She stopped and looked behind her. She scanned the people walking in every direction, garnering a couple of *tuts* as she created a sudden blockage on the path. She'd had the sense that she was being watched. Followed, maybe.

She gasped as she caught sight of the back of someone scuttling down Turl Street. The long, blonde hair billowing in the wind tweaked a memory.

Was it the lady she met yesterday?

Abigail?

10

John had slept for another eight hours, stirring a little after 9am. He felt spent, physically and mentally, despite nearly fourteen hours asleep, split between his living room chair and bed. He wanted to bury his head under the covers, ignore the world and then maybe his gambling debts would be just a bad dream.

He got past it and went downstairs to have some breakfast, the caffeine hit in particular making him feel a bit more human. His fingers danced across his phone screen, flicking from app to app, trying to take his mind off what he really wanted to do. Gamble some more. Online gaming just made it worse. Whilst he craved the noise and excitement of the casino, he often spent hours idling away on the gambling apps, with their promise of free spins and unlimited wins.

A phone call interrupted his angst. It was his mother. He rejected the call.

He flicked back to one of the gambling apps and lost five pounds within two minutes. He put the phone down on the breakfast bar and shoved it away. He put his head in his hands and closed his eyes. Maybe he should have answered the phone to his mother. Maybe she would help. Maybe she would protect him from the hell and damnation that would reign down if his father ever found out. He snorted in derision. Why the hell should he care what they thought? *Liars!*

He went and had a shower, a shave, emptied the bins. Boring mechanical tasks. Anything to eat away at the hours on his own, fighting the demons.

Just when he thought his willpower might fail him, his phone rang. For the second day running he was being called in. Within minutes of the clue coming out, people were crowding around the University Church on the high street and crowd control was once again on his agenda.

John heaved a sigh of relief. Work was the only medicine. He quickly put on his uniform and reported to the sergeant on scene as the same chaos ensued. The response was more organised this time as barriers were quickly placed along the roadside, removing the crowds that had spilled onto the roads. The pavements along the high street were packed for half a mile each side, as people tried to get to the church entrance to find the answer to the clue. John reflected that this sergeant was savvier than the one he'd worked with the day before, as he slowly organised the crowds into a neat one-way system, allowing them to queue on the wider part of the path at the lower end of the high street, filtering past the church and exiting towards Carfax. It took a while, but John was impressed by his organisation and determination. Unlike John, this guy was going far.

For nearly four hours, John and the rest of the team managed the crowds, the one-way system working to a point, with only two arrests of people that didn't want to wait their turn. John got involved in one of the arrests. A girl who was definitely on something. It broke up what was otherwise a fairly boring task.

The crowds were manageable by late afternoon, and they began to move the barriers, whilst making sure that public order was maintained. John was asked to stay until six and he found himself people watching, fascinated by the different groups and individuals who were playing the game. Whilst it was fair to say that the majority were young or middle aged, he was amused by a group of pensioners who spent most of the time shouting at each other, trying to be heard above the traffic and noise from the smaller crowds that were now around the church.

Just as John was about to sign off, he noticed a woman, on her own, waiting patiently to read the board that appeared to have the answer to the clue. He screwed his face up, trying to think where he'd seen her before. A vague memory flashed into his mind. The more he thought about it, the more he doubted his apparent recollection, but there was something about her that he recognised.

John continued to watch her. After she read the sign, she entered the answer in her phone, accompanied by a reaction he'd seen regularly that afternoon. A mini fist pump. This was followed by a look of disappointment, which John couldn't reconcile. A few minutes later she began to walk back up towards Carfax.

John glanced at his watch. It was time to finish, and he radioed to say that he was off shift. He began to walk in the same direction as the woman, although by now he was at least one hundred yards behind her. Suddenly, he noticed she'd stopped and was looking back down the street. John wasn't sure what alerted him to it, but he noticed a young girl cutting across the human traffic walking up and down the street, causing a stir with the people she bumped and shoved to dive down Turl Street.

As he reached the entrance to Turl Street, he glanced down it. The girl was running. He looked back up the high street. The other girl was still there. Now he could see her face. She looked perturbed.

John walked back to his flat, ordering a pizza on the way. When he got in, he searched the internet for the answer to the church clue, realising he'd forgotten to take a look at the board before he left. Thinking about why he hadn't stopped to solve the clue brought back the curious incident on the high street.

Was he imagining what he saw? Was something going on with those two women?

11

The door to the bedroom opened. After the incident in the living room, she had wasted no time in threatening him with the spear, forcing him back into his luxury 'prison' as he got used to the daily ritual of food being brought in on a tray. A weapon of some kind ever present. Tonight, she had the gun again, pointing it at him as she entered the room.

She stared at him, handcuffed to the bed. She pulled out her gun and walked towards him, undoing the handcuffs. "Now move and go to the bathroom before you piss yourself over my nice bed linen."

For a second Walter thought about launching himself at her, but she was ready for him.

"Ah, ah, ah. Don't even think about it or a bullet goes straight through your head."

The fight drained out of him, and he slowly walked to the bathroom. She retrieved the tray of food from the corridor and placed it on the small desk at the far end of the room. As he emerged from the bathroom he glanced at the tray.

"I want some alcohol."

"I'm sure you do. Must be terrible to have this sudden abstinence. What is it now, three days dry?"

He went to pick up a glass of water, but his hand was shaking so much he gave up. "Please. Just one glass, of anything. I need to calm my nerves."

She started laughing, a manic laugh that made Walter fear for his life. She seemed so intent on making him pay for something. There was a deadness in her eyes, like a shark waiting to attack.

He let out a primal scream and ran towards her. She fired at his feet, the sound echoing in the large, high-ceilinged room. He stopped in his tracks. "You crazy fucking bitch."

"Now now, Walter. Be a good boy and have some respect for your host. It won't be long now."

He'd thought long and hard about the time he'd spent with her and was still perplexed as to why she was acting this way. He decided to try and get back on her good side.

"What have I done to you? We were tight, right? I mean we had a laugh, didn't we? I'd really like an opportunity to make this up to you. Whatever it is you think I've done wrong, just tell me and I can sort it out."

She stared at him for a moment, revelling in his fear. Eventually she spoke. "You'll get an opportunity to make this up to me, Walter. Don't you worry about that."

With that she turned and left, locking the door behind her.

Walter shook his head. He couldn't work out what it was, but there was something different about her. She didn't seem like the same bubbly, up-for-a-laugh woman he'd spent all those hours with in the pub. She was darker, intense, full of loathing.

He sat down and began to shovel the food into this mouth. She was waiting for something, and Walter didn't like to think about what that meant for him.

When he finished the food, Walter began to pace around the room, like a caged tiger. Three days without alcohol was taking its toll. He had never experienced withdrawal before. He never stopped drinking long enough to find out.

He wasn't in the same room he'd originally woken up in. This one had bars on the windows, stopping any attempt at escape via that route. The only other route out of the room was the door, which was kept locked. He peered out of the window through the bars. All he could see was countryside.

His mind was racing. Where was he? Why had he been told the woman holding him here against his will was dead, and what had he possibly done to her to make her act in this way?

He stretched his mind to try and recall the events of the night that led up to his abduction. He had been in the Jericho Tavern as usual, the same people, the same banter. Nothing unusual. He was sure he'd left at closing time like he normally did but didn't really remember walking home.

He screamed out loud at no one in particular. Was this what she was doing? Forcing him into some ill conceived drying-out clinic? He shook his head. Apart from bringing up his meals, she had hardly spoken to him. There were no doctors, no therapists, no group sessions to pour out your deficiencies.

No, this was something different, and he didn't like it. She seemed cold and calculating. A ticking time bomb.

12

For the second day running Rachel sat in the staffroom eating her lunch, glued to the local news. Her friend Kaley was with her. "Are you into all this nonsense?" she said as the local news reporter began to update on the story.

Rachel was trying to listen. "Er, yeah, hold on a minute. I want to hear what's going on."

The Oxford Mystery game that has captivated thousands of Oxfordshire residents has taken a new twist today when the supposed missing person behind the #whereswalter was identified. He has been named locally as Walter Cribbens, a plumber from the Jericho area of Oxford. Friends say that Walter is a heavy drinker and is in the Jericho Tavern most evenings, but he has not been seen for three days. His employer has confirmed that Walter has not turned up for work in the same period and all attempts to contact him have failed. There is no answer at his flat and neighbours say they have not seen him. If anyone knows of his whereabouts, the local police have asked to be contacted on 101 with the Unique Reference Number (URN) 2541/2205. Fans of the game have also been besieging social media, asking why no further clues have been released, fuelling speculation that the organiser is running scared of the police scrutiny. More on this story as we get it.

"Wow," said Rachel, "this is all getting a bit weird."

"You don't honestly believe this is real, do you?" said Kaley.

Rachel frowned. "Oh, I don't know. I guess I'm just enjoying the distraction, as I don't have much else going on in my life at the moment."

Kaley grimaced. "Oh dear, still not getting any?"

"Kaley, please, don't be so crude."

Kaley sighed. "For God's sake, girl, we need to get you back out there. I'll tell you what, let's hit the town after work and we'll see if we can hook you up."

Rachel yawned. "I can't. I'm so tired."

Kaley stood up. "Too bad. I'm not taking no for an answer. I'll meet you in the bar at Malmaison at seven and we'll go from there."

Rachel didn't have time to object as Kaley sped out of the room. "Oh, what the hell," she muttered to herself as she checked the Oxford Mystery app for the umpteenth time. There was still no fifth clue.

Rachel did her best to glam up and got to the Malmaison a few minutes after 7pm. Kaley was already on her first glass of champagne. "Hey, babe, glad you didn't stand me up."

"I guess you didn't give me much choice."

They sat in the lounge, a couple of glasses of champagne soon despatched. "We should probably eat something," said Rachel. "I'm not good drinking on an empty stomach."

"Yeah, you're probably right. How about Thaikkun? I'm up for something spicy."

Rachel grunted her agreement but was distracted by a figure walking out of the bar area. "What is it?" said Kaley.

"Um, I don't know. How weird. I'm sure that was the girl I bumped into the other day."

Kaley leant forward but couldn't see her. "Ooh, is she a hotty?"

Rachel grimaced. "Yeah, she's fucking gorgeous, but I thought I saw her again yesterday, and I couldn't help feeling like she was following me."

Kaley almost spat out the mouthful of champagne. "You what? You've got a full-on stalker."

"No, no, I don't think so. I must be imagining it."

Rachel brushed it off and they made their way to the restaurant. They had a lovely meal, and just before they were due to move on, Rachel decided she needed the bathroom. Just as she got back to their table, Rachel froze.

Kaley looked at her, concern etched over her face. "Are you alright, babe?"

Rachel didn't answer. She started to walk towards another table, across the other side of the restaurant.

"Are you following me?" Rachel bellowed, trying to be heard above the noisy diners.

The girl she aimed the question at stopped what she was doing and looked at her, quizzically. "Oh, hi," she said. "Sorry, we met the other day, but I can't remember your name."

Rachel felt a wave of embarrassment wash over her. "It's Rachel. And you're Abigail."

"That's right," the girl replied. "What was it you said? I couldn't quite hear."

Rachel wanted the ground to open up and swallow her, but she couldn't shake the unease so repeated the question.

Abigail's expression changed from the happy, bubbly persona that Rachel had briefly seen to one a lot more serious. "Why on earth would you say that?"

Rachel steeled herself against the growing embarrassment as the tables around her became quiet, nosily listening in to the drama. "Well, I saw you near Carfax on Tuesday; I saw you down the high street yesterday, scuttling down Turl Street when I turned to look back at you, and now I've seen you in both places that I've been tonight."

Abigail put on a confused, slightly hurt expression. "Well, I live in Oxford. I've just finished my degree and have been staying in college. I'm always around the centre of town."

All eyes were now on Rachel. "Oh, right. Fine. I'm sorry."

With that, Rachel scuttled back to her table, unceremoniously grabbing Kaley's arm. "We need to leave. Now!" As they walked out of the restaurant, Abigail gave her a little wave.

Rachel glanced wide-eyed at Kaley before getting outside as quickly as she could.

13

Rachel was walking so fast that Kaley could hardly keep up with her. She didn't slow the pace, navigating back up George Street and into Broad Street, not stopping until she dived into the entrance to the White Horse pub. She ordered two glasses of wine, not bothering to ask Kaley what she wanted, before sitting down at a corner table.

For a second, Rachel stared into space, absent-mindedly sipping the wine. Eventually, she realised Kaley was looking at her, open-mouthed with shock.

"Are you going to explain what just happened back there?"

Rachel groaned. "I've made such a tit of myself. That's what happened."

"Who was that girl you confronted?"

Rachel rubbed her face. "I met her on Tuesday. I was looking at the crowd around Carfax, after that first clue came out. It was chaos, so I was watching from a distance, when I realised she was standing next to me. We had a brief chat and then she walked away."

"Okay, so what turned you into psycho bitch?"

"It's what I told you. Over the last couple of days, she seems to have been everywhere that I've been. Down the high street yesterday and tonight in the Malmaison and at the restaurant."

"So, you assumed she was stalking you?"

Rachel fought back tears. "Oh, Kaley, I just don't know. Why am I being paranoid about this? I mean, she basically hit on me the first time we met."

"You what?"

Rachel looked embarrassed. "Well, she said I was gorgeous, or something like that."

"And you did what?"

"Nothing. She walked away."

Kaley shook her head. "You really need to get some. The lack of sex is turning you into some nutter."

Rachel frowned. "The problem is that, as stunning as that girl is, I can't shake the feeling that she is playing a game with me. I mean, why would someone like her be interested in me?"

Kaley stood up. "Enough. I'm going to get us some more drinks and then we are going to hit the nightclubs and find someone that is up for a one-night stand. Anything to get you out of this pit of self-pity."

Kaley came back with some more drinks and Rachel's mood lightened as Kaley's infectious enthusiasm for life pulled her out of the doldrums.

More drinks followed and the nightclub wasn't far behind. For Rachel, the rest of the night was a blur.

14

As the first melodies of her ringtone stirred her from a deep sleep, Rachel tried to process why her head felt like a herd of wildebeest were stomping through it. Her mouth and throat were dry, and she struggled to generate enough moisture in her mouth to stop her gagging. She tried to move her head on the pillow, but pain coursed through every sense that was slowly waking up.

She desperately wanted to reach for her phone to turn off the increasingly loud alarm that was ever present when she had to work, but every movement made her groan. "Work," she muttered to herself. How on earth was she going to even get herself off the bed, let alone get to work.

Mercifully, the alarm stopped and she lay still, hoping that somehow her body would heal and allow her to rise. She kept her eyes closed, hoping that would help, but as she tried to replay how she had got in this state, she felt movement on the other side of the bed.

She opened her eyes wide, not daring to roll over and see who was there. Her brain went into overdrive. Who the hell was in her bed and why couldn't she remember the hook-up? Her head was still thumping, but she willed her body to start moving, to at least get in a position where she could get a clue who it was.

She felt light-headed as she began to roll over, every movement feeling like some pain-ridden slow-motion replay. As the figure began to come into view, Rachel stifled a scream. She put her hand to her mouth, her brain scrambling to make sense of it. How had this happened?

She was in the pub with Kaley after the incident in the restaurant. They started drinking heavily. There was a nightclub in there somewhere and then… nothing. She couldn't remember a thing. So, how had this girl ended up in her bed. Her supposed *stalker.* And where was Kaley? How had she let this happen?

Rachel tried to sit up without waking her, desperately trying not to be sick as each movement sent several pain receptors off. She took it slow but eventually dragged her chronically hungover body into the bathroom. She locked the door and dialled Kaley's number. After a few seconds she answered, her voice as gravelly as Rachel's.

"Hello."

"Kaley, what the fuck. How the hell is that girl in my bed?"

Kaley groaned. "Whoa, not so loud, Rach."

"Fucking hell, Kaley, I'm completely freaking out here. The girl that I accused of following me is in my bed. How did you let that happen?"

There was a brief pause before Kaley let out a pained laugh. "Ah, yes, I remember now. She was in the nightclub and geez she is so fit."

"Oh my God, Kaley, I was right, she's stalking me. How on earth was she in the same nightclub as us?"

"She seemed nice, Rach. She began dancing with us and I don't remember you objecting. We had a few more drinks and she and her mate were a right laugh. By the end you were so out of it that she offered to take you home."

"And you let her?"

"Hey, babe, I said my main task last night was to get you some, and it looks like I succeeded."

Rachel was struggling not to throw up as the horror of the previous evening unfolded. "I've gotta go, Kaley. I need to sort this out. I'll see you at work in a couple of hours."

Rachel disconnected the call. The room was spinning, and her head was thumping. She drank some water, her stomach lurching with every gulp. She grabbed the sides of the sink, letting the nausea ease. After a few minutes she steeled herself to leave the bathroom and confront the situation.

She gingerly walked back into her bedroom. Abigail was still asleep. As Rachel wrestled with her emotions, there was a sudden sharp intake of breath as Abigail started to come round. A few seconds later Abigail's eyes fluttered and she slowly opened them, wincing at the light. She groaned. "Oh my God, we went hard last night."

Rachel stared at Abigail, not saying a word. She had woken up in her bed, seemingly unfazed by the situation, like this was an everyday occurrence for her. "You alright?" said Abigail.

Rachel frowned. "I… I… don't know what to say. You're… um… here… in my bed."

Abigail laughed and propped herself up on one elbow. "I guess this was your version of an apology, after your hissy fit in the restaurant."

Rachel didn't know whether to laugh or scream for help. "But, I don't understand."

"What do you think happened here?" enquired Abigail.

Rachel put her hand over her face. "My God, I'm so embarrassed. I have absolutely no recollection of how we got here or what we did."

"Hey, don't sweat it. Nothing happened here. I saw you in the nightclub with your mate and tried to talk to you, but you were pretty much out of it. By the end of the evening, you could hardly put one foot in front of the other. Your mate got you in a taxi, back to your place, and I said I would go with you to make sure you got home okay. I helped you indoors and up to bed. I was worried about you, so I decided to stay. Just like besties having a sleepover."

Rachel examined every inch of Abigail's face. She couldn't believe that such a beautiful young woman was lying there, looking after her.

"Thank you for looking after me, but I need to get to work."

Abigail pouted. "Oh, that's a shame. I was rather hoping we could spend some more time together. I mean, you can't be in any fit state to work. Can you?"

Rachel sighed. "Probably not, but I can't bunk off with a hangover."

Abigail pouted in disappointment.

Rachel couldn't deal with it. "Look, I'm sorry. Thank you for looking after me, but I need you to leave. I have to get ready for work."

Abigail shrugged, getting out of the bed, not trying to hide her naked body. Rachel averted her gaze and left the room to shower and dress, hoping to God that Abigail had gone by the time she returned.

15

John was back on his normal shift as a neighbourhood officer. His patch was around Osney, the train station and up to Park End Street. The morning briefing had been interesting as the skipper focused on the Oxford Mystery game. There was general confusion as to why no clue had come out the previous day, fuelling speculation that the game may have been stopped due to the police scrutiny. But all city centre resources were warned to be on standby in case another clue was released. It was also noted that the Jericho team were continuing to make enquiries about this apparent missing person, Walter Cribbens. Neighbourhood teams were asked to keep an eye out on patrol, as some speculated that the guy could have just fallen in the river or keeled over in a hedge somewhere, based on his reputation of being a serial drunk.

John walked his patch, but nothing untoward happened. No crime and no Walter. As he began to walk back to the station at St Aldates, ready for his lunch break, his personal mobile beeped. He stopped and looked at the message, groaning when he saw it was from the Oxford Mystery game. He clicked on it.

Clue 5: the first of its kind it can surely be, and it's further down the High for you to see. Coffee, tea or a bit of cake, find this place and progress you will make. Enter the year it started to continue the story and carry on towards your glory.

John immediately got on the radio to his skipper. After a brief conversation there was a general shout-out for all available resources to get to the high street. No one seemed to be able to work out exactly where the clue was referring to, but the capitalisation of the word *High* in the previous clue had led people there. John cursed his luck. Another lunch break he wouldn't get. He nipped into a shop and grabbed a sausage roll, eating and walking.

It took him about fifteen minutes to get halfway down the high street, meeting up with other police resources that were congregating in the area. The same sergeant that was at the last incident was supervising and started briefing the team. At first there didn't seem to be any crowds gathering, but within twenty minutes, several groups had started to arrive outside the Grand Café.

It was now becoming a well-rehearsed operation as the sergeant radioed for a van to bring the barriers and they were quickly placed all along the road about five hundred yards on each side of the café. The owner of the café was perplexed, seemingly unaware that his premises was the location of the mystery game's latest clue, though he soon saw the potential for a good day's takings.

Although the crowds were large, the proactive nature of the local policing response meant the disruption was reduced and the same one-way system was introduced. By the end of John's shift, the crowds were manageable, and he remembered to get the answer, which was inscribed on the window. The café was opened in *1650*.

He was surprised when the app congratulated him on completing another day of the Oxford Mystery trail. It seemed like whoever was running this game was trying to build the tension by only releasing one clue at a time. From the brief look he'd taken at social media, it was working. Every clue was building the online world into a frenzy with a growing divide between those that thought it was a scam and the people determined to be the ones to solve the mystery and claim the fifty grand.

As John began to walk home, he realised there was something new in the message. The *#whereswalter* was still there, but this time there was an additional line on the message.

It read:

TO WIN £50,000 YOU WILL ALSO NEED A CODEWORD. TODAY YOU HAVE BEEN AWARDED THE LETTER C.

John frowned. What on earth did that mean?

16

Rachel wasn't sure how she'd got through the morning shift. A chronic hangover and what she guessed was no more than four hours asleep had contributed to a hellish morning. Thankfully, she wasn't required for any operations, spending her time on theatre scheduling and other boring paperwork, fuelled by endless cups of coffee. She knew she should eat something, but she decided not to risk it. She was still in a mood with Kaley and was relieved when she wasn't in the staffroom when Rachel took her break.

She switched the TV on and wasn't surprised to see the Oxford Mystery game as the headline story once again. She'd received the clue a little after 11am and, watching the news report, it was now obvious that the answer was the Grand Café on the high street. She found the date by a quick internet search and entered it into the app. It seemed that this was the only clue coming out that day. She read the daily message, interested that another element of the mystery had been added. A codeword and the award of a letter C.

The rest of the shift passed slowly, like every minute was doubled just to make sure she suffered for her overindulgence. She got home a little after 6pm, pinging a cottage pie in the microwave, as hunger overtook hangover. As she sat in the living room, the TV on purely to break the silence in the flat, she couldn't help feeling uneasy.

The fact that Abigail had been in her flat, knew where she lived, unnerved her. She felt strangely violated. Whatever Kaley said, Rachel had not invited Abigail into her home and definitely not into her bed. Rachel couldn't process the mindset that thought that was okay.

She cleared her dinner things away and went back into the bedroom. She'd left in such a rush that the bed was still crumpled where they had both lain. Kaley seemed convinced Abigail was just some super fit, carefree girl who was genuinely into Rachel.

Rachel forced herself to smooth the bed covers down, mentally erasing the images of Abigail lying there, but it didn't work. She grabbed the duvet, removing the cover, wrenched off the bedsheets and took off the pillowcase covers. She bundled them up, moving back into the kitchen and shoving them in the washing machine. She watched the drum begin to move, listened as the water began to fill the machine. It was like she was washing away the memory.

She went back into the bedroom and remade the bed with spare bedding. When she finished, she sat on the bed, looking around the room. There was still something that didn't feel right. She tried to replay the events of the morning. She'd told Abigail to leave and ducked in the shower. By the time Rachel had finished in the bathroom, Abigail had left the flat. So, why did Rachel still feel her presence? Like some live ghost experience.

Suddenly she spotted it. One of the drawers at the bottom of the wardrobe was not fully shut. She opened the drawer. It was a mess. The underwear she kept there not neatly stored like it usually was.

As she put her hand in to tidy it up, she felt something hard.

There, lying at the bottom of the drawer, was a kitchen knife.

17

Kaley raced round to Rachel's flat. She could barely make out what she was saying on the phone. Hysterical screams had been interspersed with the occasional word. Mercifully she had a key to the flat, a product of plant watering duty when Rachel had been away a few times.

Kaley found Rachel sat on her bedroom floor, next to her wardrobe, sobbing her heart out, her arms wrapped around her waist in an attempt to comfort herself. Kaley grabbed her, cuddling her to within an inch of her life. The sobbing slowly subsided as Kaley held her close.

Kaley risked easing her grip and gently cupped Rachel's face. "Oh, babe, what on earth is this all about?"

Rachel's breathing was heavy, and it took her a minute to say anything. Kaley waited, concern etched over her face as she let her friend calm down enough to speak. The first thing Rachel did was a gesture, pointing towards the open drawer in her wardrobe. Kaley turned to look at where she was pointing, a frown appearing as she didn't know what she was seeing. "What is it?" Kaley said.

Rachel began to shake, her hand clasped over her mouth as she stifled more tears. Eventually she managed to string a few words together. "Look inside the drawer."

Kaley peered in. "What the fuck! What is that doing in there?"

"Well, I didn't put it in there!" screeched Rachel.

Kaley was so confused. "I don't understand."

"That girl. Abigail! She must have put it in there. I told you she was a fucking psycho."

Kaley released her grip on Rachel and sat back. "Is that your knife?"

Rachel's eyes bore into Kaley. "Yes, it's from the knife block in the kitchen, but I didn't put it in there."

Kaley's mind started racing. "I know. I believe you. My God, Rach, I'm so sorry. If that's true, that's seriously fucked up. I mean she seemed like such a nice girl. There wasn't anything about her that made me concerned."

Rachel didn't reply, taking in deep breaths, trying to stifle more tears.

"We should phone the police," exclaimed Kaley.

Rachel frowned. "And say what? That a girl that I apparently invited into my home has put a kitchen knife in my knickers drawer. I think they've probably got more important things to worry about than that."

"Okay, why don't you grab some things and come and stay with me tonight? We've got a day off tomorrow and we'll go and do something nice. Try to forget about all this."

Rachel sighed. "Thank you, that would be nice."

They pottered about, getting the bedding out of the washing machine, throwing away the milk, packing a few things in an overnight bag. Small, domestic things that helped them both stop thinking about the implications of what had just happened.

It was a little after 9pm when Rachel and Kaley left the flat. The bad memories shut away.

18

John wasn't sure why, but the first thing he did when he woke up was grab his phone and check the balance on his bank account. He closed his eyes in horror when he saw the number staring back at him. There was still another two weeks to payday, and he had less than a hundred pounds left in his account. He had three credit cards, one of which was certainly maxed out, with the others not far behind.

He was grateful for the overtime he'd done due to the mystery game, but he wouldn't see that money until the end of the following month. The card of his new Gamblers Anonymous sponsor was on the side. He knew he should ring her, but pride was getting in the way.

He cycled through his options. He could go into the bank and ask to extend his overdraft. He could ignore it and wait for the bank to contact him. He could phone his mother back and beg for money. He rubbed his face in frustration. None of these were realistic options.

He scrolled to the main screen on his phone. There were three online gambling apps staring back at him. He held his finger on the first one. The options popped up on the screen. He pressed *uninstall.* He repeated the action on the other two. He let out a deep breath. A small step.

He glanced at the time. He had less than an hour before his next shift started. He was just about to close his phone when a notification popped up. It was from the Oxford Mystery game. His reaction to it surprised him. He stifled back tears, his stomach lurching. The thought of having fifty thousand pounds to reset his life was a dream. He knew he was being unrealistic. Even if the mystery game was not a scam, the chances of him winning the money seemed like a pipe dream. He knew more than anyone about addiction, and the mystery game was pushing those buttons, removing all rational thoughts. He clicked on the message.

Clue 6: opposite the place where you were the day before, is a royal lane for you to explore. Follow the lane until its end, to find a bridge around the bend. On this bridge that some say sigh, two figures are there if you look up high. Enter the name of this angelic creature and another clue will surely feature.

John read the clue a couple of times. The last clue directed players to the Grand Café on the high street. His knowledge of the city meant the first part of this clue was easy. The royal lane was Queen's Lane, which was indeed opposite the café. He tried to play through the rest of the clue but couldn't recollect what was at the end of the lane. He shrugged and got out of bed. Today's clue had come out earlier than usual, but by the time he got in, he was sure the skipper would have them tasked out to manage the crowds.

When he got in, he was surprised to find that the skipper wanted him on his usual patch. The local policing area (LPA) commander had expressed concern that neighbourhood policing was being compromised as all local resources were constantly being redirected to handle crowd control in different parts of the city. The central resourcing team had created a reactive taskforce from neighbouring LPAs to provide greater resilience.

As he set off to patrol his patch, the slower pace didn't help him manage his demons. Whilst crowd control had been boring, it at least meant he had to stay alert for any hint of trouble, not giving him a second to think about anything else. As he slowly wandered about, the occasional engagement with members of the local community didn't do enough to stop him thinking about gambling. All he could think about was reinstalling the apps that he'd deleted. He was a long way from being okay.

19

Rachel and Kaley slept in late, grateful that their scheduled day off had landed conveniently as they sought to recover from a traumatic twenty-four hours. Rachel had calmed down a lot, but Kaley could tell that she was still edgy. As they ate breakfast, Kaley watched Rachel as she fiddled with her phone, a smile suddenly appearing on her face.

"What's up, babe? It's nice to see that smile back on your face."

Rachel grimaced. "The latest clue has come out from that mystery game."

Kaley obviously didn't hide her scepticism as Rachel reacted. "Hey, don't do that. At the moment this bloody game is about the only exciting thing in my life."

Kaley pouted.

"Oh, you idiot. Stop the emotional blackmail. Being with you is obviously exciting and I'm so grateful for everything you've done for me over the last few days, but at least let me get lost in this game."

Kaley stood up and kissed her on the cheek. "Alright, babe, I'll indulge you in this little mystery game fantasy.

Does that mean you want to go into town and follow the rest of the sheep?"

Rachel gave Kaley a light punch on the arm. "Yes, and for that, you've got to come with me."

As they travelled on the bus into town, Rachel had worked out that the clue started at Queen's Lane. They got off halfway up the high street and Rachel dragged Kaley over the road. There didn't seem to be that many people around the entrance to the lane, but as they followed the instructions on the clue, eventually emerging onto New College Lane, they could hear a crowd. When they turned the corner, a large crowd was gathered under the bridge that connected two parts of Hertford College. Rachel reread the clue; the word *sigh* referred to the fact that people called this Oxford's version of the Bridge of Sighs.

They wrestled their way through the crowds, realising that the answer to the clue was on the other side to where they'd come from. A glance up at the bridge gave Rachel the answer. The angelic creature the clue was referring to was a *cherub*. She entered the clue in the app and got the same congratulatory message as the previous days. The game had got into a routine of only releasing one clue a day.

Kaley did her best to show interest. "Did you get it right, babe?"

Rachel frowned. "Yeah, but it looks like this is the only clue they are going to give today."

Kaley smiled. "Oh well, you are just going to have to put up with me for the rest of the day."

Rachel didn't respond. She was still staring at her phone.

"You alright?" Kaley enquired.

"Oh, yeah, sorry. It's just this message is a bit weird.

It's given us another letter to this so-called codeword. The letter U."

"Eh, what's that all about?"

"I dunno. There seem to be multiple aspects to this game. We keep answering these clues, there's this missing Walter guy that no one seems to have found and now we've been given a C and a U to some codeword."

Kaley couldn't hide her disdain, which this time made Rachel laugh. "Okay, I get the message. Time to do something else."

Kaley linked arms with Rachel and dragged her back towards the centre of town. "Right, I'm hungry. Let's go eat. I fancy something spicy."

They walked towards one of their favourite Thai restaurants in Hythe Bridge Street. Just as they were near the entrance, they saw a police officer walking towards them. Kaley stopped and nudged Rachel. "Speak to this guy. Tell him about what happened in your flat."

At first Rachel was like a rabbit in headlights, not wanting to accost a police officer in the street, but as he got closer, he stopped, like he recognised her.

"Hi," he said, "do I know you?"

Rachel's heart sank. "You what?"

The officer smiled. "No, don't worry. I don't mean in a bad way, it's just I think I saw you a few days ago at Carfax and then I saw you the next day on the High Street. I assume you are doing this mystery game?"

"Oh right, yes. I guess you were one of the police officers trying to deal with all these crowds."

"That's right, but… I don't know, I'm sure we've met before that."

There was a brief awkward pause in the conversation, as the officer seemed to be cycling through his memory banks. It was interrupted by Kaley nudging Rachel in the ribs. Rachel frowned at the mild assault but got the message. "Er, can I ask your advice about something?"

"Sure, fire away."

"I… God this is so embarrassing… I hooked up with some girl a couple of nights ago. I was so drunk that I really don't remember anything that happened, but the next evening I realised one of the drawers in my wardrobe was slightly open and when I looked inside, one of my kitchen knives was in there."

The officer frowned. "Really? I'm guessing you didn't put it in there."

"I know I was blind drunk, but I don't think I would have done that. The thing is, I'm convinced this girl has been following me and, despite the fact that I apparently invited her back to my place, I'm scared that she was the one that left the knife in there."

"Is she a blonde?"

Rachel recoiled. "Yes! How would you know that?"

"Well, after I saw you in the high street, my shift was just finishing so I was walking back up towards Carfax. I think you were about a hundred yards ahead of me. Anyway, I noticed that you stopped and were looking down the street at something. The next thing I see is a blonde woman dart down Turl Street. When I got to the entrance to the street, she was running down it. I thought it was odd at the time."

Rachel put her hand to her mouth, looking at Kaley, wide-eyed with shock. "You see, Kaley, I wasn't lying. This officer saw it too."

Kaley winced. "I didn't not believe you, but as I said before, when I met her in the nightclub she seemed like a nice girl."

Rachel looked back at the officer. "Do you think she was the one that left the knife in my drawer?"

The officer shrugged. "I have no idea, but if you want to make a formal report about this, you can always come back to the station with me and then at least we have it on the system if anything else should happen."

Rachel welled up. "God this is so ridiculous. This woman's got me frightened of my own shadow and I don't really know if she's the psycho stalker I've been imagining."

The officer smiled sympathetically. "Look, come back with me to the station. I think we should document this, just in case."

Rachel looked at Kaley, who gave her a reassuring nod. "I think the officer is right. Let's do this first, babe. We can eat afterwards."

With that they began to follow the officer back to the police station at St Aldates.

"I'm Rachel, by the way, and this is Kaley."

The officer smiled. "Nice to meet you. I'm John."

20

Walter lay on the bed, staring at the patterns in the wood on the roof of the four-poster. He started to create stories in his mind from the shapes he saw. People's faces, animals, clouds. Anything to take his mind off his incarceration.

Days without alcohol had been tough. The withdrawals were painful, physically and mentally, but as he lay there on the fifth day since his kidnap, he was suddenly feeling better. More alert, his senses somehow heightened. The problem was, it was messing with his head. He knew that drying out was a good thing, but not being able to enjoy this new-found freedom was a total head-fuck.

He got off the bed and looked through the barred windows. He pondered if this was what it was like for people in prison. A view of the outside world that just couldn't be enjoyed. Mindless routines, mainly based around food, and nothing to stimulate you. He snorted at the irony. When he was bored at home, he drank. It's what he did. If he ever got out, he wondered whether a sober life could be maintained. Could he find other things to do?

As he once again tried to reconcile why his captor was treating him this way, he began to wonder whether this was her intention all along. They'd been friends. Admittedly, only drinking buddies, but nonetheless, a friendship had developed in the six months he'd known her. Was this her way of helping him stop drinking?

Walter shook his head at the thought. She wasn't acting like his friend. There was something different about her. She'd changed from that don't-give-a-shit, carefree spirit he'd spent so much time with to someone with a deep sense of loathing. There was a darkness in her that he'd never seen before. He shivered at the prospect of what she was waiting to do to him.

A second later the noise of a key turning in the door pulled him back to the present. He tried a different tack.

"Thank you," he said to her.

The woman shot him a confused look. "What for?"

"For drying me out. I can see that locking me in this room has just been your way of helping me out. Finally, after five days, I'm feeling much better. More alive. I can't remember the last time I felt like this."

There was a brief pause before she started to laugh. A dark, evil laugh that shook Walter to his core.

"Oh dear, Walter, I don't give a shit how you feel. You are a pawn in my game. A step towards my main objective."

"What have I done to you?" he screamed. "Tell me!"

"Here's the problem, Walter. The fact that you don't know just makes it worse."

"Explain then and perhaps I can make it up to you."

The unnerving smile that she reserved for these moments was back. "Don't you worry about that. In a couple of days, you will be able to make this right. Patience, Walter. Patience."

With that she walked out, chuckling to herself. Walter couldn't stop himself. He began to cry.

21

Rachel thanked Kaley for being a good friend. Talking to the police officer and getting the incident recorded on their systems was a step forward. She knew she had to go back to her flat. The day and night with Kaley had been great, but another workday beckoned and she had to get back to normal routine.

It was nearly midnight, and she was grateful for the street lighting in the centre of Headington as she walked to her building, scanning every face as she walked the short distance to her flat. She got a few confused stares as her gaze lingered too long on certain people, especially anyone that bore even the vaguest similarity to Abigail.

Rachel went into the flat and walked straight into the bedroom. The drawer was still open. She picked up the knife and took it back to the kitchen, placing it in the spare hole in the knife block. No emotion, just a clinical task to put it back where it lived.

She made herself a cup of tea and went into the lounge, turning on the TV to watch the local news. The Oxford Mystery game was still holding its own as one of the top stories. Crowd shots around the Bridge of Sighs were complemented by the reporter updating on the latest search for Walter Cribbens. It seemed that several apparent sightings had proven not to have been him. The reporter was also speculating on the mystery letters that were accompanying the end-of-day messages, with most people concluding that many more letters were to come before that part of the game made any sense.

Rachel's eyes were heavy, the stress of the last couple of days catching up with her. As she bolted awake, she realised she must have lost the battle to stay awake because her phone was now reading 1.01am.

As she tried to reorientate herself, she noticed a notification on the screen from an unknown number. She clicked on the message.

At first, she didn't know what she was looking at. The video was blurry, the sound distant and tinny. Her heart froze as she realised the word LIVE was flashing in the corner. She sat up, transfixed to the screen. Whatever this was, it was being recorded now. A second later, she screamed, as the front door to her flat came sharply into focus, accompanied by heavy breathing. Rachel put her other hand to her mouth, terror coursing through her body. She willed herself to stand up and walk towards the door, craning to listen for whoever was outside.

She stood frozen to the spot, the video still running but the focus not changing. The camera was fixed on the door to her flat and the breathing could still be heard. Rachel's brain was racing through her options. Should she open the door and confront whoever was there? Should she shout out and warn them off? Should she phone that police officer as he'd given her his card to contact him if anything bad happened again?

As she agonised over what to do, the video suddenly stopped and a piece of paper was pushed through her letter box. Rachel almost dropped her phone in terror but grabbed the note and read the contents.

I love you, Rachel.

Just as she was trying to take in what she was reading, her phone rang. Someone was trying to connect via a video call. She was in total turmoil but clicked the green button to accept the call. She stifled a scream as Abigail's face appeared on the screen.

"You alright?" she asked. "You look like you've seen a ghost."

Rachel was wide-eyed with fear. "What… what are you doing?"

Abigail frowned. "I'm in my room in Oxford. I couldn't sleep. I was worrying about you. You seemed really shaken up by me being in your bed the other morning. I just wanted to ring to apologise if what I did was inappropriate. I was only trying to make sure you were okay."

Rachel's brain was racing. What on earth was happening? She had to get Abigail off the phone.

"I'm fine, thank you. No need for an apology. I appreciate your concern, but I have to get to bed. Work in the morning."

Abigail smiled. "Okay. Night night."

As the call disconnected, Rachel stared at her phone in disbelief.

If Abigail was in Oxford, who the hell was outside her front door?

22

Rachel jumped as the door to the staffroom opened.

"You alright, babe?"

It was Kaley joining her for the daily ritual of a quick lunch before work beckoned again. Rachel didn't hold back and poured out everything that happened when she got home.

"Why didn't you ring me?" exclaimed Kaley.

Rachel fought back tears. "I was so scared. I didn't know what to do, and when Abigail phoned, my theories about her being my stalker were shredded. I mean, if it wasn't her outside my door, then who the hell is persecuting me?"

Kaley gave her a hug. "You need to call that police officer."

Rachel grimaced. "I know. I almost did last night but, in the end, I was safe in my flat. Once I'd stopped shaking, I just went to bed, not that I slept much."

As Rachel went back to her lunch, forcing herself to eat something despite the rising nausea, she turned the sound up on the TV. The Oxford Mystery was featuring on the news again.

There is massive controversy today as thousands of people appear to have received a message from the Oxford Mystery app, stating that they have not been successful in reaching the second stage of the game. Members of the public have besieged social media and local news organisations to complain at their treatment, citing the fact that they have answered all the clues correctly, their culling from the game seemingly entirely random. We have been asking people to contact us if they are still involved in the game and a small handful have approached us saying they have received the next clue. It seems the mystery game is living up to its name.

Rachel grabbed her phone, ignoring the sigh from Kaley. She opened the app.

"Oh my God, I'm still in it! Look, I've got the next clue."

Kaley huffed. "Huh, seems like you've been one of the lucky ones."

Rachel was transfixed to the words on the screen.

Clue 7: now let's find a famous venue, where musical extravaganzas are on the menu. Just off the Broad, this place by Wren, has wall engravings not made by pen. Roman numerals are high on one wall, enter the last five so you can win all.

She looked at Kaley. "I'm going to take this as a good sign. This game is the only thing that's keeping me sane, and if I've made it to the final group, my chances of winning fifty grand have just risen exponentially. I'm going straight downtown after work. You can come if you want."

Kaley frowned. "I can't, babe, I've got Pilates tonight."

Rachel shrugged. "No worries."

Kaley recoiled. "Are you sure? A minute ago, you thought you had a serial killer on your trail."

"I'm fine. I'll call that police officer and tell him what's happened, but I'm not going to stop my life because someone's trying to shit me up. No, this game is all I need at the moment."

Kaley pouted.

"Oh, for God's sake. I always need you, Kaley."

*

Rachel headed straight for the Sheldonian Theatre when she got off the bus, curious to see whether crowds had gathered at the location the latest clue referred to.

It seemed as though the so-called cull of players had worked. There was no one there.

She entered the roman numerals XVIII that were on the inscription the clue referred to.

It worked. She got another congratulatory message.

23

John was four hours into his shift, touring his neighbourhood on bike and foot. The day had been full of the usual low-level crime. Shoplifters, bike thefts and a bit of drug dealing. His role was mostly after the fact, getting the PCSOs to do most of the legwork with the victims, with very little chance of catching the perps. He updated the intelligence databases with what the victims or witnesses had been able to tell them. He knew at best it might help to create a fuller case against these people, if they ever managed to nab one of them.

In between the jobs he kept thinking about the game. He needed to go to the Sheldonian Theatre, as he was certain that was the location the seventh clue was referring to. It mentioned something about Roman numerals on the building, but he couldn't find the answer on the internet. He'd seen the controversy on the news about people being kicked off the game, and he couldn't believe his luck that he still had a chance of winning fifty thousand pounds. The thought made his stomach lurch. If it happened, he would stop gambling. He had to.

He had two PCSOs on shift with him so made an excuse and messaged them saying he had to go back to the station in St Aldates. Instead, he walked up George Street towards Broad Street. He tried to walk along with a confident air, but he was paranoid he was going to meet one of his colleagues and have to explain away why he wasn't on his patch. In his full police uniform he wasn't exactly inconspicuous.

He began to walk along Broad Street, keeping a watchful eye out, but none of his colleagues were around. He reached the small gate that led to the Sheldonian Theatre and walked through, peering up at the side of the building. He couldn't see any Roman numerals so walked around the left side of the building. There was nothing there, so he went to the rear of the building. He found what he was looking for and followed the inscription along the middle bit of the wall. He found what he thought was the answer and entered them into the app. It worked.

Just as he was about to turn around and get back to his patch, a voice made him freeze to the spot. "Officer."

John discreetly put his phone in his pocket and turned around, almost gasping with shock when he saw who it was. He hadn't met him before but knew his face from all the pictures on the intranet and in the press. It was Assistant Chief Constable Geoffrey Barnett.

"Sorry, sir. I was just looking at this amazing architecture."

The ACC pulled a face that said he wasn't pleased. "I think the good public of Oxford would prefer you concentrated on your job rather than being a tourist."

"Of course, sir. I'll get right back to it."

"What's your name, son?"

John was now facing away from the ACC and cursed under his breath, gritting his teeth in the process. He was already in trouble with his skipper and couldn't afford for the ACC to be dobbing him in. He made a decision, turning briefly to address the ACC.

"It's Robin Jones, sir."

*

John was in the locker room taking off his kit at the end of the shift. Since the run-in with the ACC, he'd got back to his patch as fast as he could and wandered around in a daze until it was time to finish.

The ACC incident and the lie he told him were feeding his demons. All he wanted to do now was get on a train to Reading and gamble all night.

As he struggled with what to do, the door to the locker room burst open. His skipper was stood there, his face a worrying shade of crimson.

"Holy fucking shit, John. What have you done now?"

John's heart sank. He guessed he'd been rumbled but tried to ride it out.

"Sorry, skipper. I don't know what you mean."

The skipper's face reddened some more, and he walked towards John, grabbing him by his shirt and pulling his face towards his. "I've just had the chief super on the phone, asking why the ACC was onto her, reporting an officer he met today who was in dereliction of his duty."

"Okay, but what has that got to do with me?"

His skipper gave him a shove. "You know fucking well what it's got to do with you. I mean, Robin Jones, for fuck's sake. We don't even have an officer with that name on this LPA. Did you really think you could get away with lying to an ACC?"

John bowed his head. "I… I… didn't think he would even remember me."

"He took your collar number, you stupid arsehole. When the chief super told him we didn't have a Robin Jones, he gave her your number. Needless to say, the boss wasn't happy when she realised you'd lied."

"What happens now?"

"You're suspended. Indefinitely. The Professional Standards boys will be doing an investigation. With all your other problems, John, you're toast. Now fuck off out of here before I stick my size tens up your arse."

John pulled himself away from the grip of his skipper and walked away. As he left the police station, there was only one place he wanted to be.

He bought a train ticket to Reading.

24

"Hello."

Rachel looked up at where the voice had come from, stifling a gasp as she saw who it was.

"I… I…"

"Are you okay?" Abigail said. "You seem really edgy."

Rachel frowned. "Why are you everywhere I go?"

Abigail looked hurt. "My college accommodation is just over there. I was just on my way back to it when I saw you sitting on this bench enjoying the evening sun."

"Oh, sorry."

"It's fine if you want to be left alone. I'm just still feeling a bit guilty about staying over the other night. I thought I was doing the right thing, but I can tell it made you uncomfortable."

Rachel sighed. "No, you were very kind to make sure I was okay, although you're right, I do find it hard to have people in the flat since…"

Abigail sat down next to her as Rachel's sentence finished in a sob. "Ah, the ex, I'm guessing," said Abigail. "Been there, done that."

Rachel composed herself. “Well, sort of. It’s just been a really difficult year.”

“I’m a good listener.”

Rachel huffed. “No, it’s all still a bit raw. I’m not ready to offload to a complete stranger.”

Abigail pouted. “I’m not a complete stranger. I mean, I’ve almost seen you naked.”

Rachel put her face in her hands. “Please stop. I’m mortified that I got in such a state that you felt you had to do that and seeing *you* naked is an image I’m struggling to shake.”

Abigail leant in towards her. “I’m happy to give you another look. Why don’t you come back to my place, and we can see what mischief we can get up to?”

Rachel was sinking into the piercing blue eyes that were fixed on her face, a palpable energy coursed between them. Lust. There was a moment. A moment when Rachel thought she was going to let herself get drawn into the fantasy that was Abigail, but she quickly shook it off.

Rachel pulled away, sucking in air, getting her brain to reset. “I’ve got to go. It was nice to see you again, but I’ve got work tomorrow and I need an early night.”

With that Rachel stood up and walked away, not looking back, avoiding the possibility of getting drawn back in. As she sat on the bus on the way home, the note came back to mind. Who was outside her flat and why had they slipped that note under her door? It wasn’t Abigail. She was at home when she called a few minutes after the note was delivered. It didn’t make sense.

The thought made her shiver, but it reminded her to ring the police officer. He told her to report any new instances so they could build up a picture of the perpetrator. She looked in her bag and found his business card: *PC John Bamford.* She called his number, but it went straight to voicemail.

She got back to the flat without further incident. The lobby was clear, and her flat was how she'd left it. She made herself a hot chocolate and sat on the sofa watching the local news. The Oxford Mystery had been relegated to the third story of the day, the frenzy abating now that the game was down to a few lucky players, some of which were being interviewed about the latest clue and speculating on their chances of winning.

It prompted Rachel to pick up her phone and open the app. She was still in the game, but she had no desire to laud her good luck in the media. She read the end-of-day message again. It was mostly the same type of message, with the hashtag and a promise of more clues to come. But she missed the fact that another letter to the codeword had been given. *You have been awarded the letter Y*, it said.

She read out the letters in her mind, *U, C and Y.*

25

The wheel spun. Red or black. Red or black.

It was black. John pumped the air. Another win. He was up. Back on black. The wheel spun. Black again. "Come on!" he shouted to no one in particular. More on black. Another win.

John looked at the growing pile of chips in front of him. He knew he should quit. He knew he should cash in and walk away. His life had hit rock bottom. As an isolated incident the lie to the ACC would have got him a slap on the wrist but the rest of his growing disciplinary record was not going to help his case. He was sure he was for the boot, meaning money could become even tighter. He needed to cash in.

The waitress bought him a glass of whisky. He downed it in one. Sweat started to form on his brow. His heart began to quicken. *Ladies and gentlemen, place your bets.*

He shoved the whole lot on black. The wheel spun, the ball whizzed around the edge, slowing down, bouncing over the ridges of the numbers. John watched as the ball hopped about as everything seemed to happen in slow motion. The ball landed on a number.

It was red.

*

John lay staring at the featureless concrete ceiling. The thin mattress he was lying on was doing nothing to ease his discomfort. The smell of the metal toilet in the corner of the cell made him gag. He rolled away from it.

As he lay looking at the wall, he knew this was the definition of rock bottom. Why had he carried on gambling? He was ahead. He had actually made some money. He should have cashed in and walked away, but the urge to carry on was overwhelming. All rational thought had left him. It was all about red or black. He was on a roll. Black, black, black. It had to work again.

When the ball landed on red, his world collapsed. He had fleeting memories of what followed. Screaming at the croupier, grabbing at his chips, security bundling him away from the roulette table, a fight with one of the guards and then… the final humiliation. Being arrested by his colleagues.

The isolation and time to think was not helping. He wondered what his mum and dad would say if they could see him in this state. He let out an ironic laugh. It was their fault this all started. His childhood was okay, fairly uneventful as they grafted to put food on the table, proud of their working-class roots. But any reverence and respect he may have had for their part in his upbringing was blown away when he returned from police training college. He wanted to celebrate passing the training and becoming a real police officer, but instead his mother decided to drop a bombshell. The man that he thought was his father, the man that had been there since his birth, was a fraud. He didn't know why they chose that moment to tell him, but his mother admitted to having an affair, resulting in a pregnancy that led to his entry into the world. They discovered that his other *dad* was unable to father children, which is why he knew that his wife had strayed when she fell pregnant. John could never understand his decision to stay with his mother. He hated them both for what they'd done. His mother a cheat. His so-called father a weak, pathetic man. And his genes populated by a faceless bastard who never wanted to know anything about him.

The betrayal ate away at him. He tried to concentrate on being a good police officer, but the pain wouldn't go away. A casino visit with a bunch of friends was all it took. It was the fix he needed. It took him out of himself and eased the pain. The problem was he couldn't control it.

He never bothered to find out who his real father was. It didn't matter. Shutting away the pain was the only way he knew how to deal with it, as his life spiralled into self-destruction.

He wasn't sure exactly how long he'd been in the cell, but he knew being arrested whilst under suspension was going to be the final straw. As he lay wallowing in self-pity, he heard the clink of keys opening the cell door, reluctantly rolling over to see who it was.

John's heart sank. It was his LPA commander, Chief Superintendent Wendy Hawsley. "Come," she instructed. He was led to one of the interview rooms.

As they sat down, he didn't wait to be spoken to. "Am I under arrest?"

The chief super looked at him, barely able to contain her rage. "No."

"So, what's this about?"

She shook her head. "You are a member of my staff, PC Bamford, and when I get a call to say that a serving police officer in my LPA has been arrested, I want to know what the hell is going on. Is that okay with you?"

John shrugged.

"You have just been suspended and now I find you charged with disturbing the peace in a casino. Are you trying to breach every single one of the Professional Standards you signed up to as a serving police officer?"

John shrugged again.

"Your lack of response is not helping your case. If there is something you want to tell me, something that will help your case, I suggest you tell me now."

There was a tense stand-off. John stared at the disapproving face of his top boss. "I've got a gambling problem."

She nodded. "I guessed as much. Your disciplinary record is not great reading, but I could see that your misdemeanours seemed to follow your days off. Why did you not raise this with someone? If not your skipper, why not the welfare team?"

"It's not an easy thing to admit."

"What about your parents? Brothers? Sisters?"

"Only child and I've fallen out with my parents. I haven't spoken to them in years."

She sighed. "I'm sorry to hear that. I can't deny that you are in a whole heap of trouble, and I can't guarantee that you will survive this. It will be up to PSD and HR to decide your fate but, if you show some remorse and get some professional help, there may be a chance."

"I've been to a Gamblers Anonymous meeting."

"That's good, but I guess it didn't stop you last night."

"No. When I was told about your call from the ACC, I knew I was in deep shit. This is how I deal with stuff like this. It numbs the pain. Takes me out of myself."

The chief super suddenly stood up. “Whilst I have some sympathy for your plight, PC Bamford, I am afraid this situation is now out of my hands. I have smoothed this over with the casino and you will not be charged with anything. I hope some time in the cells will have brought you to your senses and that you will continue to seek professional help. You are still on indefinite suspension whilst this latest situation is investigated. I think the chances of you ever pulling on a police uniform again are low, but I hope that whatever happens, you sort yourself out.”

John rubbed his face. He knew she was right.

She walked to the door and stood propping it open. “Come on. Get out of here. You’re free to go.”

John collected his belongings from the custody sergeant, exiting the custody suite as quickly as he could. He didn’t need any more of his colleagues to see him in this state.

He headed for the train station and was relieved when once again one of his credit cards allowed him to buy a ticket.

As he opened his phone, he saw that there was a voicemail message. It was from the girl he’d seen around Oxford a few times, the one with the so-called stalker. She asked him to give her a call, but the realisation that he was going to let her down as well overwhelmed him.

He began to cry.

26

Rachel forced herself away from the ward, dragging Kaley to the coffee shop on the ground floor of the hospital for lunch, desperate to offload about her run-in with Abigail.

"Aha," said Kaley, "so you do like the knife-wielding psycho after all?"

Rachel grimaced. "For crying out loud, don't say that."

"But it doesn't change the fact that when she was offering you a roll in the sack, you considered it, you dirty bitch."

Rachel laughed. "Oh, Kaley, you do have a way with words. Don't ever not be my friend, will you?"

"Course not, babe, you ain't getting rid of me anytime soon, but stop deflecting. Are you gonna shag this girl or not?"

"No! Christ. She was the only one that could have put that knife in my bedroom drawer. The girl's unhinged. I mean, why would someone like her be interested in me anyway? It just doesn't make sense."

Kaley frowned. "Now that right there is why you haven't gotten any for… how long is it now?"

Rachel sighed. "I don't even know."

"Look, I don't know what this Abigail creature is up to, but whether it's her or someone else, you've got to move on."

"I know, but there's something else and you're going to think I'm paranoid."

Kaley smirked. "I'm getting used to sad, mad Rachel. Hit me with it."

Rachel paused for a second, not wanting to say the words out loud. Like in that film *Beetlejuice*, where once the name was said, you couldn't put it back and chaos reigned.

"It's this Oxford Mystery game." Rachel ignored the ever-present sighing from Kaley when the game was mentioned.

"I think I told you that apart from solving the clues on the mystery trail and this weird hashtag, they've been awarding letters to a codeword over the last three days."

"And?" said Kaley impatiently.

"The letters we've been given so far are U, C and Y."

There was a pause. "Is that supposed to mean something to me?" said Kaley.

Rachel rubbed her eyes. "I must be going mad, but what if the next letter is an L?"

Kaley shook her head in frustration. "I'm sorry, babe. Stop talking in riddles. What are you trying to say?"

"The letters. U, C and Y. If you add an L at the beginning, what do you get?"

"Er, well, Lucy." Kaley frowned. "I'm still not following."

"I'm sure I've told you this before. My last serious relationship. Her name was Lucy."

"And this is relevant, why?"

Rachel blew out a breath. "Look, I know this sounds completely barmy, but all this shit with Abigail, the person at my flat door, the note. It all started happening when I began to play this game. And now, the codeword could be spelling out the name of my ex. Someone is playing with my head."

Kaley let out an exasperated scream. "Have you completely lost the plot? You've been given three letters that just happen to be in the name of your ex. You've no guarantee that the next letter is L and, even if it was, there are other words that can be made if more letters are given. Lucky for instance. And if it isn't L, how about juicy or yucca. Also, if you look at it cryptically, could the letters be hiding a phrase?"

Rachel looked confused.

"You, see, why. It could be part of a phrase with other clues to follow."

"Oh, yeah, clever."

Kaley looked at Rachel wide-eyed with frustration. "I mean, do I need to go on?"

Rachel sat staring at the angry face of her friend. After a few seconds, she bowed her head. "Oh, I'm sorry, Kaley. I don't know what's wrong with me. This whole situation has made me jumpy and irrational. Maybe I should stop playing this stupid game."

Kaley's anger hadn't dissipated. "Yes, maybe you should."

They finished their lunch, trying to change the conversation to lighter subjects. As they walked back to the ward, Rachel's phone beeped.

It was the latest clue from the Oxford Mystery. She ignored it and put her phone back in her pocket.

27

John slept until after midday. The mental exhaustion of the last few days had caught up with him and he didn't want to get out of bed. His police shirt was hanging on the handle of his wardrobe. He rolled over, not wanting to be reminded of his failures.

His phone beeped. It was a message from the Oxford Mystery game. The latest clue.

Clue 8: if this mystery trail has you hot and bothered, then the local market has got you covered. Move along the Broad and into Turl, then into the Market where the clue will unfurl. The flags outside will adorn, the date the market was originally born. Enter the date and you will complete, this mystery trail, an amazing feat.

John sat up, reading the clue a few times. He was fairly sure he knew where the clue was directing him to. The realisation he was still in the game and was a step nearer to fifty thousand pounds galvanised him. He did the mechanical things people do: shower, shave, eat. Within an hour, he was stood outside the Covered Market on the high street side, the first line of the clue giving a clear indication that this was the place.

John looked around the entrance, but he couldn't see the flags that were referred to in the clue. He read it again. He suddenly realised that the capitalised words were street names and that by the nature of the game this was a mystery trail. Reference to *the Broad* was referring to Broad Street where the last clue had been solved. He realised that the clue was directing you from the Sheldonian, down Turl Street and then into Market Street.

He couldn't help but get excited, grateful for something good in his life. He'd worked it out. He was on the wrong side of the Covered Market. The clue was directing him to Market Street. He began to walk through the market, the eclectic mix of shops always a fascination to him. He passed the booth offering milkshakes in more flavours than you could imagine, a leather goods shop, several places selling amazing-smelling food, a butcher, a fishmonger, a grocer. He always felt that this was the real beating heart of the city. Not the flashy, in-your-face shops in the Westgate. Just amazing independent businesses earning a crust. His guilt rose. He really wanted to buy something from every shop, but his financial plight would not allow it.

He pushed on and emerged into Market Street. The flags were there, high up on the wall by the entrance to this side of the market. He read the clue again. It asked for *the date the market was originally born*, which indeed adorned the flags. He entered *1774*.

It worked. A message came up congratulating him on completing the mystery trail. For a second, he held his breath. Had he won? Were his financial woes over? Was another message going to come up, congratulating him on his win?

He realised there was a NEXT button at the bottom of the screen. He clicked it and the screen took a second to refresh. He was manically staring at the screen, willing it to confirm his win, but as the next screen finally came up, he was disappointed to see another message.

Enter the codeword to continue the game.

John wasn't sure what to do. The app had a menu item that allowed you to look back at all the previous clues and messages, so he began to scroll back through them. He realised that the last three days' end-of-day messages had given a letter towards the codeword. The three letters were C, U and Y.

His brow furrowed as he concluded that no word could be made out of those three letters. After a moment of frustration, he realised he hadn't looked back at the congratulatory message he had just received. Sure enough, when he read it again, another letter had been awarded. The letter L. He ordered the letters in his mind.

After a few minutes he realised there was only one word it could be.

28

John had stewed all day. For a fleeting second, he thought he'd won the money. He'd solved the final clue and entered the correct codeword. But, as he held his breath, waiting for the thrill of winning, his bubble was burst as the game simply congratulated him on entering the correct answer. Clicking on the NEXT button just brought up another clue.

Clue 9: if you want to be one of the final few, then now it's time to solve this clue:

roses.engine.begins 29/5 17:45

John didn't know what it meant. The words *final few* spurred him on, but as he sat in a pub, drinking a pint of bitter, he became more agitated as the answer eluded him. He'd worked out that the last bit of the clue was a date and time, but given that it was less than twenty-four hours away, the stress of missing out on the money grew. What confused him more was the lack of a dialogue box to enter an answer.

As he thought about buying another pint, his phone rang. It was his Gamblers Anonymous sponsor. As reluctant as John had been to call her, speaking to her about the events of the last couple of days proved to be a relief. He was even more pleased when she said she was just round the corner and would join him for a drink.

They chatted, they laughed, and all the while John felt relieved that he had something else to distract him from gambling. The more time he spent with her the more he realised how cute she was. The job had put paid to any sort of long-term relationship. Soulless sexual encounters had been the order of the day, but this woman seemed different. Maybe it was because she understood his demons. Sponsors were addicts that had been clean for more than a year and, in John's eyes, she was doing a great job.

He wasn't sure whether it was the copious amounts of alcohol they were consuming, but he was falling for her with every pint. He fixed her with a lustful gaze.

"We shouldn't do this," she said.

John feigned surprise. "What?"

Her smile broadened. "I'm supposed to be your sponsor. I'm here to talk you down when the gambling urge overwhelms you. I'm here to empathise and give you ways to cope. I'm not supposed to get romantically involved."

John was conscious his speech was beginning to slur, so he tried to right himself, but his brain seemed disconnected as he blurted out the first thing that came into his head. "We could just have sex. Doesn't mean we have to be romantic."

She laughed. "Does that line work on all your conquests?"

John sighed. "Oh, God, I'm sorry. Just ignore me, I'm just…"

She filled in the gaps. "You're just in a bad place. I know, which is why we need to get you to bed."

John did a wide-eyed grin.

"No, your bed. Not mine."

John shrugged and opened his phone. The Oxford Mystery app was still open.

"Ooh," she said, "are you playing that mystery game? Are you still in it?"

John grunted. "Yeah, seems like I'm one of the few that have got this far but this latest clue has me stumped."

She grabbed the phone and looked at the clue. "Well, that's easy. It's What3words."

"Eh?"

"You know, that What3words initiative where every location has three words attached to it, so you can tell people like emergency services exactly where you are."

"Oh, yeah, how stupid that I didn't see that."

She tapped away on her phone. "It's referring to the car park at Shotover Country Park. I reckon you need to be there at 5.45pm tomorrow."

"Bloody hell," exclaimed John. "Do you think that's where the money will be?"

She shrugged. "Well, there's only one way to find out."

29

Rachel was still shaking. The screeching had subsided now Kaley had dropped everything and was in her flat, holding her close, allowing the hysteria to slowly ebb away.

Eventually, Rachel pulled away from the embrace, her snotty, tear-stained face a picture only a true friend could love. She ignored the pitiful look on Kaley's face.

"You see? I was right. What the hell is going on? Why is Lucy the codeword to this game?" asked Rachel.

Kaley frowned. "Look, it might just be a coincidence. Maybe it's the name of the game organiser. I mean it's quite a common name."

Rachel stared at Kaley, not knowing how to respond. The parcel she'd found when she returned to her flat caught her eye. She grabbed it and unwrapped the ornament.

"How do you explain this?"

Kaley smiled. "Looks like you have a secret admirer."

"No, Kaley. That creepy note was put under my door and now this has turned up. It's not a coincidence."

Kaley put on a serious expression. "Okay, let's say for a minute that I'm prepared to indulge this fantasy of yours. Tell me your theory."

The challenge stumped Rachel for a second. "Um…"

"You see, you're being irrational. You're joining dots that don't need to be joined."

"No, Kaley, the bottom line is that my recent experiences with Abigail coupled with these creepy love tokens are not normal, and now my ex's name appears on some random mystery game."

Kaley shook her head. "Listen to yourself. You just said the mystery game was random. Tens of thousands of people started that game, so why would the codeword being your ex's name be anything other than a coincidence?"

Rachel said nothing, tears welling in her eyes.

Kaley ploughed on. "Now, Abigail apparently leaving a knife in your knicker drawer is weird, but she hasn't done anything since that moment to cause concern. As for these love tokens, as you put it, maybe whoever is lusting after you is a bit shy, and this is their weird way of trying to get your attention."

There was a brief pause before Rachel's demeanour changed. She let out a big sigh, putting her head in her hands.

"Oh God, you're right. I've just realised who this could be."

"Who?"

"You know Lauren, the health care assistant that helps in the recovery ward, she keeps chatting to me at every opportunity. Until you said it, I hadn't really thought about it, but she is incredibly shy, and I think she's into me."

Kaley punched her friend lightly on her arm. "See, you little chick magnet, you've got them falling at your feet."

Rachel poured out the last of the wine and took a big gulp. "I'm sorry, Kaley. What a mess. What can I do to make it up to you?"

Kaley finished her wine in one go. "Hey, nothing, babe. What are friends for if not to be around when their bonkers bestie has a meltdown?"

It was getting late and Kaley went home, leaving Rachel to her own devices. She knew she needed to sleep but instead she navigated to the Oxford Mystery app. The congratulatory message was still there. She realised there was a NEXT button, which she hadn't activated. She didn't waste another second and clicked on the button.

The final clue came up. She smiled and got ready for bed.

30

Walter stirred from another sleep. It was light outside, but he'd lost all sense of time, the incarceration messing with his daily rhythms. The odd thing was he felt so energised. The detox from alcohol was making him feel better every day, and despite the hours being locked up, he was finding an inner calm that he'd never experienced before.

His captor was still acting strangely. He wanted to thank her for forcing him to be clean, but she seemed uninterested in what was happening to him. She'd been a good friend, and he kept thinking this was her way of helping him out, but now she was angry and distracted every time they spoke. She was waiting for something, and for some reason Walter was part of her plan. He'd tried not to think badly of her, but there was a darkness in her that he hadn't seen when they were drinking together.

He got up and started doing some stretches. He'd been exercising at regular intervals to pass the long hours with no human contact. He was feeling fitter. The more he reflected on his imprisonment, the more he realised he had to change his life. When he got out of here, he was going to do it. Sort himself out.

As the positive vibes washed over him, he heard the daily ritual of the key being turned in the lock, which normally indicated food was on the way. The door opened and she stood there, holding a spear.

"Come on, Walter. It's time for you to help me out."

For a second, Walter didn't move.

"Shift it!" she shouted.

"Why? What are you going to do to me?"

She strode into the room, thrusting the spear close to his throat. "I don't have time to discuss this, Walter. Move now or I'll thrust this spear into your windpipe."

Walter leant back from the threat. "Okay, okay, calm down. I'm coming."

He stood up and she guided him out of the door. They turned left down the hallway, passing several other bedrooms. They got to the top of the staircase, descending into the main entrance hall, retracing the steps Walter had taken on his first day.

She told him to turn left at the bottom of the stairs, along the ornate, high-ceilinged corridor, eventually emerging into the large sitting room. The first time he'd been in this room, he was distracted by the shock of seeing her. Now the full grandeur of the place was revealed. The room was filled with antique furniture; a grand piano sat resplendent in the corner. There was a large cocktail cabinet full of decanted spirits over to the right and beautiful summer sun streamed in from the grand floor-to-ceiling windows on the left.

Walter stopped and turned. "Wow, is this all yours?"

She frowned, giving him a painful nudge with the spear. "Yes, it's the family pile, but we don't have time for small talk. Go and sit down in that chair over there."

Walter studied her face. There was something wrong. The dark rings under her eyes, coupled with permanent frown lines and a simmering anger in her tone, were a combination that made him shiver. The girl he knew was not like that, but now she stood glaring at him, hatred in her eyes.

"Come on," he said, desperately trying to reconnect with her, "whatever you're angry about, I'm sure we can sort it out."

She jabbed the spear towards him. "Move!"

"Okay, okay, chill out." Walter moved towards the chair and sat down, staring her down. "What happened to you?"

A dark, evil laugh emanated from her. "Oh, Walter, you're just making it worse. You keep asking that question when you should know the answer."

Walter held his hands up in mock surrender. "So, I'm a fucking idiot. No change there."

They stared at each other. Palpable tension in the air. As Walter watched her face, a sense of dread washed over him.

The last thing he saw was her face etched in fury as she thrust the spear towards him.

31

Rachel hadn't told Kaley about this latest development in the game. She felt a bit guilty. Kaley had been at her beck and call for a while now, but Rachel needed some space. She knew it was unkind, a relationship that was all one way in terms of emotional support, but it couldn't be helped.

The taxi picked her up bang on time and, after a few minutes, they were already close as they drove up the long, steep hill towards the Shotover car park. She scanned the area as they bumped their way up the narrow uneven road. All she saw was the odd person walking their dog. As the taxi reached the brow of the hill, the road levelled out and eventually opened out to a large square car park. She leapt out, paid the taxi driver, and immediately looked around to see if there was anyone else that looked like they might be involved in the game. There were a few cars left in the car park. A couple were being loaded up with dogs and children, but otherwise there wasn't anyone else about. Rachel looked at her watch. It was 5.35pm.

She couldn't help but reflect on how different this was

from the first day playing the game. The thousands of people crowded around Carfax, the noise, the hysteria, all on the promise of winning fifty grand. But now, despite the few people going about their business, she was alone. She pulled her light jacket around her stomach. The summer heat had subsided quickly, and she felt cold.

She thought about ringing a taxi, giving up on the charade, but just as her resolve was beginning to wane, she spotted another taxi driving into the car park. She waited with bated breath. The car door opened and a man got out. He looked shocked when he spotted her.

They walked towards each other. "What are you doing here?" he said.

"Er, I'm playing this mystery game and the latest clue led me here," replied Rachel.

"Huh, me too."

"Sorry, it's John, isn't it?"

"Yes, that's right."

"I tried to call you the other night."

"Oh, yeah, I know. I'm sorry about that, but…"

Rachel waited for him to finish the sentence, but he was gazing off into space.

"Are you okay?"

John shook his head. "No, not really."

Nothing else was forthcoming so Rachel pushed it. "I'm a good listener."

John did a pitiful laugh. "I'm not sure we've got long enough, suffice to say that I've been suspended from my job, which is why I didn't phone you back. I can't help you at the moment."

"Oh, shit, I'm sorry to hear that."

"Don't be sorry. I deserve it. My personal life is an absolute car crash at the moment so I thought I would play this game to get away from all my troubles. Fifty grand would really sort me out."

Rachel huffed. "No shit. I think we could all do with that sort of money."

John grimaced. "Anyway, I feel guilty about not being there for you. Did you have another run-in with the psycho blonde?"

"Sort of, but there has been lots of other weird shit going on and I was getting more and more paranoid that someone was trying to shit me up, especially when the codeword to this game is the name of my ex."

"Oh."

John's reaction crystallised it. He'd tried not to show his scepticism at what she'd said but his body language gave it away. Rachel put her hands to her face. "Oh, God, I know. My friend came round last night and made me realise I was being totally irrational and that there has been a sensible explanation for everything that has been going on. In the end, I did what you did and decided to focus on the game, which now feels like a good plan as we seem to be some of the last people involved."

John looked around the car park. "Yeah, that is odd. I was expecting more people to be here."

"Me too. Do you really think we've been lucky enough to be the final two?"

John's face lit up. "I hope so, then we know at least one of us is going to be rich."

As their optimism grew, a large people carrier drove into the car park and circled behind them. They looked at each other, their minds asking the same question. *Was this for them?*

A few seconds later they got their answer. A man got out and walked towards them. A deep Scottish accent boomed from his mouth. "Are you laddie and lassie here for the Oxford Mystery game?"

Without any thought, Rachel blurted out a response. "Yes, yes, we are."

The guy gave a subtle smirk. He opened the sliding door on the side of the vehicle. "Get in."

John got straight in, but Rachel didn't move. John sat in the vehicle staring back at her. "Are you coming?"

Rachel didn't move, shaking her head. "Are you mad? Didn't your parents ever tell you not to get into cars with strangers?"

John laughed, mockingly. "Are you for real?"

Rachel didn't move. "No," she said, "I can't do it."

Just as John was about to respond, the driver got out of the car and came around to where Rachel was standing. "Look, missy," he said, "this is your only chance to win the money. If you don't get in the car now, the game ends here."

Rachel looked at the driver. "No, I'm sorry. This doesn't feel right."

The driver shrugged. "Okay, but that means you need to get out as well."

"What?" shouted John.

"I'm sorry, laddie, but my instructions are that you both have to get in the car, or none of youse do."

John looked at Rachel. "What the hell are you doing?"

"This is not right, John. Why can't you see that?"

"See what? We've got the chance to win fifty grand and you're standing there having some irrational crisis."

"It's not irrational. How is it possible that we meet up in the midst of all the weird shit that has been happening to me recently and now we are the only ones left in this game? That just doesn't make sense. Something is really off with this situation."

John just huffed, not moving from his seat.

"Come on, lassie," the driver said, "I haven't got all day."

Eventually, Rachel let out a big sigh and got in the car.

32

The mood in the car was tense. John seemed annoyed with Rachel, putting his head against the rest and closing his eyes. Rachel let it go and gazed out of the car window.

The guy drove back down the hill and turned right into the Quarry area of Headington. Towards the end of the road, he took the tight, snaking road that thread its way past beautiful houses, all built with the light-coloured stone that was this area's signature building material. He went past a couple of pubs before he emerged onto the dual carriageway. He traversed the large roundabout heading off on the road towards London.

He drove along the A40, turning off just before it became the M40, taking the road that ultimately led to Thame. He drove along the road, taking the next available right. They were heading for the countryside. Another twenty minutes of driving through roads that became more rural and narrower with each turn, eventually led them to an entrance, with stone pillars on either side of a roadway that stretched as far as the eye could see.

"This is it," Rachel whispered to herself. She looked at John. His eyes were still closed, so she jabbed him in the ribs.

He came to with a jolt. "Uh, what's going on?"

"We're here," Rachel said, a sense of panic creeping into her voice.

"Where's here?" he replied.

"I don't know. Somewhere remote. I don't like it."

John shrugged and looked out of the window. The car made its way along the road, which seemed to go on forever. A small forest lined the road on both sides as squirrels and other assorted wildlife zipped in and out of the trees. After about a mile, the forest gave way to open countryside with fenced-off fields on both sides. It was beautiful but they weren't looking at the views because as the road widened out the sound of gravel crunching under the tyres told them they had reached their destination. The driver stopped the car.

They peered out at the eerie façade of an imposing manor house.

Rachel looked at John. "Now do you believe me?"

"What? This is obviously where we compete to win the money. Come on!"

"Have you not watched any films? Nothing good happens in spooky manor houses."

John got out of the car and looked back at Rachel. "You are properly nuts. There is fifty thousand pounds waiting for one of us behind those doors and you're having a Scooby Doo moment."

Rachel jumped out of the car. "Stuff you, John."

The simmering tension was broken by the car driving away. They looked at each other and back at the entrance door. John began to walk towards it without a word. Rachel was still seething but followed.

They opened the large door to the manor house, going through a small entrance lobby before emerging into the grand entrance hall, their footsteps echoing off the marble floors. They marvelled at the scene. A wide, sweeping carpeted staircase was right in front of them. To their immediate left was a large closed door. To their right was a long corridor, which seemed to have rooms feeding off it on both sides. At the end of the corridor, they could just make out the light of another room.

John immediately tried the door to the left. It was locked. He made for the stairs. "Come on. Let's explore."

Rachel watched as he bound up the wide stairs. She followed, reluctantly. As he reached the top of the stairs, John had stopped, staring down the corridor. "What is it?" whispered Rachel.

"I… I'm sure I just saw someone, go into that room at the end of the corridor."

As John continued to stare, Rachel bundled past him. "What are you doing?" he said.

"I'm tired of this already. If someone is playing games with us, I'm going to bloody well find out what is going on."

John shrugged his shoulders and began to follow Rachel down the corridor. As they reached the last door on the right, Rachel immediately tried the handle. Locked. She put her ear to the door. "I'm sure I can hear someone in there." She started to bang on the door. "Open up. If there's someone in there, stop pissing about. We've solved your stupid hide-and-seek game."

They strained to listen for any response. They waited. There was nothing.

They stood there for a few more minutes but nothing changed. Rachel grunted and started back down the corridor, trying every door as she passed. They were all locked.

Rachel went back to the top of the staircase, stopping suddenly as she heard music coming from down the corridor. John moved past her. "I guess we go this way then. Follow the music."

They got to the bottom of the stairs and began to walk along the corridor, passing three more locked doors. Two on the left and one on the right. They continued with an increasing sense of unease at every step.

They carried on to the end of the corridor, which opened out to a large, well-lit room adorned with numerous pieces of furniture. But any feelings of awe they may have been experiencing were replaced by the distraction of what was in front of them.

Rachel's screams could have woken the dead.

33

John rushed towards the body, instinctively putting his fingers to the man's neck to check for a pulse. He didn't expect anything, given the man had a six-foot spear embedded in his chest.

John realised that Rachel was standing just behind him, her hand to her mouth stifling further screams as tears of horror streamed down her face. He looked back at her. "I think we've found Walter."

"What?" she replied, meekly.

John stood to one side to reveal the full horror of the scene. In his lap was a piece of paper, with one word on it.

#whereswalter

Rachel began to pace the room. "Jesus, I fucking told you this was all wrong. Why didn't you believe me?"

John ignored her. "We need to call the police."

"You are the police!"

"I… I can't deal with this."

John pulled his phone out of his pocket but just as he was about to dial, they heard a commotion outside. The sound of sirens was followed by the crunch of gravel as several vehicles arrived outside the house.

They hardly had time to react before they heard boots pounding down the corridor and men shouting instructions. Within seconds the room had filled with armed police officers, pointing their weapons at Rachel and John.

"Get down on the floor. Arms behind your head."

John immediately complied but Rachel stood, frozen in fear. "What… what the hell is going on?"

The officer repeated the command.

"We've done nothing wrong. We've just found—"

The officer interrupted her pleas and repeated the command, closing the gap between them.

Shaking with fear, she eventually complied, wincing as an officer grabbed her arms and handcuffed her. He pulled her up to a standing position as John was being manhandled in the same way. Despite her shock, Rachel was not about to let it go.

"What the hell are you doing? We're playing this mystery game and have just been delivered here. We don't know anything about this man. He was dead when we got here."

"Shut up, Rachel," shouted John. "Don't say another word."

Rachel glared at John as he bowed his head, resigned to whatever fate awaited them. Just as she was about to protest further, the officer who'd been aiming a gun at her started to read them their rights.

Rachel felt like she was having an out-of-body experience. The words he was saying didn't make sense… *arrested, murder, anything you do say may be used against you…* like she was in some bad cop film. She started to scream at them but all that did was hasten their departure from the manor house, as they got ceremoniously bundled into a custody van. John wouldn't look at her. Her screams intensified but everyone just got on with their jobs and ignored her.

She was bundled into a seat at the back of the van, with John on the other side. Two officers sat with them, still locked and loaded like they were escorting a couple of major terrorists. Rachel's breathing became laboured. As the van began to drive away, she gasped for breath.

Her world went black.

34

Clank.

Rachel's brain tried to process what the noise was.

Clank.

Was this a dream? She had her eyes closed. Horrible images flashed in her head. A nightmare. An involuntary shudder brought her further back to reality. She frowned and opened her eyes.

Clank.

This time the noise bolted her fully awake. She tried to raise her right arm.

Clank.

The full horror of what happened came streaming back. It hadn't been a nightmare in her sleep, one that could be shaken off as her overactive brain made her sleeping hours adventurous and a little bit dangerous. No, this was a real nightmare. Rachel was handcuffed to a hospital bed.

As she tried to regain full cognisance of her surroundings, the soothing tones of a nurse were accompanied by a short examination.

"What is this? What's going on?" she pleaded to the nurse. Her questions were ignored.

When the nurse left, a man in a smart suit came into the room.

"Miss Keen, do you remember what happened?"

"Who are you?"

"I'm Detective Inspector Yin and I should remind you that you have been arrested on suspicion of the murder of Walter Cribbens."

Rachel's head was still woozy, but she wasn't about to let that stop her. "You what? I had nothing to do with that guy's murder!"

"I should advise you that you are still under caution and that anything you say now can be used in evidence against you."

"Good, because you've got it all wrong. We were playing the Oxford Mystery, and a taxi brought us to that house as the next stage of the game. We found that body a few minutes before you arrived."

"Miss, I am simply trying to establish that you are aware that you are under arrest for murder. As soon as the doctors discharge you, you'll be taken to the custody suite in Abingdon, where you will be retained and interviewed in the morning. I suggest you get some legal representation. I can supervise your one phone call before I leave."

*

Kaley turned on the local news as she sipped her cup of pre-bed cocoa. She was looking forward to a day off, a lie-in followed by a good old fry-up. The national weather forecast was still on, promising more erratic summer weather.

She sipped at the steaming cup, fighting the urge to nod

off. As the intro music for the local news started, she tried to focus, keen to see what was going on. The headline story almost made her spill her drink.

There has been a significant and disturbing development in the Oxford Mystery game. The craze that gripped the county recently appeared to have fizzled out with the few remaining players seemingly reluctant to make themselves known publicly. But, in a shocking development, the police have issued a press release stating that they have found the body of Walter Cribbens in a manor house, deep in the Oxfordshire countryside, the man at the centre of the #whereswalter. Police state they've arrested a thirty-two-year-old woman and a twenty-six-year-old man on suspicion of murder. They were arrested at the scene of the crime. We'll bring you more on this story as we get it.

Kaley immediately grabbed her phone. She realised she hadn't seen Rachel as their shift ended. They'd often leave together, heading for the bus stops, but today she was nowhere to be seen. Kaley checked her messages. Nothing from Rachel. She glanced back up at the TV screen, but the newsreader had moved onto another story.

A thirty-two-year-old woman. Kaley couldn't fathom it. Rachel was still playing that stupid game, and she was thirty-two. That had to be a coincidence. Kaley shook it off. If Rachel had been messaged about another step in the game, she would have told her. Wouldn't she?

Kaley cocked her head to one side. Rachel didn't know anyone called Walter so why would she be accused of killing this missing dude? She shook her head. It couldn't be. There would be some other explanation.

She navigated to her contacts, jumping out of her skin

as her ringtone began just as she was about to phone Rachel, who was now calling her.

"Babe," Kaley beamed, "I was worried about you. Have you seen the news?"

"Kaley, just listen. I'm in real trouble."

35

John lay on the barely adequate mattress in a police cell at the Abingdon custody suite. Déjà vu. This one smelt better than the one he'd just been in at Reading Police Station, but the starkness of the walls and the CCTV camera in the corner of the room reminded him how far he'd fallen.

He'd been checked in by a custody sergeant he knew, the pitiful looks he'd received not helping his mental state. Other officers he knew had been hovering around the station, as he became a sideshow. He'd said nothing once his rights had been read. He knew enough about the system to know that it was better to wait for legal representation. He had no one he could call, certainly not his parents, so he took up the offer of having a solicitor appointed for him. He was due to be interviewed in the morning.

He tried to readjust his aching spine as he stared up at the ceiling. Being arrested a second time in three days, whilst under suspension, was another nail in his coffin. But murder? No. What on earth had just happened? How had a large squad of armed police turned up the minute they discovered the body? It was a classic set-up, but he had no credit with his police colleagues. He was a scumbag in their eyes. A failed officer who had no self-control. He could imagine their accusations. A corrupt cop who turned to murder to fund his gambling habit.

He put his hands over his eyes, stifling back tears. He knew he was innocent, but there would be no one on his side. The door to his cell suddenly opened and one of the custody officers left him a tray of food and a bottle of water. He didn't want anything but forced a bite of a limp sandwich and guzzled half of the water.

He shook off the self-pity, as his emotions switched to pure anger. He was an addict, but he wasn't a murderer. What possible evidence could they have when he and Rachel had barely been in that house for five minutes? He pondered what had been happening to her. Some of what she said had sounded odd. The knife in the drawer, in particular, was not the action of a sane individual, and he had seen the girl she was worried about acting strangely that day in the high street. Could that be it? Was this all about Rachel and he was caught in the crossfire?

The more he thought about it the more confident he became. The duty solicitor would have him out of here by lunchtime. There wasn't a single thing they could pin on him. He was sure of it. If his brief association with Rachel was at the heart of this problem, he could explain that away in seconds. He'd taken her statement. Colleagues would be able to see that he was merely doing his job and the fact they had both got to the final stages of the Oxford Mystery game was pure coincidence.

He felt more settled and lay down, trying to make the best of a bad situation. He would be alright.

*

John was woken at 8am, with another tray of food that purported to be breakfast. The custody sergeant informed him that the duty solicitor was due in at 8.30am before his formal interview at 9am.

The meeting with the solicitor was functional. He agreed with John's assertion that his arrest was flaky at best. At 9am, he was sat in an interview room with DCI Yin and DS Baxter, officers he vaguely knew from the local policing area CID team.

Yin repeated the charges for the recording. John confirmed he understood. Questions were asked. *How did he know Rachel Keen? Why were they at the manor house? Why did they kill Walter? How much money had he gambled away?*

John initially took his solicitor's advice and said the bare minimum, denying any charges and generally being difficult but, after half an hour of going over and over the same questions, he lost his rag, garnering a disapproving look from his solicitor.

"Look, I'm a serving police officer and should be treated with more respect. You have no evidence to convict me of anything. Why don't you examine what that woman is up to? She's already reported concerns about her safety, and if anyone is deep in this shit, it's her. And explain how a squad of armed officers got to that house minutes after we arrived. Who made the call to justify that response? It's a set-up. Can't you see that? We were taken to that house by a taxi, having got to the latter stages of this mystery game. Find that driver and he will confirm that we had no idea where we were going, so how can we be accused of premeditated murder? That guy was dead when we walked in that room and I bet the ME will tell you that he'd been dead well before we got there, so why don't you get your facts right before accusing me of murder?"

The rant seemed to work. There was silence as the two officers just stared at him. Eventually, Yin closed his notebook and stood up.

"We are verifying the validity of all the evidence, Mr Bamford, but I am satisfied that you are not a flight risk, so you will be bailed until we complete our investigations. I don't need to remind you that you are suspended from duty, so please do not attempt to make contact with any serving officers. The LPA commander has informed me that she will be in touch to check on your welfare, but the only other contact you will have with the police will be with me or DS Baxter here. We will contact your solicitor if we need to interview you again."

John looked at his solicitor, who nodded his agreement. He fixed Yin with a fierce stare. "Please don't hesitate to interview me as many times as you want, because I'm innocent. I'll look forward to making a complaint to the Professional Standards Department about your incompetence and the wrongful arrest."

The solicitor put his hand on John's arm, trying to persuade him to move out of the room.

John got processed out of custody without another word.

He stood outside Abingdon Police Station, appreciating the feel of the sun on his face. His anger simmered.

He was going to find out what the hell was going on.

36

Rachel sat in the interview, arms crossed, staring at the ceiling. The police officers were introducing themselves, but their words were not registering. The solicitor Kaley had organised was sat next to Rachel, looking serious and professional, but at that point she could have been anyone.

Rachel tried to focus, subconsciously gripping her stomach as it churned away. The officer started talking, but she just changed her focus from the ceiling to the wall over the officer's shoulder. The only thing she was thinking about was how they thought they could pin a murder charge on her.

She was conscious that the officer was repeating the questions and that her solicitor was intervening when Rachel didn't answer. Eventually, Rachel started talking without any cognisance of what questions he'd been asking her.

"Can you explain to me how a bunch of armed officers turned up at that manor house the minute we found that body?"

She looked at the officer's face, realising that it was the same guy who had seen her in the custody cell the previous evening. He didn't look happy. "I asked you a question, Miss Keen."

Rachel frowned. "I don't care. Answer my question."

She noticed a glance between the two officers and the semblance of a smirk on her solicitor's face. There was a brief pause, followed by a sigh from the lead officer.

"We had a call that there had been a murder at that property."

Rachel gasped. "There was someone in the house when I was being driven away. Did you speak to them? Did they make the call?"

She noticed the glance again.

"Miss Keen, there was nobody at the house."

"What? You are joking. As we drove away there was a figure silhouetted in one of the bedroom windows."

"I can assure you we searched that house from top to bottom. There was no one there."

"Are you calling me a liar?"

"Er, no, but maybe you imagined it. You were probably quite stressed at the turn of events and the mind can do strange things under those circumstances."

Rachel leant forward, resulting in her solicitor placing her hand on her arm, which she ignored. "Oh, so you're a fucking quack now."

"Please mind your language, Miss Keen. We are not here to be abused just for doing our job."

Rachel leant back, letting out an exasperated scream. "Doing your job. Ha! I did not imagine that person. It's obvious they were behind whatever shit is going on here. Don't you see that this is a total set-up and for some reason it's linked to that stupid Oxford Mystery game?"

The officer sighed again. "Okay, Miss Keen, I'll indulge you. Tell me your theory."

Rachel paused for a second, wrong-footed by the change of direction. "Er, well, I've been playing this mystery game like most of the population of Oxfordshire and have been lucky enough to be one of the few people that has got to the latter stages. The last clue directed us to Shotover car park, where we were picked up by a taxi and taken to the manor house. We had no idea where we were being taken."

"When you say we, I assume you are referring to Mr Bamford?"

Rachel frowned. "Yes, if Mr Bamford is the guy I knew as John."

"Yes, a police officer currently on suspension. How well did you know him?"

"Hardly at all. He took a statement from me about some strange things that had been happening with a girl I met but otherwise we were both surprised when we met again in the car park."

"Really. Can you explain why you had his personal phone number?"

Rachel couldn't believe it. Their questions were going in a bad direction. Accusatory, like they had something on her. She tried to ignore it.

"If you bothered to read my statement you will have seen that the girl in question left a knife in my knicker drawer."

"We did bother to read it, and it seems as though she was in your flat voluntarily, looking after you due to severe drunkenness."

Rachel was steaming but responded through gritted

teeth. “That’s not how it was, and John gave me his number so I could ring him anytime I was scared. That woman was strange, and I was frightened of what she might do.”

“It’s not standard police procedure to give out personal phone numbers, which suggests he saw you as a friend.”

“So, what difference does that make?”

“Stop leading my client to incriminate herself.” Rachel shot a look at her solicitor, confused by the intervention. The solicitor carried on. “Please stop this line of questioning, Chief Inspector. You are trying to suggest that my client and Mr Bamford were somehow in cahoots for this murder when it’s clear they hardly knew each other.”

The DCI leant back in his chair, pausing for dramatic effect.

“Okay, let’s get to the meat of this issue. Can you explain how your fingerprints are on the murder weapon?”

Rachel felt light-headed and put her hand on the desk to steady herself. “That’s… that’s impossible.”

“We have a clear set of your prints around the handle of the spear that killed Mr Cribbens.”

Rachel looked at her solicitor, tears not far away. Her solicitor advised her to say nothing. There was a stand-off before the DCI squinted in concentration and pulled out an evidence bag.

“Okay, it’s noted that you refused to answer the questions about the fingerprints, so can you explain how this item was around the victim’s neck?”

Rachel slumped in her chair. All the fight had gone. The item was one of her favourite possessions.

37

A silk scarf. It was hers.

Rachel realised the DCI's eyes were boring into her. "Miss Keen. Can you explain why your scarf was found on the victim?"

For a second, Rachel thought she could ride it out. "How do you know it's mine?"

The DCI sighed again. "It's covered in your DNA."

"Oh."

"So, once again, please explain how this came to be around the victim's neck."

Rachel leant forward, less threatening this time, trying to close the space between them in an attempt to improve the intimacy of the conversation. "Look, that is my scarf, but it was taken by my ex when we split up. I've not seen it for ages."

"What's her name? Your ex."

"Lucy. Lucy Beaufort."

"Beaufort!" the DCI exclaimed.

"Yes, is that significant?"

The DCI looked at his DS. "Er, well, the manor house

is the Beaufort family home. It's apparently been in their family for over three hundred years, but the place appears to have been empty for a while and we can't find any members of the family to help us with our enquiries. Do you happen to have contact details for Lucy?"

Rachel's voice began to crack. "Er, I'm afraid not. Lucy is dead. She committed suicide six months ago."

The DCI leant forward. "Are you trying to tell me that despite dating one of the family, you have never been to that house?"

"No, never. She lived in a flat in Oxford and we spent most of our time around the city. She never once mentioned that her family had a massive country pile."

The DCI frowned. "I'm finding that hard to believe. We find you in the family home of your ex, next to a dead body that has your scarf wrapped around its neck and your fingerprints on the murder weapon. I'd say that was an open and shut case. Wouldn't you?"

"But I didn't do it. We were taken to that house as part of the Oxford Mystery game. We didn't know where we were being taken and that was the first time I set foot in the place."

"It still doesn't explain the scarf or how your fingerprints are on the murder weapon."

Rachel was close to tears. "Someone's setting me up. Can't you see that? I don't know how or why, but ever since I started playing this game, weird things have been happening. All the stuff with this Abigail person, I've had weird love notes sent to my home and now I've been lured into some trap with a freaking dead body. I mean, you can't make this shit up."

The DCI frowned. "All very noble, Miss Keen, but maybe there's a simple explanation. You killed Walter Cribbens. Plain and simple. Someone saw you going into the house to commit murder and called us. We find you at the murder scene with forensic evidence all over the victim. Case closed."

Rachel slumped down in her chair. "I'm done. You're clearly not prepared to accept my side of the story so I'm not saying another word. You will not be able to convict me on the evidence you have so go for your life. I'll see you in court."

The DCI stopped the recording and stood up. "You will be retained in custody until we have completed our initial investigations."

Rachel watched as the two officers left the room, wincing at the pain coursing through her head. The stress was too much. She couldn't spend another night incarcerated in this horrible place. She looked at her solicitor. "Why won't they let me go?"

The solicitor tried a sympathetic smile. "They think they've got a serious case here and are quite entitled to retain you until they decide whether to formally charge you. But don't worry, I'm working on getting you out on bail. Just be patient."

"I'm sorry," said Rachel.

"What for?"

"I said too much."

"No, you did okay, although try not to swear at police officers as that doesn't really help."

"Sorry."

"Stop apologising. Despite the fingerprints and the

scarf, their case is flaky at best. We've not seen the ME report yet, which will be critical at establishing a time of death. If what you say is right, that body must have been there for a while before you got there, meaning the timeline will be in your favour. Also, the fact you didn't know where you were being taken by that taxi means they will find it hard to prove premeditated murder."

"But how are my fingerprints on the murder weapon when I didn't touch it?"

"I don't know. Can you think of any way that someone could have got hold of your fingerprints? With a bit of basic forensic knowledge, it's quite easy to lift a fingerprint off a glass or something similar and place it somewhere else."

Rachel put her head in her hands. "No, no, no!"

"You have something."

"Abigail. It's got to be her. She was in my flat overnight. Who knows what she did when I was comatose?"

"Okay, good, when it comes to it, we'll subpoena her to attend court."

"And the scarf. How has someone got hold of that, when my ex is dead?"

"Did she have any siblings?"

"No, she said she was an only child. I know her mum passed away some time ago, but I thought her dad was still alive."

"Hmm, this is all very odd, and we are going to need to look into this scarf issue. I'm tending to agree with you that this mystery game is not all it seems. There are too many coincidences for my liking, and I can see some credibility to your theory that everything that's been happening to you is somehow linked."

Their deliberations were interrupted by the custody sergeant. Their time was up, and Rachel was bundled back into a cell.

She lay on the bed and shut her eyes. All she could think about was Lucy.

38

DCI Yin and DS Baxter sat in the CID office, drinking coffee, the caffeine hit perking them both up.

"What did you make of that?" Yin said.

"Well, she's a feisty one, I'll give her that, but I reckon it's all bluster to try and deflect from her guilt. I mean, we have her at the crime scene, with links to the family that own that house and forensic evidence on the body. What else do we need?"

Yin frowned. "I wouldn't be so confident, Sergeant. It still doesn't really explain why she killed a random stranger, and the point she and Bamford made about not knowing where they were being taken is a problem for us to prove premeditation."

"Hmm, we are struggling to find that taxi driver. So far, the team haven't been able to find a cab firm that picked anyone up from Shotover car park."

Yin frowned. "Keep the team on that. It's vital evidence either way. What about the woman that called it in?"

Baxter huffed. "Same problem. All we have is the 999 call. There was no one else at the property when the armed response team arrived, and the house is miles away from any other dwellings."

"But she said on the call that she saw our two suspects going in the house with a gun and a spear?"

"Yes."

"So, where's the gun?"

"Hey, guv, sounds like you are trying to plead a case for the defence."

"Not at all, Sergeant, but if we can't close these loopholes, we are not going to be able to charge either of them; our case is going to fall at the first hurdle."

"Okay, guv, I'll go and get the team to double their efforts."

With that Baxter left, leaving Yin staring at the case file. He wasn't about to let a killer go free, but there was something odd about the scenario. The pieces didn't fit together, and he was worried that he was going to have egg on his face. He knew they had done the right thing in arresting the pair, but his initial optimism that they had a solid case was waning rapidly.

He was just about to refill his coffee cup when an email pinged into his inbox. It was the ME report. He took a second. This could be it. This could be the one piece of evidence that proved or disproved his case.

As he began to read the report, his heart sank. The ME was unequivocal in his conclusion. Walter Cribbens had been dead long before Keen and Bamford got there.

He put his head in his hands. The suspects had been right. On the face of it, this looked like a classic set-up, but the execution was clumsy. Surely anyone trying to get the suspects in the frame for this would have known the time of death would not stack up.

He reread Rachel Keen's statement. At the time the ME estimated the murder took place, she was at work. This had been verified by his team. John Bamford's alibi for that time was not verified as he'd been home alone.

In his desperation to find some way out of this, Yin began to ponder whether Bamford had been to the house to kill the guy earlier in the day and then played the part of a finalist in the mystery game. He'd met Keen, so could he have planted the fingerprints? Yin didn't know every aspect of Bamford's fall into disgrace, but he'd clearly done enough bad things to get suspended. Maybe plotting an elaborate murder was just another bad judgement on his part. A rotten cop to the core.

He read the ME's report a couple more times, cursing as he finished the final read-through. He had no choice. He would not be able to charge them at this point. They needed more time to investigate the anomalies because, at the moment, they did not have a case that the CPS would support.

He messaged Baxter to get the team together. Next, he made two phone calls that he didn't want to make, to Keen's and Bamford's solicitors. They were now officially bailed until they could complete further investigations and would not be charged at this juncture.

The last thing he did before his team streamed back into his office was to message the custody sergeant to let Rachel Keen go.

It hadn't been a good day.

39

Rachel's heart was racing as she listened to what the custody sergeant was saying. They were letting her go.

"You're… you're not joking," she said, her voice wobbling with emotion.

"No, madam, you are free to go. DCI Yin will be in touch with your solicitor if he needs to speak to you again."

"Am I in the clear?"

"No, madam. You are being bailed to allow the officers to complete their investigation. If they feel they have a case against you, they will be in contact, and you will need to attend court to enter a plea against the charges. Your solicitor will be able to explain this to you in a bit more depth."

Rachel left the station in a daze. She felt dirty and desperately wanted to get out of the clothes she was in. They felt somehow tainted by her time in the cells, and she wasn't sure she could wear them again. It was early afternoon, but she needed a shower and a large glass of wine.

She phoned Kaley.

Within a few hours, Kaley had brought her back to her flat. She'd showered, changed her clothes and made good inroads into a bottle of white wine.

Rachel tried not to be mean to Kaley, but she couldn't help but lace her next comment with an accusatory tone. "Now do you believe me?"

Kaley grimaced. "Alright, alright, so it looks like your psycho stalker bitch is exactly what you thought she was."

Rachel refilled her glass. "I'm sorry, Kaley, but what if they charge me with murder? I can't go to jail."

Kaley grabbed her hand. "Look, babe, from what you said, the evidence won't stack up. That body was there before you found it and you had no idea where you were being taken so they can't prove premeditated murder."

"But my fingerprints and scarf. I mean, how fucked up is that?"

Kaley blew out a breath. "It must have been Abigail that got your prints when you were out of it. It's the only explanation."

Rachel shook her head. "But why? What have I done to that girl? I've never met her in my life."

"Are you sure? If you think this is somehow connected to your ex, was she part of the social circles you two moved in?"

Rachel put her head back. "Oh God, I don't know. I'm sure we've never met."

Kaley tried a sympathetic smile. "What about this scarf?"

"I'm fairly sure my ex took it when we split up. She knew I loved it, so I'm certain she took it to upset me."

"But she's dead. How did that scarf end up on a body in her family mansion?"

Rachel shook her head. "I have no idea. For some reason, I'm being set up and, at the moment, Abigail is the only lead we have. We need to find her and get her to tell us what is going on."

"Don't you think you should leave that to the police?"

"You are joking! They are trying to convict me of murder. They are hardly going to work to prove my innocence."

Kaley threw her hands up in mock surrender. "Okay, Miss Marple. Your call."

As Rachel drank her wine, Kaley noticed the note that had been shoved under her door was still there. "What about this?" she said. "Do you think this is connected and not from your pretty little work buddy?"

Rachel glanced at the note. "Who the hell knows? I don't know which way's up at the moment."

As they fell silent, the wine working to numb the stress, Rachel's phone rang. She listened to the person on the other end without a word, disconnecting the call after about a minute. She threw the phone down and stared into space.

"What is it, babe?" exclaimed Kaley.

"That was the boss. I've been suspended. Seems as though having a suspected murderer dealing with patients isn't a good look."

"Oh, babe, I'm sorry. That's so fucked up."

Rachel sighed. "I'm done. I just need to sleep. If I'm going to prove my innocence to every bastard that's doubting me, I need to rest and be ready for the fight tomorrow."

Kaley took the hint and left, giving her friend a huge hug that she hoped would sustain her overnight. Rachel began to get ready for bed, but progress was interrupted by her phone ringing again.

She answered it.

"Rachel, it's John. We need to talk."

40

Mid-morning. The sun was shining; the birds were chirping away; but John and Rachel sat sipping their drinks on the top floor of the Westgate, oblivious of everything as they tried to process what the hell was going on. The dark rings under both their eyes were a sign that sleep had been at a premium over the last couple of nights.

"I don't appreciate being drawn into your drama," said John, accusingly.

"You what?" exclaimed Rachel. "Why do you think this is all about me?"

"Well, it isn't about me. My life might be an absolute car crash at the moment, but I'm no murderer."

"Nor am I!" The volume of Rachel's voice garnered some furtive looks from passers-by.

"Look," said Rachel, softening her tone, conscious that she needed someone in her corner, "I have no idea what is going on here, but we need to work together if we are going to sort this out."

John frowned. "That is why I called you."

Rachel tried not to get riled by John's bolshiness, taking a moment before speaking again.

"Right, let's start again. I'm sorry if this is anything to do with me, but we are both in the shit, regardless of why."

John nodded, a pained smile appearing on his face.

"Honestly, if I think too much about the fact that I have a murder charge hanging over my head, I might just lose the plot, so I need to focus on something."

John leant forward. "Okay, I agree. I'm in deep trouble already. I've been suspended from my job because I have a gambling addiction. I lied to one of my bosses and got arrested for affray in a casino in Reading. A conspiracy to murder charge might just be the final nail in my coffin, so yeah, I'm with you, otherwise I might just throw myself off the nearest bridge."

There was a pause.

John frowned. "Sorry, did I say something wrong?"

Rachel blew out a breath. "No, not really, but please don't talk about suicide."

"Why?"

"I know I'm being paranoid, but I'm sure what has been going on is something to do with my ex. She committed suicide six months after we split, and I can't help but feel a bit responsible. Our split was bitter and horrible."

"Huh, so who might still be holding a grudge against you for her death? Did she have any family?"

"No, I don't think so. As far as I know she was an only child. Her mum definitely passed away, but I think her father is still around."

"Have you met him? Is he the sort of man that would do this?"

"No idea. I never met him and, until yesterday, I didn't know that the manor house we were lured to was her family pile."

John's ever-present frown seemed to deepen further. "You what? Are you trying to tell me that you're connected to that house?"

Rachel wasn't sure she liked his tone but moved past it. "Well, yeah, I guess."

"Holy shit. That's not good."

"You figure. How about my fingerprints being on the murder weapon and my scarf being round the dead guy's neck?"

John's mouth fell open; his face dropped. "Jesus Christ. That DCI must think all his Christmases have come at once. Evidence stacked up against you and a corrupt cop in tow. Fuck! You can't make this shit up."

Rachel grimaced. "I know and, as I stewed in that cell, I didn't think I'd see the light of day, but they can't place us at the scene when the murder was committed."

John rubbed his face. "They can't place you there because I guess you were at work, but I have no alibi. I was at home, sleeping off a hangover."

Rachel reached over and grabbed John's hand. "Look, I've been to hell and back in the last forty-eight hours, but my friend made me realise that the only way to deal with this is to prove we are innocent. We weren't there. We didn't kill him, and we didn't know where we were being taken when we got to Shotover. We just need to knock down a few more hurdles and then we can focus on who the hell is behind this."

John gave a brief smile. "Okay, Sherlock. Where do we begin?"

41

DCI Yin was hauled into the chief superintendent's office. She was a worrying shade of red.

"What on earth is going on?" she shouted. "We've got the press going nuclear about this murder and now I find out that you've released our two main suspects. They're demanding to know what we are doing to protect the public against these so-called murderers, alongside every conspiracy theory under the sun about this mystery game. People are freaking out that they played a game that meant they could have ended up as a corpse and are branding that *#whereswalter* as one of the sickest things anyone could do. They want to know why we haven't tracked down the nutter that has been running this game."

Yin didn't respond, not sure whether her rant had finished.

"Well?" she shouted.

Yin steeled himself. "I'm sorry, ma'am. I know this is a mess, but we couldn't keep them in custody, as a key piece of evidence came in that meant they almost certainly weren't at the scene when the guy was killed."

"What evidence?"

"The medical examiner's report said the guy had been dead at least eight hours. Miss Keen was at work and Mr Bamford was at home, although he doesn't have anyone that can corroborate that."

She shook her head. "What is John doing getting mixed up in this? When I hauled him out of that cell in Reading, I thought he would keep a low profile, but now I find him facing a conspiracy to murder charge. He must have breached half the list of Professional Standards with all his antics over the last few months."

"For what it's worth, ma'am, I don't actually think either of them are involved. This does look like a classic set-up. We arrested them both because we had an apparent eyewitness who saw them going into the house with a spear and a gun. When the armed response officers attended the scene, they did what any sensible officer would do and detained them. When the crime scene people found her fingerprints on the weapon and a scarf tied around the neck of the victim with her DNA on, we thought we had a strong case. However, the medical examiner's report and the fact they both claim they were playing that game, having no idea where they were being taken, seems to work in their favour. We simply don't yet have a case that the CPS will support."

The chief super sighed. "What about this mystery game? Are we sure it was part of this apparent set-up, and why haven't we been able to track down who is running it?"

"It does seem likely that it is squarely part of this conspiracy. All attempts to track the person running this game have failed. Our tech experts have been unable to trace them online. They clearly know a lot about cyber security as they've been bouncing their IP address across multiple countries. We're still trying, but I can't guarantee that we will find them."

The chief super's face had turned back to its normal colour, but Yin could sense her anger was still simmering.

"Look, ma'am, we've put a large team together and are chasing down several leads. As well as trying to find the person running this game, we are trying to locate the person that made the 999 call, the taxi driver that took them to the house and the owners of the manor house. We are also taking a deep dive into the private lives of Miss Keen, Mr Bamford and the murder victim. If they are guilty, we will find the evidence to bring them to justice. I promise you."

She cocked her head. "Promises. Huh. I hope your optimism is well placed, Chief Inspector, because at the moment we are looking like incompetent fools."

There was a brief silence, which told Yin the meeting was over. He stood up, hoping he wasn't showing signs of disrespect. She ignored him and began to tap away on her laptop. As he walked out the door, she shouted after him, "Find me something quickly, DCI Yin. I don't want to do a press conference looking like an idiot."

Yin walked away. He needed a break in the case. Now.

42

"Let's start with this mystery game," said Rachel. "Is there any evidence to suggest that there are other people still playing it?"

John and Rachel scrolled through various online news feeds but found nothing other than the stories about their arrest.

"This is so upsetting," Rachel said as she read one of the local news items. "How have they found out that I'm a nurse and you're a copper? That wasn't released by the police. Was it?"

"No, but these bloody journalists have contacts all over the place. I wouldn't be surprised if it was one of my colleagues that leaked it. At least our names aren't mentioned."

Rachel stared at John, not convinced that was really something positive in their current predicament. She reset.

"Okay, so it doesn't look like the game is continuing, adding fuel to my theory that the game has somehow been an elaborate set-up."

"Go on."

"Now, I know this seems ridiculous, but let's assume that the game was set up to lure me into a trap, being caught with that poor man's body and incriminating evidence all over him. That means that whoever is behind this started the game as a smokescreen, knowing that the promise of fifty thousand pounds would get people interested. The trail was a nice touch, getting people obsessed with solving each clue, adding to the theatre of the thing. But the critical clue that this was not all it seemed was when thousands of people were suddenly cut out of the game. They dressed it up as a random culling of numbers, but I think it was a deliberate act to leave me as one of the last players."

"So, why am I involved?"

"I don't know. Maybe to try and add a bit of authenticity to the scenario. To make me think I'd been lucky to get down to the last two. Either way, the fact that the codeword was Lucy, the name of my ex, can't be a coincidence."

John rubbed his eyes. "Lucy's a very common name. I used to know a Lucy before—"

Rachel didn't wait for him to finish the sentence. "But the house. It's her family home. It's no coincidence."

John frowned. "Huh, yeah, that does seem to rather endorse your theory. If the manor house we went to hadn't been connected to your ex, we might have been able to explain it away. Either way, it does seem like someone is trying to get to you."

Rachel took a sip of coffee. "But why? If my ex was still alive, I could imagine that she might cook something like this up."

"It's got to be this Abigail person then. If we are going full conspiracy on this, the fact she met you at the beginning of the game, wheedled her way into your flat and kept popping up at odd times, means she has to be part of it."

Rachel sighed. "I agree. My friend Kaley tried to rationalise all her actions as normal, and for a moment I could see that it was a possibility that she was just a nice person, but I saw the silhouette of someone at an upstairs window of that house."

"Really?"

"Yes, I'm sure of it. The police claim there was nobody in the house, but they were there. I didn't imagine it."

"Okay, are you assuming it was Abigail?"

"I don't know. It just doesn't make sense. Even if Abigail is involved, what beef has she got with me? I've never met her before."

"We need to find her. What do you know about her?"

"Er, well, she's an Oxford Uni student. She said she was staying in accommodation off Broad Street. That was the last time I bumped into her."

"Hmm, not much to go on. You don't know her surname or which college she's in."

"No."

John put his head back and closed his eyes for a second. "What else?" he said, re-engaging in the conversation.

"The taxi driver," said Rachel. "He must be a key witness for us. He can tell them we didn't know where we were being taken."

"Yes, good idea. Can you remember which taxi firm he was from?"

Rachel cocked her head, trying to recall. "Actually, I don't remember there being anything on his cab."

"Yeah, you might be right. Maybe he was a private hire."

"Either way, we have to find him," she replied.

The conversation paused as they finished off their coffees.

"We have to go back there," Rachel said.

"Where?"

"That manor house."

"It's a crime scene! That's the easiest way to get hauled back to custody."

Rachel leant forward. "The answers are in that house. I'm sure of it. We'll just have to bide our time. Surely they'll leave the scene once it's processed. Won't they?"

John smiled. "I can see you're going to do this with or without me."

Rachel let out an ironic laugh. "Yeah, you're right."

43

Rachel was back in her flat with Kaley watching the local news, a ghoulish curiosity compelling her to see whether her infamy was growing. John was right. Their names weren't out there, but she knew the glare of publicity might lead to further leaks and her exposure. She shuddered at the prospect.

They weren't the top story, which she initially thought was a good thing, but when a picture of the dreaded manor house appeared on the screen as the second news item, her heart sank. After an initial summary of what had happened, the news item flicked to the face of a stern-looking police officer. She was giving a statement about the case. The label under her face said she was Chief Superintendent Wendy Hawsley.

I'm here to provide an update on the murder of Walter Cribbens at a manor house in the Oxfordshire countryside. As per our previous statement, we did arrest two people on suspicion of murder, but we've had to release them on bail whilst we complete further investigations. I can assure you that they continue to help us with our enquiries and do not present a danger to the public. We are continuing to investigate possible ties between the murder and the Oxford Mystery game, and we urgently need to speak to the organisers to assist us in solving this case. We are also appealing for a taxi driver, who took our two suspects from Shotover car park to the manor house on Tuesday evening, to come forward and help us to clarify the circumstances behind his involvement. I would ask members of the public to call 101 or contact Crimestoppers if they have any information pertaining to the case. I will update you further in due course but will not be taking any questions today.

With that the camera cut to the reporter on scene, who started to recap on the case and speculate on what the officer had said.

Rachel huffed. "At least I'm not a danger to the public."

Kaley rubbed her hand. "Too right, babe. You wouldn't harm a fly."

As Rachel watched the rest of the news, she absent-mindedly chewed her nails.

"You're plotting. I can tell. You're not about to let this lie. Are you?"

A brief smile spread across her face. "I can't let this go. Someone is trying to mess my life up, and I'm not about to roll over and let them beat me. I thought my time with Lucy was just a bad memory, but I'm convinced someone is trying to take me back there."

Just as Kaley was about to offer some words of support, Rachel suddenly bolted upright from her slouched position.

The news was nearly at the end of its broadcast but suddenly a *BREAKING NEWS* banner flashed up on the screen with the manor house in the background. They were transfixed as a reporter showed an Instagram post entitled WINNER!!!!!

They sat there open-mouthed as the video that accompanied the post was played. A woman was holding a cheque for fifty thousand pounds, beaming from ear to ear as she celebrated being the winner of the Oxford Mystery game.

It was a face they both knew.

44

John paced the room. These were the worst times. Alone, in his own head, his world crumbling around him. Gambling numbed the pain. A short-term fix but never a solution. He picked up his phone and called his sponsor. She answered straight away.

He found himself yearning her company but knew he was blurring the lines. She was so hot. Why had he been given someone that was stirring lustful emotions in him when he had so much more to process? She helped, guiding him through his crisis and neatly sidestepping the boundary crossing.

He grabbed a beer from the fridge and sat in his living room, trying to focus on something else. He began to think through what Rachel had said. If they were going to find Abigail, he needed a colleague who wouldn't mind taking some risks. But who? Most of his immediate team had grown tired of his antics. His mind wandered. There was only one person. She was based in the intel team and was always sweet on him. John had never been in a place to do anything about her mini infatuation, but maybe now was the time. He scrolled through his phone, sure that she had given him her personal mobile one of the many times she had dropped hints that he needed to ask her out. He found it. *Isla.*

He phoned and she picked up straight away, speaking before he could say anything. "Oh my God, John. How are you? I heard what happened. That's so fucked up."

They spoke for a few minutes before agreeing to meet in a pub down in town. Half an hour later, John was sipping a beer as Isla stared back at him, a mix of joy and concern spread across her face.

"I'm in trouble, Isla."

She grabbed his hand. "I know. People are being really horrible, calling you all sorts of things."

John grimaced. "Thanks!"

"No! Sorry, I didn't mean to upset you, but you need to know that people have you convicted before giving you a chance."

John sighed. "Don't worry about it. I've brought most of this on myself, but I'm no murderer."

"Course you aren't. You're one of the sweetest people I know."

John shook his head. "That doesn't stop me being an idiot though. You know I gamble. I have a problem."

Isla put on her best sympathetic face. "I know. People have been gossiping about you."

"Well, it's all true. My gambling is out of control; I lied to an ACC and got arrested in a Reading casino for disturbing the peace."

Isla tried not to laugh, just grunting a stifled *Oh.*

John shook his head, a wry smile spreading across his

face. “Maybe that’s what I need to do. Just laugh about it, otherwise I’m going to crack up.”

Isla fixed him with a more serious expression. “What do you need, John? I’m guessing there’s no one else in your corner?”

John shrugged. “Well, I guess my solicitor is trying hard and the girl who got arrested with me, Rachel, seems pretty determined to get to the bottom of this.”

“Okay, that’s good, but what can I do?”

John took in a deep breath. “I don’t want you to lose your job, but I need information. The kind of information you may only get from police systems.”

Isla smiled. “You do know I can find almost anything in the cyber world. Dark web, normal internet. Police systems really aren’t the panacea of information you think they are when it comes to deep intel gathering.”

“Okay but I might need you to tell me if something is breaking in the case.”

“Hmm, that could be difficult, but give me a flavour of what you need.”

“Well, there’s a girl we need to find called Abigail who’s been stalking Rachel. All we know is she’s at Oxford University and lives somewhere near Broad Street. We also need to track the taxi driver who picked us up from Shotover car park and took us to that manor house. We can’t remember anything about it other than the make and model of the car and the possibility it was a private hire rather than a cab from a regular taxi firm. Finally, we need to know more about that manor house. It seems to be the family home of Rachel’s ex but, despite her claiming to see someone silhouetted in the window, the police claim there was no one there and they can't find any surviving relatives that appear to own the place."

Isla smirked and cocked her head. "Well, well, Mr John, seems like you are going to owe me big time if I do this for you."

The frown lines appeared again. "I know this is asking a lot."

Isla sat back in her chair. "Sex."

John recoiled. "You what?"

"Sex. That's my price. I've been dropping you hints for nearly two years now that I want to do the dirty with you and you're either gay, stupid or really bad at picking up signals."

John's face reddened. "I think I'm probably two out of three."

There was a brief embarrassed silence before John realised Isla had an expectant look on her face. "Oh, you mean now."

Isla laughed. "Well, I'm up for it, if you are."

John stood, bumping the table as he did. Flustered. Isla stifled a laugh, John shaking his head at her as he continued to act like a clown. She stood up and kissed him passionately.

"Now calm down. Let's go and have some fun and then I'll see about getting that information for you."

45

Rachel stared open-mouthed at the image on the TV news report.

Abigail.

She was holding a cheque for fifty thousand pounds and jumping up and down like an excitable puppy. The reporter was urging her to contact them so they could do a proper interview about her win, the Instagram post being the only thing that had been released. The news item flicked back to pictures of how the Oxford Mystery all started, with the crowds at Carfax, and then charted each step in the game, finishing with their arrests and how there was now a big question as to how all these incidents were linked.

All the while, Rachel stood in utter disbelief at what she was watching, glancing occasionally at Kaley, who just sat stony-faced, not knowing what to say.

As the news item ended, Rachel slumped back in her chair. "What the hell is going on?"

Kaley grimaced. "Oh, babe, this is so fucked up. Did she ever give you any indication she was playing the game?"

"No, although I guess at the beginning everyone was

playing, and I did meet her first at Carfax, and then again on the high street, so it's feasible she was doing it."

Kaley sighed. "But you don't think this is a coincidence. Do you? I know when I tried to rationalise her behaviour you didn't really believe what I was saying could be true."

"You're right. From the minute I met her, that girl has been playing me, with her pretty face and perfect body, pretending she was into me and playing the oh-so-innocent victim whenever I challenged her about stalking me. This is no coincidence. Someone is trying to ruin my life, and this is just the latest sick act in whatever game these people are playing. This is a total charade, and I just can't believe..."

Rachel tried to fight it, but the tears came. Long, convulsive sobs that Kaley tried to soften by hugging her friend tightly. As the emotional outpouring began to wane, Kaley fixed Rachel with a firm gaze. "What do you want to do?"

Rachel brushed the tears away. "I need to phone John."

She tried. No answer. Rachel glanced at her watch. It was nearly 10.30pm.

There was a small amount of wine left. Rachel picked it up and drank it straight from the bottle, wiping her mouth with her arm, like some cowboy in a wild west saloon. She noticed Kaley's amused expression.

"Don't judge me. At the moment, I don't know which way is up, so if I want to down wine straight from the bottle then I will."

Kaley put her hands up in mock surrender. "Hey, babe, no judgement from me."

Rachel tried John again. Still no answer.

"How can we find that bitch?"

"Beats me," replied Kaley. "All we seem to know is that she's an Oxford Uni student living somewhere near Broad Street. Could you go to the university admin people and pretend you're a friend trying to track her down?"

Rachel shook her head. "I can't see that working. They aren't going to give out personal information to some random stranger, especially now she's apparently Little Miss Rich Bitch. They'll probably think I'm after her money."

Kaley began to tap on her phone, eventually shoving the Instagram post they'd just seen on the news in Rachel's face. "Where is she in this video?"

Rachel watched it a couple of times, getting angrier with each watch. "I don't know. That could be a garden in one of the colleges, but there's nothing there that really stands out."

They slumped back into their chairs.

After a minute or so, Rachel piped up. "No, there's one thing I need to do first. I'm going back to that manor house."

46

John stirred, conscious of movement on the other side of the bed. Isla was still there. She'd stayed all night. The sex had been great. Twice, if he remembered correctly.

He lay there watching her sleep, the gentle rise and fall of the duvet a weirdly relaxing sight, a far cry from his recent stresses and strains.

John was so out of practice he didn't know what to do. Should he wait for her to wake up and have sex again? Should he get up quietly and bring her breakfast in bed, and then have sex? Or was that way too presumptuous? Maybe the sex had been bad. Maybe she'd just put up with his fumbling attempts at lovemaking. But then they'd done it more than once, so she must have enjoyed it a bit.

He watched her a bit longer. She was dead to the world. He went for the breakfast option. He didn't have much in but managed to rustle up poached eggs on toast, coffee and orange juice. As he walked back into the bedroom with the tray of breakfast, she was sat up, her long blonde hair sitting seductively on her shoulders and her breasts exposed, as perky as John remembered them. Things immediately began to stir as he stood there with a tray of food and an obvious bulge in his boxers.

Isla smiled. "Well, well, I wonder what I should put my lips round first."

The sex was fast and passionate. The eggs were lukewarm by the time they finished but they didn't care. Much-needed sustenance.

"Well, Johnny boy, you can add great sex to your list of talents. I think you might just have convinced me to help you."

John wiped a last piece of egg from the side of his mouth, a slightly hurt look on his face. "Oh," he said. "Is that it then? I've passed my test. Been used and abused and now you're dumping me."

Isla frowned. "Whoa! Someone's got issues." Her happy-go-lucky expression soon returned, and she moved her hand inside his boxer shorts. "No, my dear John, I'm not dumping you. I'm going to shag you until your cock falls off. If that's all right with you?"

John was trying to get used to her sexual confidence, something that most girls he'd been with hadn't had. It was refreshing and exciting. But just as he was wondering whether he could do it again so quickly, he was distracted by a beep on his phone. There was a brief look of disapproval from Isla as John glanced at the device. "You going to get that? Might be something important."

John looked a bit embarrassed but picked up the phone. He had two missed calls from Rachel the previous evening, but the most recent beep was a text message from her. He opened it and let out a massive sigh.

"What is it?" said Isla.

"No, no, no," John exclaimed. "What is she doing?"

Isla leant in to read the text.

"Oh, is that wise?"

"No! I told her that going back to that manor house is a really bad idea. I'd be surprised if the police are even finished processing the scene. If she rocks up and they're still there, she's going to get arrested for disturbing a crime scene."

"What should we do?"

"Oh shit. Get dressed quickly. We need to see if we can head her off at the pass."

As they drove out of the centre of Oxford, Isla was searching the news items trying to get an exact fix on where the manor house was. John cursed himself for sleeping most of the way the first time they went there but did have a vague recollection of its location.

They drove around the ring road and set off on the route towards London. Eventually Isla found it and began to direct John onto roads that got more and more rural.

He sensed they were getting close.

"Let's hope we're on time and can stop her making the stupidest mistake of her life."

47

She thought about the manor house, the opulence in every room reminding her of everything she hated about her family life. Her father, constantly absent from her life, always travelling, buying more and more tat to display in this cold, soulless place. She knew it was expensive tat but all the same, it just made her feel like she was living in some museum of foreign antiquities rather than a warm, loving home.

Her mother tried hard but she had no idea how to love, how to show affection. Physical contact was at a premium. She left the family home at sixteen, a product of this upbringing and a sense she could never compete with her much cleverer sibling. Better grades, better attitude. Just better. She tried to forge a life for herself, initially working in dead-end jobs to pay for a crappy room in a crappy bedsit, whilst the rest of the family continued to live in the lavish surroundings of the grand manor house. She struggled, but slowly she found her place in life, a few relationships here and there but nothing that ever stuck. She knew it was a result of not knowing how to love, how to commit.

Her family were dead to her, until she found out that her mother had passed away. She felt nothing but had a strange compulsion to go to the funeral. Her father and sister tried to pretend they were pleased to see her, but she got in and out as quickly as she could. Her father's passing changed things. Her sister was different. The perfect child was broken. For the first time in her life, she was needed but, to her dismay, it didn't last long.

It started slowly, but her sister began to fall apart. She started doing things she'd never done before. Drinking, drugs, gambling. All of a sudden, her sister was sending her messages every time she was in trouble. In a police cell, after being arrested for being drunk and disorderly. Beaten up by a drug dealer for failing to pay her debts. Waking up in a stranger's bed, not knowing where she was. The vices got worse. She attached herself to people who just wanted to help her fall deeper into the hole she was digging for herself.

There was an inevitability to what happened next. Her sister committed suicide. The ultimate betrayal. The easy way out. Just as she thought she was going to forge a new life with her sister, the emptiness returned. Alone, once again.

The need for revenge began to brew; each day she woke up, the memories of her sister made her more and more bitter. Time was not healing. She needed closure, and ruining the lives of the people who had hurt her sister was the only way she could move forward.

She was a ghost in this tragic story, her father cutting her out of any family inheritance. A final bitter act on his part that said to the world that he only had one daughter. She'd changed her name in an act of spite.

Her sister didn't make a will, which was a problem as

her father had left her everything. She knew the solicitors handling the case would eventually find her. There was no way her father could eradicate birth records and, if the timing was right, she would reveal herself and claim the inheritance. But the burning desire to exact revenge on those who had led her sister to take her own life was the priority. Everything else would have to wait.

She replayed the moment she plunged the spear into Walter's chest. He was barely worth her anger, but his part in her sister's tumble into total despair deserved recrimination. He was such a waste of space that no one would miss him. One down, two to go.

48

Rachel sat in her car, looking at the façade of the manor house. She'd had no problem remembering the route, having been transfixed by every twist and turn of the first journey to this place. She'd been ready to hotfoot it out of there if any police were still hovering around, but thankfully the place was deserted.

The discussion with John hadn't really formed much of a plan, other than a mutual desire to find out what was going on. He hadn't answered when she rang.

She stepped out of the car and took in the full scale of the grand manor house. The dark clouds in the sky made it look eerie and imposing. A screech of a crow made her jump. She brushed it off and walked towards the large front door, framed in a stone archway.

The door was open. She hovered on the precipice. She stopped and listened. All she could hear was the variety of wildlife noises coming from behind her.

She stepped slowly through the door into the marbled entrance hall. She instinctively looked right towards where Walter had been murdered and the scene of their unceremonious arrest.

She pulled her cardigan around her. It was a warm day, but being in this house was chilling her to the bone. Physically and mentally.

Rachel gazed up at the stairs, before slowly climbing them. The door at the top to the right was locked. The long corridor she ran down when John thought he saw someone was the opposite way.

She was jumping at every creak, every tiny noise.

The beep of her phone made her scream. It was a message from Kaley.

Where are you, babe? I'm worried you are going to do something stupid.

*

John looked at Isla anxiously as they sped along a narrow rural road, deep in the Oxfordshire countryside.

"The entrance is two hundred yards on the left," she said.

As John turned into the tree-lined entrance road, the memories came flooding back. He might have dozed off on the way, but he remembered Rachel nudging him awake as they turned in. The trees seemed somehow darker and more imposing, like they were closing in on them. Some of the wildlife stopped and stared their way, almost as though they'd never seen such a sight. There was a brief spatter of rain on the window.

"All we need now is the thunder and lightning," said John, "and then we can have the full Scooby Doo experience."

"Okay, raggy," said Isla in her best Scooby Doo voice.

John smiled, a brief respite from the deep-seated fear he had for Rachel's wellbeing. As he got closer to the manor house, he slowed, arching his neck to see if there were any police vehicles still present. The last thing they needed was to walk straight into a police presence that would surely have them back in custody before they could say *let's split up and look for clues.*

As John drove from the last bit of the entrance road onto the gravel surrounding the house, his emotions were mixed. There was no police presence, but a car they assumed was Rachel's was there – she wasn't in it.

They got out of the car. "Come on," said John.

They walked through the front door, their shoes echoing off the marble floor, the noise making John wince. He hesitated, unsure whether to go up or down. The door to the left was locked, so he moved right, towards the room where Walter had been found. They searched the rooms in that end of the house, but there was no sign of Rachel.

"Should we call out for her?" said Isla.

"No, for some reason I feel like we are not alone. We've already announced our presence with our clonking feet on that bloody entrance hall. I'm not inclined to give any more clues as to where we are."

They crept back towards the staircase, satisfied that the downstairs search had proved fruitless. John urged them onwards, despite his gut doing somersaults. They went up the grand carpeted staircase, slowly but surely, Isla slightly behind John as they both kept an ear out for any noises.

At the top of the stairs, John tried the door to the right. It was locked. He turned to look down the hallway. "Come on, I think these are all bedrooms. We need to search each one."

They walked along side by side, Isla trying the doors on the left and John the ones on the right. Every one was locked. As they got three quarters of the way down the hallway, Isla stopped. "What's that?"

They stared at long gouges in the wooden flooring, right outside one of the bedrooms. The door was locked. "This house just gets weirder by the minute," said John.

They continued to the end of the corridor, and just as they thought they were going to draw a blank, the handle on the last door on the right turned.

Isla gasped as John stood frozen to the spot, his hand gripping the handle tightly. "Go on," urged Isla.

John opened the door. Isla screamed.

Rachel was sprawled on the bed. Unconscious.

Worse than that, the word *bitch* was clumsily scrawled on her forehead.

49

"Call the police. Call an ambulance. Do something, John!"

John hadn't moved from his spot in the doorway.

"John!" screamed Isla.

"We can't call anyone."

"What?"

John turned and gripped Isla, hands on her upper arms. "Look, she can't be found here. Nor can I. This is the scene of the murder we are charged with. If we're found here, we are going straight back to custody and will probably cement the case against us."

Isla's stress levels were peaking. "You what?! I thought you said the case against you was flaky at best. A set-up, you said."

John sighed in exasperation. "It is, but if we're found here it's going to look like we are tampering with evidence, compromising a crime scene… or something. God, I don't know. We just have to get out of here."

Isla wrestled herself from John's grip and rushed over to the bed. "At least check she's still alive for God's sake."

John did as he was told as Isla looked at the word scrawled on her forehead. She touched the red lettering, worried at first that it might be blood. She gasped in relief. "It's just lipstick." Isla grabbed a tissue out of her pocket and rubbed it away. She looked at John.

"She's alive," he said, "but out cold. How do you propose we move her?"

"God knows."

John seemed distracted.

"What is it?" screeched Isla.

"Whoever did this must still be in the house."

Isla looked at John in disbelief. "Are you for real? One minute you're stressing about getting out of here and the next you want to chase a ghost in a spooky house."

John walked back to the doorway and looked up and down the corridor. There were no sounds, no sign of anyone else. He walked back into the room. "I don't know. We do need to get out, but Rachel came back here because she was convinced she saw someone in the window when we were being driven away. The police said no one was in the house, but it's obvious that she was right. Whoever is setting this up must be hiding somewhere in the house."

Isla just shook her head. "Do something, John. Make a decision, because I'd rather not spend a minute longer in this creep fest than I have to."

John stood for a minute, his eyes darting between Rachel and Isla. "Shitting hell. Come on, we need to try and move her. As much as I want to nail this bastard, life is going to get much worse for both of us if we are caught here."

They moved over to the bed. "Right, you grab her legs, and I'll take the weight of her body," said John. They tried to move her, but the softness of the bed was not helpful. They manoeuvred her so her legs were dangling over the side of the bed as John came round to haul her body up and off the mattress. John's leg buckled as he tried to take the weight, sending them sprawling backwards onto the carpet, Rachel unceremoniously landing on top of him.

He pushed her off, gently rolling her onto her back. Suddenly, there was a soft groan. "She's waking up," said Isla.

"Rachel, Rachel," shouted John.

The groans got louder as Rachel began to stir. Slowly her eyes began to flutter open. After a minute, she gasped as John loomed over her. "It's okay, Rachel, take your time. It's John."

"Where… where am I?" Rachel said.

John grimaced. "You're in the manor house. Don't you remember?"

The scream from Rachel made them jump. She hauled herself up onto her elbows, scanning the room. "It was her, John."

"Who?"

"My ex. Lucy. She's alive!"

50

John stared wide-eyed at Rachel, trying to comprehend what she was saying. "You what?"

"The person who's behind this. The person in this house. It's Lucy. My ex."

"Eh?" exclaimed John. "You said she was dead."

"What can I say? I was exploring the house. I got to the top of the stairs and heard someone shout my name. I then got a message from Kaley and, as I was reading it, someone struck me on the head. As I fell, I saw her. Lucy."

"Are you sure it was her?" said Isla.

Rachel looked at Isla. "Who the fuck are you and what are you doing here?"

John interjected. "Don't be rude, Rachel. This is Isla. She's my—"

"Fuck buddy," Isla interjected.

Rachel raised her eyebrows. "Okay, but that doesn't explain why you're here."

John's tone became more annoyed. "She was with me when your text came in. We jumped in the car as soon as we got it to try and stop you doing this."

"Doing what? Proving I was right! Proving that there was someone in this house when we got arrested? Let the police come and we can prove we're innocent."

"Don't be naïve, Rachel. If you're found here revisiting the scene of the crime, they'll have you back in custody, and do you really think that whoever is in the house is going to be here when the police turn up?"

"Not whoever. It's Lucy. I saw her. She's alive."

John moved away from the confrontation and went into the bathroom. Rachel hauled herself up and sat on the bed.

"I'm sorry," said Isla.

"What for?" replied Rachel.

"For all this. John's right. We were just trying to help. I have a talent for finding information that, let's just say, can be hard to find. I agreed to help find this Abigail person, your taxi driver and look into the family background of the people who owned this house."

"Oh, but you're…"

"Shagging. Yes. That was my price."

Rachel smiled. "Wow. Go girl."

"Well, what can you do? I've been practically offering it to him for two years now and he never picked up on the signals, so I thought, *fuck it. Now he needs me, I need to get my fun.*"

For a second Rachel forgot where she was, amused and impressed at Isla's confidence to get what she wanted.

"Do you have a picture of her? Your ex?"

Rachel grimaced. "No, I deleted them all in a fit of pique. You know. The kind of irrational thing you do when you have a painful break-up."

"Oh. Well, never mind. I can certainly look into the circumstances around her apparent suicide and the death records to see if there is anything untoward, if you are sure that was who you saw."

Rachel frowned. After her initial hostility she was warming to Isla. Just as she was about to say something else, John came out of the bathroom. "What are you two doing?"

"Just talking about Lucy. Isla's going to see if she can find anything that can explain why she's alive."

Rachel ignored the sceptical look on John's face, moving over to the door. "Come on," she said, "let's get out of here."

As she got to the door, she gripped the handle and stopped.

"What is it?" said Isla.

Rachel turned round, a look of horror on her face. "It's locked."

51

The three of them stared at each other in disbelief, trying to take in the implications of the locked door.

"Shit!" said John, walking over to the door to check that Rachel was right. "Bloody hell, there is someone in this house."

"We have to get out of here," said Isla, a hint of panic in her voice.

John shook his head. "I don't know. If there's someone here, we need to find them. They may be our only chance to prove our innocence but, on the other hand, if they've called the police, we're toast."

Rachel didn't comment but started to walk around the room, studying the walls intently. Rachel began to touch the walls, feeling around the panels inlaid into the fabric of the room's structure.

"What are you doing?" said John.

"I know it's a cliché," she said, "but I wonder whether an old place like this has secret passages. Come and help me look."

John and Isla looked less than convinced but started to

copy what Rachel was doing. "Any luck?" said John, after about a minute of searching.

Rachel didn't answer at first, but suddenly she gasped, pushing at a panel towards the far corner of the room. The panel pushed inwards to reveal a space behind the wall. She turned to the others, an excited look on her face. "See! Not a cliché after all. Come on, this might just be our way out of here."

She disappeared into the space. John and Isla quickly followed her. As they entered, Rachel turned on her phone's torch to light up the darkness. They faced a stone wall, covered in cobwebs, with a passage running to the right. "Come on," said Rachel, not offering the other two any opportunity to contribute an opinion on her actions.

They moved precariously along the passage, stumbling often as the uneven flooring and dim light made progress difficult. They passed several makeshift doors that they thought must be the entrances to other bedrooms. Rachel pushed on, convinced her sense of direction was going to bring her out at the other end of the house. After what seemed like a never-ending trek along the passageway, tensing up at every potential stumble and brushing cobwebs out of their faces, they reached a turning. It led to a set of stairs that went down. "This is it," whispered Rachel. "I reckon we've come to the far end of the house and these stairs lead down to the ground floor."

John and Isla nodded their agreement and followed Rachel down the stairs. The passageway continued, and after a short way, a door appeared to their right. Rachel stopped and looked at them both. "Go on," said John. Rachel pushed at the panel, and it moved inwards, making a screeching sound that made them all wince. She took a tentative look around the panel and realised they were in the corner of the main living room, where Walter had been murdered. Rachel walked into the room, satisfied there was no immediate danger. John and Isla followed, their faces etched with fear and concern.

None of them needed any prompting to charge down the main hallway towards the front door. Mercifully, no one stopped their progress. But, as Rachel went for the exit, John stopped her. "Don't you want to find this person?"

Rachel glared at John's hand on her arm, swiping it away. "No, John. We have to go."

They ran towards their cars. Rachel fired up the engine and wasted no time in slamming her foot down on the accelerator, wheel spinning on the gravel as the car fishtailed towards the main drive. Rachel looked in her rear-view mirror. John's car was right behind her.

She drove as fast as she reasonably could, scattering the odd bit of wildlife that didn't move fast enough, not expecting the type of noisy intrusion to their otherwise tranquil life.

As she got near the end of the driveway and the junction with the main road, she could hear sirens.

52

Rachel instinctively swung her car round to the left as she exited the driveway from the manor house, paying little regard as to whether there were other vehicles on the road she was joining. The suspension on her little car squealed in complaint at the rough treatment and, for a second, Rachel thought she was going to lose control of the vehicle as it lurched from side to side. She screamed as the car bounced around, but eventually it righted itself and began to move forward in the direction she wanted. She hoped to God that she'd been right; that the increasingly loud sirens were coming from the other direction.

She glanced nervously in her mirror and saw that John and Isla had followed her. She held her breath as she reduced her speed, not wanting to bring attention to herself if the vehicles that she was sure were there for her, happened to be coming in their direction.

She had no idea where she was but kept driving down the twists and turns of the minor road they were on. As each minute passed, she became more confident that they had got away. The sound of the sirens was fainter than before.

She began to look for somewhere to stop, so she could calm her racing heart and talk to John, but she suddenly came to a junction. The signpost signalled that Thame was left and Chinnor was right. She went left.

As she drove along the more substantial road, she was just about to get on the phone to John to tell him she was going to stop when its urgent ringtone made her jump a mile. It was an unknown number.

"Er… hello," she said, a nervous pitch in her voice that she failed to hide.

"Miss Keen, it's DCI Yin."

"Oh, hi."

"Are you okay? You sound distressed."

"No, no, just driving and an animal just ran out in front of me. It shook me up for a second." There was a brief pause. Rachel winced at the lie she'd told. She really was an idiot, she thought to herself. Lying to a police officer. Weren't they trained to spot when people were not telling the truth?

Eventually he spoke. "Oh well, as long as you are okay."

"Is there something I can do for you?" Rachel said, as she tried to bluff it out.

"Yes. Look, I know you are technically still on bail for a charge of murder, but I wondered whether you could come in and see me – entirely on a voluntary basis – to help us with our enquiries."

Rachel didn't know what to say.

Yin carried on. "I can make the request more formally through your solicitor if you would prefer, but either way I could really do with a chat."

"Has something happened?"

"Yes."

“Something positive from my perspective?”

“Yes, but I’d rather talk about it face to face. Can you come in and see me now? At St Aldates Police Station.”

Rachel’s mind was racing but she thought it made sense to comply. “Yes of course. I need to drive home and get a bus into town. I’ll try and be with you in an hour.”

As the call was disconnected, she noticed a layby was coming up and she indicated to stop in it. John pulled in behind her.

She told them about the call, the drama at the manor house seemingly a footnote in that current moment.

“Come to my house later,” Rachel said. “We need to review everything that’s happened today, including whatever this police officer has picked up.”

John and Isla agreed and began to get back in their car.

“Come at seven and bring some wine,” shouted Rachel after them.

She got back in her car and began to drive home, curious about what DCI Yin had found.

53

Rachel waited patiently at the front desk of the St Aldates Police Station. She wasn't sure whether she was being paranoid, but some of the police officers milling about the station were giving her dirty looks. She'd been taken to the Abingdon custody suite, so there was no reason that people should know her face but, for some reason, she felt exposed and vulnerable at their scrutiny.

Mercifully, the door to the side of the front desk opened, and DCI Yin stood there, beckoning her inside. His expression was deadpan, just as he'd been when he formally interviewed her. It didn't help her paranoia.

He led her into his office and offered her coffee, which she gratefully accepted. After a nervy few minutes, he sat down opposite her and launched in.

"Miss Keen, thank you for coming in so quickly. I really do appreciate it. I want to restate that this conversation forms no part of any formal investigation we are undertaking in respect of your murder charge and will not be recorded."

"O… kay," she replied nervously.

Yin took a sip of his coffee. "The thing is, Miss Keen, there has been a development in the case."

"Oh."

"We found the driver that took you and Mr Bamford to the house, and he has confirmed that you had no prior knowledge of where you were being taken. He also confirmed that he is a private hire driver and only got the booking the day before from a woman who had never booked him previously."

Rachel leant forward, trying to stifle her rising optimism at what he was saying. "Did you track her down? The woman who booked him."

Yin winced. "Unfortunately not. The credit card she used led us to a fake identity. It was a dead end."

Rachel leant back. "But the driver's statement works in our favour?"

Yin frowned. "I'll be honest, Miss Keen, this case has me baffled. Ordinarily, the forensic evidence that we found that links you to the murder, together with your association with the family that owned that house, would have me licking my lips at how secure the case was. However, as I'm sure your solicitor told you, the ME report has the time of death many hours before you both got there, and the driver's statement does indeed remove any suggestion of premeditated murder on your part."

"So, you believe I'm innocent?"

Yin held his hands up. "Whoa. I didn't say that. It would be remiss of me not to follow every thread of evidence before we can get to that conclusion, but I accept that our case against you is much weaker than it was when we first arrested you."

"So, what do you want from me?" A hint of annoyance entered her voice.

"Tell me about the Beaufort family."

Rachel frowned. "Well, not much to say. I was in a relationship with Lucy for two years. We split up a while ago and I heard she committed suicide about six months ago. She never talked about her family that much, but I gathered that her mother passed away just before we met, and I believe her father's more recent passing may have been a factor in her life falling apart. As far as I know she was an only child."

Yin turned a couple of pages in a file he had in front of him. "The thing is, the father died about five months before Miss Beaufort's suicide. The solicitor handling the estate said she inherited the lot. By all accounts she became an incredibly wealthy woman. Can you think of any reason she may have taken her own life?"

"I've no idea. Our split was messy, and there have been times when I've wondered whether everything that has been going on was someone trying to get back at me for her suicide."

Yin shook his head. "But who? The solicitor says Miss Beaufort died intestate, and they can't find any living relatives that could now inherit the fortune."

Rachel shrugged.

"Also, this scarf bugs me," he said.

"How so?" Rachel replied, concerned at where the conversation might be going.

"Miss Beaufort is dead, and you admitted that she gave you that scarf. It seems feasible that the scarf was in the family home, and whoever killed Mr Cribbens used it to implicate you in his murder."

"I'm not following."

"Whoever did that must have an intimate understanding of your relationship with Miss Beaufort. It can't have been a coincidence that it was tied round the neck of the body. Someone is trying to take you down in the most brutal of ways."

"So, you do believe I'm innocent?"

Yin raised his eyebrows. "I think I've already answered that question, Miss Keen, but work with me here. I'm trying to be objective, but I need you to be completely honest with me."

"I am being," she shrilled. "Lucy took that scarf when we split up. She knew it was one of my favourite things, and she took it out of spite. That was the first time I've seen it since the split."

Yin refilled his coffee. "And the fingerprints on the glass. You think that was done by this Abigail person?"

"Yes and… shit, didn't you see her on the telly? She posted on Instagram that she was the winner of this Oxford Mystery game."

"And you don't believe that?"

"*No!*" shouted Rachel. "That girl has been stalking me the whole time that mystery game was in play. John and I were convinced that we'd got through to the last stages of the game, only to be framed for murder, and then she pops up claiming to be the winner. I mean, that is so far from being credible that I'm surprised you haven't brought her in for questioning."

"On what grounds? Winning a competition?"

Rachel began to fume. "Look, you asked for my help, and Abigail is a fraud. You need to find her and question her about her involvement in this case."

As Rachel's sentence drifted off, she noticed that Yin was no longer looking at her, or apparently listening to what she was saying, as he looked at something on his laptop screen.

A moment later he looked back at her, the lines on his face deepening in anger. He stood up. "Miss Keen. I need to end this conversation immediately and notify your solicitor that we need a discussion linked to your formal caution."

"Why? What's happened?"

Yin shook his head. "You need to explain to me why you've just revisited the crime scene."

54

Rachel walked out of the police station slightly unnerved by the ending of the conversation with Yin. She'd been walking back through town for barely ten minutes when her phone beeped. It was a message from her solicitor. The DCI had wasted no time in demanding a formal interview for 10am the next morning. Rachel closed the phone, fighting back angry tears.

As she continued to walk through the centre of Oxford, she realised she was on the corner of Broad Street. She glanced at her watch. It was only 4pm, but she desperately needed a drink and her favourite pub, The White Horse, was only a few minutes away.

She began to walk towards it, the summer sun beating down on her head. As she got about halfway to the pub, she stopped. Sitting on a bench, across the other side of the road, was someone she couldn't believe she was seeing.

Abigail.

She didn't know what to do. Fight or flight. Should she confront her or skulk into the shadows to watch what she did? A second later, it was too late. Abigail was waving frantically at her.

At first Rachel did that thing where you pretend you haven't seen the person or aren't sure they're waving at you. She looked around, but every time she looked back, Abigail was waving more frantically.

Fight.

Rachel's heckles were up, and she stormed over to where Abigail was sitting. "What the hell?" she screamed.

Abigail recoiled. "What's up?"

"What's up? What's up?" she parroted back.

Abigail looked upset. "What have I done? I don't understand why you're so angry with me."

Rachel got in Abigail's face. "Look, you fucking bitch. I know you are part of all this. Stop playing games."

Abigail pushed Rachel away and stood up. "My God, Rachel. What's got into you? I haven't done anything to you. I was just really pleased to see you again and wanted to celebrate my good luck. I've only gone and won that bloody mystery game. Fifty grand. Can you believe that?"

Rachel was astounded at her gall. Her mouth dropped open in disbelief, her face flushed red. "Are you trying to tell me that you don't know anything about what's happened to me?"

"No," shouted Abigail.

Rachel stared her down, examining her face, looking for involuntary twitches that would show she was lying, but there was nothing. Just the hurt face of Abigail staring back at her.

All rational thoughts had left her. She wanted to phone that police officer and get him to drag her back to the police station and interrogate her about the case. But every time Rachel thought she'd worked out Abigail's game, she just put on that oh-so-sweet little-girl-lost persona that made people feel sorry for her.

Rachel couldn't handle it. She walked away.

55

There was a sharp knock at the door. Rachel's gaze moved from her half-empty wine glass to the clock on her mantelpiece. They were bang on time. John and Isla stood there, both holding wine. Isla had a laptop tucked under her arm.

Rachel gestured them in, slumping back down in her chair, without another thought for her guests. She realised they were stood in her living room, unsure what to do. "Oh, sorry, glasses are in the kitchen."

When they returned, Rachel had her head in her hands.

"I'm guessing the chat with the DCI didn't go so well," said John.

Rachel finished her wine and poured another glass. "You could say that!"

There was a silence as John and Isla chose not to fill the void.

"They know we were back at the house."

"Eh?" said John.

"Yeah, I was having quite a nice chat with that DCI. Apparently, they found the driver that took us to that house, and he's backed up our story—"

"That's good," interrupted Isla.

Rachel ignored her. "And he seemed to be coming around to the idea that we've been set up, but then suddenly his mood switched. I think he got a message to say we'd been at the house, and he suddenly insisted that the informal chat had to end. Now, I have an interview under caution tomorrow morning where I need to explain our actions."

John rubbed his chin. "That's strange."

"What is?" asked Rachel, her tone moody and impatient.

"Why haven't I been called in on the same basis?"

"I don't know."

"Are you sure he referred to *us*, or did he just mention you?"

"What the fuck difference does it make?"

"A lot!" replied John, his voice rising. "If for some reason they only think you were there, then I don't have to answer for my actions."

Rachel sunk half the glass, whilst pinning a fierce look at John. "So, you want me to lie? You're cutting me adrift."

John softened his tone. "No, Rachel, but honestly, if they don't have me in the frame, I'd rather you kept me out of any discussion tomorrow."

There was an uncomfortable silence. Rachel eventually broke it. "I saw her."

John tried to stay with his more conciliatory tone. "I know. You said."

Rachel waved her hand and let out a loud tut. "No, not Lucy. Abigail."

"What? Where?" exclaimed John.

Rachel refilled her wine glass, another step towards what she hoped would be drunken oblivion. "Can you believe she was just sat in the sun on a bench in Broad Street? Not a care in the world."

"What did she do when she saw you?"

Rachel huffed. "She's unbelievable. Waved at me from across the street like some mental person then, when I challenged her about what happened to us, she claimed to know nothing about it. She kept going on about how she was pleased to see me and wanted to share her good news about winning the mystery game. I mean, she's got more front than Brighton beach."

Rachel hadn't noticed Isla had begun tapping away on her laptop. She cut across their conversation. "The thing is, Rachel, Abigail checks out. She's a third-year undergraduate at Lincoln College. She's just finished a psychology degree and is living in an apartment just off Broad Street, as she said. Looks like she's quite a social butterfly as she comes up under a number of the university clubs including rowing, amateur dramatics, theatre club and, bizarrely, the real ale group."

Rachel gave Isla a disapproving stare but said nothing. Isla carried on. "Look, Rachel, I accept that the whole knife in the drawer thing was weird and she absolutely is in the frame for the fingerprint evidence that was planted, but we can't prove any of this."

"Can you go deeper? You said you could find information that others couldn't. Can you do it? Can you find dirt on her?"

Isla smiled. "Of course I can." She smiled at John. "This one's paid his dues so I'm all yours."

Rachel sighed. John looked embarrassed. Isla stood up. "Come on, John, I think Rachel needs to rest."

With that Rachel was left on her own. She finished the wine. A text message came in from Kaley, frantic to know what was going on. She messaged back to say she was okay. The wine was having an effect. She put her head back in the chair and closed her eyes.

The image of a smiling Abigail kept haunting her thoughts.

She had to be dealt with.

56

"Why did you return to the crime scene, Miss Keen? That's normally the action of a guilty party."

DCI Yin had wasted no time in getting to the point. Rachel's head was thumping with the mother of all hangovers and, despite her solicitor's advice to say nothing, she wasn't in the mood for a *no comment* interview. She allowed just enough gap to make the atmosphere a bit edgy, leaning forward in an attempt to intimidate him.

"Because you're not doing your job," she hissed.

"How so?"

"When I got arrested there was a person silhouetted in that window, yet your officers claim there was no one there. I went back to prove that someone was in that house."

"And what did you find?"

Rachel shook her head in disapproval. "She was there. My ex. She bashed me over the head and knocked me unconscious."

Yin's face crumpled into a mocking laugh as he looked first at his sergeant, then at Rachel's solicitor, before addressing her. "You are trying to tell me that your *dead* ex assaulted you?"

Rachel ignored his attitude. "It was her. She came from behind me but as I fell, I saw her face."

"I shouldn't need to remind you, Miss Keen, that you are being interviewed under caution on a murder charge. This type of irrational response is not going to help you."

Rachel slammed her hand on the table, making everyone jump. "It's not irrational. It was her."

Yin's manner stiffened further. "We had a call yesterday afternoon from a person who said they saw you breaking and entering into that house. When we got there, we couldn't find anyone."

Rachel's head was still pounding, making her short on patience. "She's hiding. That house is old. Full of secret passageways."

"How do you know?"

"After the assault she incarcerated me in one of the bedrooms. I couldn't get out but found a secret passage in the wall, which eventually led me back to the front door, which by the way was open when I got there so it was not breaking and entering."

"Were you alone?"

There it was. The question. If she lied now, she knew she was committing perjury, but John was in so much trouble, could she really dob him in? The question lay unanswered as Rachel tried to read the expressions of the two police officers. Did they know that John and Isla were there? She pulled at her neckline, the heat of the room creating beads of sweat all over her body.

"Miss Keen. Were you alone?"

"To start with, yes, but I'd told some friends what I was doing and they came and helped me escape."

"Their names please."

"I'm sorry, I'm not prepared to say. They are not involved in this."

"I assume one of them was Mr Bamford."

"No comment," retorted Rachel.

Yin did a raised-eyebrow look at his sergeant. "The thing is, Miss Keen, your actions will only strengthen the prosecution case against you, and without any evidence that this fantasy story stacks up, you've just made us more determined to prove that you killed Mr Cribbens. Now, I know there are some discrepancies in the prosecution case, but if you continue to act like this, we are going to believe that you are guilty, and we will find a logical, evidence-based solution as to how you committed this murder. It is also obvious from your manner that Mr Bamford was assisting you in this escapade, meaning we will be talking to him urgently."

Rachel shrugged. "Is that it then? Can I go?"

Yin terminated the interview.

Rachel winced as the bright sun greeted her exit from St Aldates Police Station. She felt light-headed. She hadn't eaten since the previous evening, the hangover stopping any chance of breakfast. The thought of food made her stomach lurch, and she dry heaved.

She took a minute to calm herself as passers-by gave her weird looks. There was only one thing for it. She had to get home and sleep it off. She messaged Kaley to come to her flat.

She needed someone – anyone – to keep her going.

57

Rachel jumped as the sound of the doorbell woke her up. She tried to focus on her bedside clock. It was just gone 6pm and she'd slept for nearly five hours. The doorbell rang again. She hauled her exhausted body off the bed and trudged to the door.

Kaley stood there, a beaming smile on her face, holding wine and a bag of takeaway food. Her face dropped as soon as she saw Rachel. "My God, babe, you look awful."

Rachel beckoned her in. "No wine but I could eat a horse."

Kaley smiled. "Oh, I see. Getting pissed without me and suffering for it. Well, it's a good job we're besties or I might be offended."

Rachel gave a pained smile and began forking out the Chinese takeaway onto the plate, relishing the spiciness and depth of flavour as she shovelled it into her mouth. Eventually she finished gorging, sank a glass of water and sighed. "Bloody hell, that's better."

Kaley looked at her friend with concern. "Do you wanna catch me up here? Where have you been these last few days?"

Rachel rubbed her face. "Oh, Kaley, I don't know where to start. I'm completely losing the plot here. Why is someone trying to destroy my life?"

"Has something changed?"

Rachel raised her eyes to the sky. "I've been an idiot. I did go back to that manor house, where John and I were arrested."

"You what? What the hell did you do that for?"

"I saw her, Kaley. Lucy."

Kaley began to laugh but stifled the reaction as she looked at Rachel's face. "Fuck me. You're serious."

"It was her. She was in that house."

"But… but she's dead."

Rachel wailed in frustration. "I know. I know, but when I was in the house, someone hit me over the head and, as I fell, I caught a glimpse of the person's face. It was Lucy."

Kaley fixed Rachel with a serious expression. "Listen to what you just said. You were hit over the head. You were in the house that you now find out was your ex's family home. Do you think maybe you saw what you wanted to see?"

"Oh God, I don't know. That's what Isla said."

"Who's Isla?"

"Huh, John's got a *friends with benefits* arrangement going on with this girl, although I think she was the one that forced the situation. Seems she's a cyber nerd that works with John, fancies the pants off him, so offered to help us find information for a roll in the sack."

Kaley gasped. "Wow!"

"Yeah, that's what I thought, but it does seem like she can help us."

"Where does she fit into this story?"

"Well, I told John that I was going to the house, and they followed me, trying to stop me making a mistake, but it was too late. They found me unconscious in one of the bedrooms. As we tried to leave, the person behind this locked us in the room. I found a secret panel in the wall and managed to find our way out of there. We got out just in time because they called the police."

"Holy shit. So you got away with it?"

"No. As I was speeding away from the scene, I got a call from that chief inspector wanting me to go in and speak to him about the case, all off the record like. But we hadn't been talking long when his attitude suddenly changed. Someone told him what I'd done, and I was hauled back in there this morning for a further formal interview under caution."

"What happened?"

"John was right. He took a very dim view of me going back to the crime scene. Seems to have made him more determined to prove I killed that man."

"Oh, Rachel, I'm so sorry. Why didn't you call me sooner?"

Rachel began to cry. "Everything… is such… a mess."

Kaley hugged her until the crying subsided. "That's not all," said Rachel, trying to steady her breathing. "I saw Abigail."

Rachel told the story of the latest encounter and could see Kaley was less than convinced about Rachel's theories. "You don't believe me, do you? Why have you always defended her?"

Kaley shrugged. "I don't know. In the brief time I met her she seemed like such a sweet, innocent girl, just having a good time."

Rachel shook her head. "*Fuck!* Isla said much the same. She did a bit of digging and everything that Abigail said seems to check out. I just don't know what to think."

"People are missing you at work," said Kaley.

"Is that supposed to make me feel better?"

"Well, I thought a change of subject might help, and everyone thinks you've been treated really badly. Especially that cute lab tech. She keeps defending you with that *innocent until proven guilty* stuff. In fact, she admitted she was the one who left that note under the door and sent that ornament in the post."

Rachel bolted up from her slumped position, immediately regretting the sudden movement as her head continued to pound. "You what? Holy shit!"

Kaley gave her a sympathetic smile. "I know. She apologised for acting weird, but she's really shy and didn't know how else to approach you. Anyway, at least that solves one of your mysteries."

Rachel sighed, eyeing the unopened wine bottle, but thought better of it. She gazed at Kaley. "Thank you for being such a good friend. I really needed this tonight."

As Rachel's sentence drifted off, the moment was disturbed by something being posted through the letter box. Kaley went to retrieve it, turning it over and over in her hands as she brought it back into the kitchen.

"What is it?" said Rachel.

"I don't know. It's a handwritten envelope. It must have been hand delivered."

Rachel immediately bolted for her front door and rushed out into the corridor looking left and right, and then down the stairs. There was no one there. She grabbed the envelope and tore it open. As she unfolded the single piece of paper, the horror of what was written was reflected in her facial expression. She shoved it at Kaley barely able to speak, her hands shaking.

Kaley looked at the note.

Do you really think you've solved the Oxford Mystery?

58

John and Isla lay in bed, the glow of another round of passionate sex giving them some respite from all the stress.

"Have you heard from Rachel today?" she said.

John huffed. "No. Thank God. That crazy bitch is going to get us both sent down."

Isla sat up. "Wasn't she seeing Yin this morning?"

"Yeah."

"Do you think she dobbed you in?"

John rubbed his face. "I dunno. I'm in enough trouble as it is. I'm not sure she can make it much worse."

Isla gazed out of the bedroom window, watching the wind buffet the trees, her mind constantly at work. "The thing is, I had another quick look at that Abigail person. I can't find anything on her. She's squeaky clean."

John turned to look at Isla, subconsciously glancing at her exposed breasts, an action she noticed as she pulled the sheets up to cover them. "Now calm down, stud. This is serious. Rachel seems convinced that girl's out to get her, but she seems completely innocent."

John shook his head. "Ever since I met Rachel, I've never been completely sure that she's not a few sandwiches short of a picnic. Most of her ramblings seem emotional, irrational. I can't believe I've got caught up in her dramas."

Isla frowned. "Yeah, I know what you mean. She does seem a bit unhinged. I mean, didn't you think it was odd that she's apparently just seen her dead ex but didn't want to search the house to find her?"

John winced. "Absolutely. She seemed so intent on getting out of that place and yet all she's been going on about is someone being in that house. It just doesn't stack up."

Isla exhaled. "There's something else. When I asked her to show me a picture of Lucy, she claimed she'd deleted them all as a reaction to them splitting up. Does that seem normal to you?"

John frowned. "I don't know. Maybe. She does seem like a very emotional person, so I suppose it's possible."

Isla shrugged. "I need to do some digging into the family and that country pile we've just been to. I can't believe Rachel didn't know Lucy came from money, and I'm curious who was in that house. I know it can't have been Lucy, but someone was there, bashing her over the head and locking us in that bedroom. There's something we are all missing, and I'm damn well going to find out what it is."

John leant into Isla. "God, you make me horny when you go all detective on me."

Isla laughed. "Well fuck me and call me Sherlock."

As the lust began to rise once again, their passion was interrupted by a beep on John's phone. He opened the message, his face dropping as he read it.

"Shit. We've got the answer. She dobbed me in. My solicitor's just messaged to say I need to go back in for another interview with Yin and his boy wonder."

*

DCI Yin was just putting his daughter to bed when his work phone buzzed, resulting in a disapproving look from his wife. He wished his daughter sweet dreams and stepped out onto the landing.

"What is it this time?" snapped his wife.

"I need to deal with this. I won't be a minute."

He went into the study. There was a message from DS Baxter, telling him to check his email. Yin cursed. He quickly grabbed his laptop, hoping it was something quick.

He opened the email. A video file was attached. He opened it, gasping in shock, as he began to understand the implications of what he was watching. He got straight on the phone to Baxter.

"Go and rearrest Miss Keen. I want her back in custody. *Now!*"

59

Rachel lay on the lumpy mattress, a barely adequate blanket draped over her body. She stared at the cracks in the floor, tracing them from end to end. Anything to take her mind off what was happening.

She'd barely had time to process the arrival of the note when the police were banging on her door, unceremoniously dragging her back to the cells. She was barely cognisant of the reasons they'd given for doing what they did. Something about new evidence and a restating of the murder charge. Mercifully, Kaley was still with her and called the solicitor.

Two hours later she was back in an interview room with DCI Yin, DS Baxter and her solicitor. It was just gone 10pm, a fact her solicitor challenged the officers about. They didn't care.

Yin started the recording and wasted no time in getting to the point. He loaded up the video file on a tablet and turned it towards Rachel. "Miss Keen, would you like to explain this?"

Rachel's heart sank at the realisation of what she was watching. She glanced at her solicitor, who looked confused.

"Well, Miss Keen?" Yin repeated.

Rachel tried to bluff it. "What are you seeing here?"

Yin huffed. "Really? That's your response."

Rachel shrugged.

Yin put on a serious expression. "Okay, Miss Keen, let me spell it out for you. That is CCTV footage from the morning of the 29th of May. The timestamp shows you leaving the John Radcliffe in your car at 8.42am. Your original alibi has you at work from 7.30am to 5pm, meaning there was no way you could have got to the manor house to murder Walter Cribbens. We now see you leaving work well within the window of time that the medical examiner said he was killed, some eight or so hours before you and Mr Bamford were arrested. This, coupled with your fingerprints on the murder weapon, your scarf around the victim's neck and your association with the house, leads me to believe you are guilty of murder."

The room fell silent. Rachel looked at her solicitor once again. "Could we have a short recess for me to consult with my client?" he said.

"No," said Yin, "I want an explanation."

Rachel was fighting back tears but knew she needed to answer the question. She put her head down and rubbed her eyes, eventually looking back up at Yin. "I had an eye test, or at least I thought I did. I started my shift at 7.30am but asked if I could have a couple of hours off to go to the opticians in Cowley. The appointment was at 9.15am. The problem was when I got there, I realised I'd made a mistake. I'd got the wrong day. I felt like such a numpty."

Yin frowned, seemingly unconvinced by her response. "Can anyone verify that?"

Rachel grimaced. "I doubt it unless the receptionist at the opticians remembers me."

There was once again a brief pause as the officers stared her down, a tactic that Rachel concluded was to force her into blurting something out that would incriminate her. She shuffled uncomfortably in her seat, suddenly realising the note was stuffed in her pocket. She pulled it out, smoothing out the crumpled piece of paper. "If I'm guilty then explain this."

Yin examined it before passing it quickly to Baxter, making no comment.

"Well?" urged Rachel, suddenly feeling like the roles had been reversed.

Yin leant forward, trying to intimidate. "Miss Keen. This little fantasy you've created around the Oxford Mystery game is a bit desperate. The game's finished. Someone's won the money. It's old news. You have no evidence to back up your theories that someone is out to get you and has used the game as a smokescreen."

Rachel was fuming. "What about the driver taking us to the house? What about me seeing a person silhouetted in the window when I was driven away? What about someone bashing me over the head when I returned to the house? What about this note?"

Yin shook his head. "If you really want to play this game, here's my response to your delusions. You have no evidence to back up your claims that someone was in that house. We've searched the premises extensively, twice, and there was no one there. The family solicitor says they are searching for family members to settle the estate but no one has been forthcoming. The driver could conceivably be part of your elaborate plan to secure your alibi, and the note could quite easily have been produced by you, as a convenient ruse to make us think that you are being persecuted by some anonymous perpetrator."

"What's my motive then? Isn't that key to your case? Motive and opportunity. I guess you think you've now got opportunity but what possible reason could I have for killing a complete stranger?"

Yin shook his head. "We don't need to answer your questions, Miss Keen. You are the one that is being held to account here."

Rachel let out a scream of frustration. "It's clear you've made your mind up. I've nothing further to say."

Yin glanced at Baxter, who shook his head. "Okay, that concludes the interview for now. The time is 10.33pm. You will be retained in custody for a further twenty-four hours, starting from when you were booked in, while we complete further investigation and decide whether to file formal charges against you. Do you understand, Miss Keen?"

Rachel grunted her understanding, trying not to lose it at the prospect of spending more time in the soulless four walls that was the custody cell.

As she settled back in, she lay on the bed, looking up at the ceiling.

Seething.

60

Yin yawned, as he wrestled between the need to get home and appease his wife, and the stress of proving that his case against Rachel Keen stacked up. He looked at Baxter. "What do you make of her answers?"

Baxter raised his eyebrows. "Well, I guess we are going to have to check her alibi at the opticians in Cowley. If that doesn't come through, I reckon we can prove opportunity because she would have had enough time to get to the house, murder Cribbens and get back to work by the time her car was spotted on CCTV returning to the hospital."

Yin stroked his stubble, a reminder of the lateness of the hour. "Get that alibi checked first thing in the morning." He rubbed his eyes, tiredness threatening to overwhelm him, but he pushed on. "What about motive? She's right that we don't have any real explanation as to why she killed an apparent stranger."

"We are looking into any links between her and Cribbens but nothing so far. I guess it's your call as to whether we submit a file to CPS but, apart from motive, we have everything in order."

Yin stood up. "I'd like it tighter than it is. I think a defence brief could easily prove reasonable doubt on some aspects of the case, as it currently stands. Get the team back on any links with Cribbens. If we can prove she knew him, our case will be much better."

"Okay, sir."

Yin yawned again. "Bloody hell, this case is doing me in. Are we ready for the interview with Bamford tomorrow, and have we told the chief super?"

"Yes, sir, on both counts."

They both left to go home. Yin's brain was still in turmoil. He'd had to step back from charging Rachel Keen the first time she was arrested, and he had some weird guilt about charging a fellow officer with conspiracy to murder. He shook his head. Would his case and reputation really survive if he got this wrong again?

*

Kaley paced around her living room. She couldn't rest. Why had the police rearrested Rachel? What could they possibly have on her?

She realised in all the furore that Rachel had left her phone. Kaley picked it up. It opened straight away, which made her laugh, as Rachel always seemed so tech savvy, yet left her phone without a password. She knew what she had to do.

The phone rang a few times before there was a weary answer. "What?" the voice said, a hint of annoyance clear in the tone.

"John, it's Kaley, Rachel's friend. We met once when you were taking her statement."

"Oh, yeah. What do you want? It's late."

Kaley glanced at the time. It was just before midnight. "I'm sorry but I didn't know where else to turn. The police have rearrested Rachel."

She heard some mumbling on the end of the line, another voice, the friends with benefits girl she guessed.

"I can't help you."

"What? I thought you were in the same deep shit that Rachel is."

"I am, and it's all because of her, so sorry if I'm not sympathetic to her plight."

His attitude was riling her up. "I thought police officers were supposed to support their community."

"I'm suspended."

Just as Kaley was about to fire back an angry response, there was another voice on the line. "Hi, Kaley, it's Isla. Ignore old grumpy grots here. He's just feeling sorry for himself. I said I would help them both with this problem, so do you want to get together to talk?"

"Er, yeah."

"I'm working tomorrow, and I guess you are too, so how about we meet in that little coffee shop by the entrance to the Golden Cross around 6pm?"

Kaley got off the phone and slumped in her chair. She'd only known Rachel for just under a year, when she got the job in the same department. They hit it off instantly and now she felt like she'd known her all her life. But Rachel was hard work. She felt that the emotional support was always one way. She was a complex person, and it was clear that there was some baggage from the relationship with this Lucy person.

Her thoughts turned to Abigail. Rachel's attitude to this sweet girl was strange. Dark and obsessive, yet Kaley could only see good in her.

As her eyes began to lose the fight between awake and asleep, she began to wonder whether there was more to her friend than met the eye.

61

Isla was on her lunch break, tapping away at her laptop. She knew in her role that she shouldn't be doing what she was doing, but she'd made a promise to John.

She dug a bit deeper into Abigail's life. There was a stable family home in Southampton, a younger sibling and an enviable school record. The girl was clever, but Isla pondered whether that made her a manipulative schemer. Someone that could play the role that Rachel was so sure she was playing. The thought prompted her to look back at her previous notes. Abigail was a member of the amateur dramatics group. She tapped the pen she was holding subconsciously against her mouth. "Maybe," she muttered.

Isla started to trawl social media, her eyes bulging at the sheer volume of posts that Abigail was either in or had posted herself. She knew the chances of finding any clues in all the content was going to take hours. Classic needle-in-a-haystack stuff.

She closed that line of enquiry down for another day, changing over to the Beaufort family. She started off by trawling the net for the death records of Lucy Beaufort.

Eventually she found the official copy of the death certificate. It was dated just over six months ago. The cause of death recorded as suicide. Isla glanced instinctively at her work laptop. This was it. This is where she was really going to cross the line. In her role as an intelligence analyst, she was allowed access to most case files, if it helped build an intel picture of an ongoing investigation. The problem was she had no official authority to justify what she was about to do. She sighed and ignored the little voice in her head telling her she was going to get in big trouble.

Now she had the exact date of death, it was going to be much easier to find an incident reference or a case file about Lucy's demise, if the latter existed. As it was, all she found was the incident record. It seemed as though a neighbour of Lucy's had called the police, worried that she hadn't seen her. Officers attended her flat, broke in and found her dead next to an open bottle of pills. The medical examiner's report had been unequivocal. She'd taken enough drugs to kill a horse.

Isla frowned. She really wanted to believe what Rachel had told her, but unless there was some major conspiracy going on, with the police and coroners somehow falsifying records, Lucy Beaufort was as dead as a dodo. Isla did love a conspiracy, but it just didn't stack up. She sat back and tried to recall the events that had led Rachel to this point. It all seemed to have started with the Oxford Mystery game. Abigail had come into the frame. John had somehow got himself linked with Rachel and then this weird clue luring them to the manor house.

The thought prompted her to look back at the Instagram post that Abigail had written announcing that she'd won the prize. Isla watched the video. Abigail was holding a cheque for fifty thousand pounds. Isla took a screenshot, so she could check out whether the account it was drawn against was real. Ten minutes of trawling through programmes on Tor that were definitely on the edges of the law, she found the bank account. It was registered in the name of the Oxford Mystery. Isla huffed. How had the mystery game seemingly led Rachel and John on a different path, while Abigail was merrily picking up the winner's cheque? She vowed to take a deeper dive into the game, but there were other things she needed to do first.

Isla started to search for family records on the Beauforts. The death of Lucy's mother and father were both recorded within the last three years. As she did a wider search of the family, she came across some notices from the family solicitor requesting that anyone who that felt they had a familial claim on the estate after Lucy Beaufort's death should contact them by the end of June. She couldn't find anything to suggest that anyone had come forward, and the deadline was looming.

She moved onto the land registry to look at the manor house. As far back as records were available, the house had been in the family, although it was Lucy's mother, an heir to the Billingsworth family fortune, that had it originally. They appeared to have owned the house for centuries, with the titles moving into joint ownership when Lucy's mother married her father.

Isla glanced at her watch. Her lunch break was almost over, but she had the bit between her teeth. There had to be something in the dark recesses of this family's history. She thought Rachel's theory that someone was getting back at her for Lucy's suicide was a credible motive for all that had gone on.

She went into the birth records to verify that Lucy had indeed been born to her parents and that there wasn't some adoption story at play here. A few minutes later she found what she was looking for. Lucy was indeed their daughter. She sat back from the computer, frustration coursing through her, but as she looked back at the screen, she spotted something.

The page of registrations she was on had a chronological list of all births registered in that area. She hadn't spotted it the first time, too focused on finding Lucy's name.

As she stared at the entry underneath Lucy's, she gasped in shock.

Now it all made sense.

62

Isla was frantic. A name. That's all it was, but a name that completely changed the dynamic of the situation. She'd called John straight away, but his phone just went to voicemail. She'd messaged him to call her urgently but for some reason, in the ten minutes that had passed, he hadn't responded.

She was supposed to be working, another four hours of her shift ahead of her, but she just couldn't let this go. She messaged her boss to say she wasn't feeling well and was going home, but instead she stayed at her desk. The only colleague she shared the office with was on leave and her boss was at HQ in an all-day meeting.

There was something about the name she'd found that tweaked a memory. She cycled back through what she'd been searching when it came to her. She looked at the police and coroner's records. This person had identified Lucy Beaufort's body.

Isla checked her phone again to see if she'd missed a reply from John. Nothing. Her mind was racing. She had to tell John about her discovery. It was the answer they'd been looking for. Her stomach was full of butterflies, the excitement of the chase. A feeling she always got when she was building up a profile of a suspect. There was nothing for it. She was only five minutes away from John's flat. He was probably asleep, but it was time to wake him up.

Just as she was about to shut her computer down, something else caught her eye. At first her brain couldn't rationalise what she was seeing. The officer's name that had signed off the body identification. *PC John Bamford.* Isla did a double take. *How?* she mouthed. How was it possible that John had met this person, who Isla was now convinced was behind all this, but not thought to mention it? It just didn't make sense. John had listened to Rachel's story about her time with Lucy. Why did he not say that he'd been involved in Lucy's body identification and met the very person that had to be pulling all the strings in this nightmare.

A sense of dread began to consume Isla. There was something else nagging at her. She went back to the record of the original incident when the neighbour reported that she was worried about Lucy. Isla pulled up the screen that recorded which officers were the first responders.

Tears welled up. What was going on? John had been the officer who attended Lucy's property. He'd written up the incident report, had liaised with the coroners about the post-mortem and closed the case down when the body was identified. He'd met her. The name that had to be behind this.

Isla sat staring at the screen, her stomach churning. John was in so much trouble. Suspended. A conspiracy to murder charge hanging over him. Was he really that stupid? Was he really that forgetful that he hadn't retained a vital piece of information that could help him and Rachel?

She'd known him for ages. Well, maybe more like passing acquaintances. She remembered the first time she'd met him at some awful Christmas drinks thing. She was immediately attracted to him but, although he was friendly, he seemed guarded. Their paths crossed a few times as cases developed, when he submitted intel reports and the occasional word in the kitchen when coffee was beckoning. She knew she'd always been gushing in her emotional responses to anything he said but, as she said to Rachel, he never seemed to pick up on the vibe that she was massively into him. She was so confused. The sex had been amazing. He was a gentle and considerate lover. Was it right that Isla was beginning to doubt who John was?

She tried to remember everything he'd said and done when Rachel was around, desperately looking for something that might explain this away. There was nothing. For some reason, John had been more involved with Lucy Beaufort than he had let on and was keeping that fact from Rachel.

Isla screamed in frustration. John was not a bad person, but he had to realise that the person that identified the body was a key player in everything that had happened. Didn't he? Isla's brain kept cycling through everything she thought she knew, trying to find an explanation for John's actions.

In her job, she was all about facts. The evidence. She wasn't paid to speculate, but as the sense of dread grew, she realised there was one possible explanation.

John was an addict. He was squandering every penny he owned on gambling the pain away. Was it possible that this name, this person that surely held the key to this case, had got to him?

Isla shivered at the thought.

Had John been persuaded to participate in Rachel's downfall on the promise of some serious cash?

The tears began to flow. It was the only explanation.

63

Abigail looked around the room, exasperated at the amount of stuff she'd accumulated over her three years at university. Her father was picking her up in the morning and she still had so much to do. The clothes were mostly sorted, shoved into a large suitcase and a smaller duffle bag. The kitchen equipment had been loaded into several boxes, but spare bedding, towels and other household items were still sprawled around the place.

It was late afternoon, and she pondered whether she could really justify wine o'clock starting so early. She shook the idea away and fussed around some more, shoving things into random bags, when a small sachet of white powder fell out onto the floor. She picked it up, eyeing it curiously. She hadn't remembered having a spare bag of cocaine, surmising that this little package would do three or four lines. She never felt out of control with the drug. It was available at every party, as common as the wine and vodka most people downed after doing a line. She rarely had it in the flat, but that wasn't to say it didn't happen. She remembered one particular night when the boy and girl she was having a threesome with were snorting lines off her stomach. She smiled at the thought but went to the toilet and flushed it. She was sure that her father would not approve.

As she got more demoralised by the mess, someone knocked on her door. It was the postie with a package. She opened it to find a lovely bottle of white wine with a small card that simply said:

Sorry, R xx

She checked the package again, but there was nothing else. "R," she muttered. Was it from Rachel? Every time she'd met her, she seemed so emotional, unhinged almost. But, when they last spoke, Abigail felt like she might have got through to her, even though she walked away in a huff. Maybe this was her way of saying sorry.

She glanced at the time. It was nearly 5pm. "Oh sod it," she said, as she pulled a glass out of one of the many boxes that had already been packed. She was glad it was a screw top as she couldn't face finding the corkscrew. She poured a glass and sat down on the only chair that wasn't covered in stuff.

She took a sip. It tasted a bit odd, much sweeter than she was used to, but she didn't care. A free bottle of wine was great. The thought made her heart skip a beat. Here she was feeling grateful for free wine when she realised that she could now buy as many bottles as she wanted. The only problem was, the last time she checked, the cheque for fifty grand still hadn't cleared. She'd taken it to the bank as soon as she'd received it. They said it would take three days to clear, but it had now been four days. She picked up her phone and navigated to her banking app. She gasped as she saw the balance.

The cheque had still not cleared. She cursed at the time. Would the bank still be open? She called them quickly, immediately stressed by all the *press one for this, press two for that,* options, but eventually got to a person. There was a tortuous conversation about when she'd deposited it, which branch and what seemed like a hundred questions to verify her identity against the relevant account. She sipped at the wine as the lengthy conversation continued, regretting drinking on an empty stomach as it didn't settle well.

Eventually, the call taker came back, their tone suddenly changing from *Miss super customer service person* with the annoyingly chirpy manner to something much more serious. "Er, Miss Simmons, I'm afraid I've got some bad news. The cheque has bounced."

"What?" exclaimed Abigail, almost spilling her wine in the process.

"Yes, unfortunately the account that this cheque was drawn against has insufficient funds to pay this amount."

Abigail disconnected the call. What was going on? She absent-mindedly took another sip of wine. The Oxford Mystery had told her she was the winner. The cheque was delivered by courier the next day. She couldn't believe it. The whole thing had been a con.

She finished the first glass of wine and poured another. As she took a large slug of the second glass, she started to feel odd. She tried to let the feelings pass, realising that she better eat something but, as she tried to move, her body felt tired and heavy. Her limbs wouldn't move. She shook her head, trying to clear the fog that was consuming her.

A few seconds later, the wine glass dropped onto the floor.

64

It was just after 6pm as Isla sat in the coffee shop just inside the entrance to the Golden Cross shopping arcade. She was sipping a latte, having already sunk an espresso shot, like some non-alcoholic chaser. Her mind had been spinning all afternoon at what she'd found. Despite repeated calls and messages to John, he'd not responded, which meant that the only person she could talk to about this had just walked through the door.

They'd never met, but the coffee shop was nearly empty, so it seemed that Kaley had assumed who she was and wasted no time in introducing herself, seemingly relieved that she hadn't just accosted a bemused stranger. Isla was immediately jealous. Kaley was pretty with a round face, long brown hair tied back in a ponytail and a lovely summer dress clinging to a good figure. The antithesis to her unruly hair, Guns and Roses T-shirt and a height and weight disadvantage that always made Isla self-conscious.

She must have had stress written all over her face because after the brief introductions, the first thing Kaley asked was what was wrong.

Isla rubbed her face. "Oh, Kaley, I'm sorry. This was

supposed to be a nice chilled get-together where we discussed how we were going to help our dearest friends, but I'm… God… so confused."

"What is it?" replied Kaley.

"I don't know if Rachel told you, but I'm a bit of a geek, with a reputation for finding things that others can't find. Well, I decided to start digging into some of the elements of this weird situation and found a couple of things that blew me away."

Kaley tried a smile to encourage Isla to carry on.

"The thing is," Isla continued, "I knew there must be something to find around this Lucy Beaufort character, the ex that Rachel seems to be obsessing about—"

"Okay," interrupted Kaley, "I'm guessing you found something."

Isla shook her head. "No shit. I checked all the birth and death records of the family and, sure enough, Lucy's mother and father both passed away in the last few years. I also found Lucy's death certificate and searched the police incident records."

Isla kept pausing, like she didn't want to say the words. Kaley kept prompting her to carry on.

"The thing is, the person that responded to the 999 call about Lucy was John, yet in all our discussions he claims he never met her."

"Do you think he's just been a bit forgetful? I mean, I gather he has some issues."

Isla frowned. "Maybe, but he also dealt with the body identification."

"And?" said Kaley. "I'm guessing from your expression that there's more."

Isla drew in a deep breath. “When I was looking at Lucy’s birth records, to verify that she was indeed born to her mother and father, I noticed something else.”

“What?” exclaimed Kaley, losing patience with the stuttering explanation.

“Lucy has a sister, and she was the one that identified the body.”

There was another pause, ramping up the tension further.

“And what’s more, they were born only minutes apart. Lucy has a twin.”

65

John winced at the bright light as he left St Aldates Police Station. He'd been in the windowless interview room for over two hours, a deliberate police interrogation tactic to desensitise the suspect from all external factors. The late afternoon heat was still hanging around, and he started to sweat the minute he picked up the pace.

He didn't know where he was going. He was aware that there were several messages and missed calls from Isla, but he just wasn't in the mood for her.

The formal interview by Yin and Baxter had been demoralising. He didn't try to hide the fact that he'd been back to the crime scene, when it was obvious that Rachel had dobbed him in. Instead, despite his solicitor's advice to say nothing, he'd tried to make them see that his intentions were merely a mercy mission to try to stop Rachel from entering the house. They didn't seem interested in his version, going over and over the same questions, each time adding a subtle change to the angle they were taking. Trying to trip him up. Trying to see cracks in his story.

John tried to go on the offensive, challenging them about the driver's evidence. He could sense that Yin was on the defensive with that point but kept turning it around, focusing on the growing evidence they had against Rachel, a fact they claimed strengthened the conspiracy to murder charge against him.

After nearly two hours of interrogation, with an inadequate cup of brown liquid that purported to be coffee, the only thing to sustain him, he was released.

They stated that the bail conditions stood, and he got the distinct impression that Yin felt he was close to being able to post a formal charge.

John carried on walking. He needed a drink, and he needed to gamble.

*

Rachel lay on the bed in the custody cell, constantly trying to get into a comfortable position as her back began to complain about the hard surface she had subjected it to for the last sixteen hours or so. Her solicitor had told her that under the Police and Criminal Evidence Act – PACE – they could only keep her in the cell for twenty-four hours, unless they charged her or sought a formal extension from a senior officer. More likely was a release with the bail conditions remaining in place.

She knew they were checking out her alibi on the morning of the murder. It was touch and go how that would play out. She needed there to be sufficient doubt for her to be released again.

She took in a deep breath. Hoping.

*

Yin and Baxter were debriefing on the interview with John when a message came through from one of the CID team that they'd tasked to check out Rachel's alibi. The moment Yin read it he closed his eyes, throwing his head back with an exasperated grunt.

"Not good news then, boss?"

"No, Sergeant. It seems as though the opticians Miss Keen was supposed to go to that day couldn't remember either way whether she rocked up for an appointment. They confirmed that she did not have an appointment on that day but was scheduled in a week later, adding some credibility to her story."

"Come on, sir," urged Baxter, "doesn't that add doubt to her alibi and strengthen our case that she's lying and was indeed at the house murdering Walter Cribbens?"

Yin shook his head. "I need something that connects those two. She doesn't profile as a psychopathic serial killer which means, if she did it, there must be some reason she killed him. I want everything focused on finding those links and then maybe I can convince the chief super that we've got reason to formally charge both Keen and Bamford."

"Yes, sir. I'll get right on it."

Yin watched Baxter leave, a tightness in his gut telling him he wasn't yet certain of a conviction.

He reluctantly picked up the phone to the custody sergeant to once again release Rachel Keen.

66

The shock of the revelation about Lucy having a twin sister prompted Isla and Kaley to move on from the coffee shop, in search of something stronger. As they revelled in the sharpness of their respective G&T's, Kaley summarised what they were both thinking.

"Holy shit, so Rachel is right. There's a twin sister who is seeking revenge on Rachel for her part in Lucy's suicide."

"Well," said Isla, "it certainly seems so. This sister must have been the person Rachel saw silhouetted in the window of the manor house when they were arrested, the person who bashed her over the head when she went back there and the person who locked us in that bedroom. I reckon she's also behind this mystery game."

Kaley stared into space, eventually blurting out what was on her mind. "But why didn't Lucy ever mention to Rachel that she had a twin sister? Rachel was adamant that Lucy said she was an only child."

Isla shrugged. "Who knows. Maybe they were estranged and this twin only came back into the picture after Lucy committed suicide."

Kaley frowned. "Seems unlikely. I thought twins always had this unbreakable bond."

Isla gasped. "Oh crap. Sorry, complete tangent but this means what I found out about John may be an explanation as to why he's also been targeted."

"I'm not sure about that. From what you said, all he did was attend the flat she was in and find her dead, later dealing with the body identification. I can't see how he could be blamed for that. There must be something else."

They both sat in silence for a minute. Kaley broke the silence. "What's her name? The twin?"

Isla opened her laptop and navigated back to the body identification records she'd bookmarked. "Er, Maya."

"Oh. Does that mean you can now search for her across all your internetty things?"

Isla smiled at Kaley's apparent lack of tech savviness. "Yeah, give me a minute. Let's do the basic searches to see if we can find anything."

Kaley took the opportunity to go to the bathroom and get another round in while Isla tapped away. By the time she returned, Isla had a deep frown on her face.

"Bloody hell, that doesn't look like a face that's found happy things," Kaley said.

"This doesn't make sense," Isla said, "there are no records of a Maya Beaufort existing in adult life."

"Eh?"

Isla explained more. "I can find school records up to the age of sixteen, but then she drops off the earth. There are no social security records, no job history, no social media presence and no credit card records. She doesn't exist."

"How's that possible? If she used her name to identify Lucy's body, why is she a ghost?"

Isla shook her head. "I have no idea, but I'm sure John or Rachel said that the police had been in contact with the family solicitor about the Beaufort estate and claimed no one had come forward to grab the inheritance. I gather there's a lot of money in Lucy's estate, so why wouldn't her sibling jump at the chance to claim it?"

They continued to chat, throwing ideas around, none of which seemed to explain how an apparent twin was raging vengeance against John and Rachel, whilst avoiding identification. As they re-examined every avenue, Kaley suddenly thought of something. "What about this Walter person? Do you think Maya killed him because he did something to Lucy, or was he just used to frame Rachel for murder?"

"Bloody hell," replied Isla, "I'd forgotten about him. If it's the latter, you know, using him as an innocent victim to frame Rachel, then she is as twisted as fuck."

Time was getting on and they realised it was near closing time at the pub. "What are we going to do with all this?" said Kaley.

"We need to tell Rachel and John, as this could have a major benefit to their defence case. I can't get hold of the miserable bastard, and I guess we don't know if Rachel is out of custody yet."

Kaley checked her phone. There were no messages. But as she was about to click her phone off, a local *Oxford Mail* breaking news notification came through. She clicked on it out of curiosity, immediately gasping and putting her hand to her mouth.

“What is it?” enquired Isla.

“Er, shit. That girl. Abigail. She’s been found dead in her uni accommodation.”

67

John stirred from a fitful sleep. The side of his face was sore and, as his eyes fluttered open, he realised he was lying on the floor in his living room. The soreness was down to him lying on the rough carpet, a position he did not remember getting into. His thumping head reminded him how much he'd drunk the previous evening after the police interview. He remembered walking aimlessly around the centre of Oxford, trying to clear his mind, but pub after pub lured him in, until he erased the short-term memories. He had no idea how he'd got back to his flat, but the fact that he ended up on the floor suggested he barely made it.

He slowly hauled himself off the floor, dragging his hungover body into the kitchen and drinking a glass of water. He stood for a second wondering whether it was making him feel better or was going to prompt something worse. He managed to take a few deep breaths, stopping himself from throwing up. He leant against the kitchen counter, his mind never far away from playing through the tragedy that was his life.

He couldn't believe how, as a police officer, he'd managed to get himself so much on the wrong side of the law. The gambling, the catalyst for the lying, the bad decisions and ultimately his suspension. But why couldn't people see he wasn't a murderer? He just wouldn't do that. Ever since he met Rachel his world seemed to be dragged deeper into the dark void. She was toxic.

He was sure he'd met her previously, a while before the day she accosted him in the street about her Abigail obsession, but he just couldn't remember when and where. Whatever the reality, Yin seemed to have the bit between his teeth, convinced that they were in it together and guilty as charged. His solicitor seemed vaguely competent and kept reassuring him that the fact no formal charges had been brought was a good thing. It meant they did not have a solid enough case to go in front of the CPS.

John's default reaction to stress over the last few years had been to drown himself in the noise and anonymity of the casino. He had no idea whether the money had run out. He just didn't care.

In the last few days he'd been considering his options. Could he run and hide? Go to some foreign country where he couldn't be found. It wasn't like he was public enemy number one. Surely they would just give up on him. He contemplated going back home to Leeds, but he couldn't bear the prospect of the judgement and disapproval from his parents. His mother would undoubtedly label him a particular failure for not delivering her any grandchildren. He didn't care. He wasn't like them, and they didn't deserve anything from him.

The beep of his phone reminded him of the numerous messages from Isla. She was nice and the sex had been a welcome release from all the stress, but he couldn't see himself with her. As he drunk another half a glass of water, he knew he had no choice but to face the music.

As his brain began to wake up and his thumping headache began to ease, there was one thing he knew he had to do. He needed to distance himself from Rachel. He wasn't a police officer anymore. He had no obligation to her.

The thought of Rachel sent his brain spinning again. What was it about her that he recognised? Also, the Lucy thing. There was something in the deep recesses of his memory banks that kept telling him he was part of this story. He knew someone called Lucy but, as he'd said to Rachel a while ago, it was a common name. She'd never shown him a picture of her, so he had nothing else to go on.

John was embarrassed at his lack of recall. The last ten months or so had been particularly bad. Work had become a mechanical task, turning up and getting through each shift with the minimum of fuss, so he could go off and gamble some more in his downtime. If he had met Rachel or Lucy in this time, he was ashamed to admit that he probably barely acknowledged their existence. In the early part of this dark period he was on response, attending all the immediate 999 calls. The nature of the job meant you went from one emergency to another, with barely time to think. He was relieved when, around five months ago, he was moved to the neighbourhood team. The pace was better but, if anything, it just gave him more time to gamble.

He managed to stomach a piece of toast and some strong coffee. As he began to contemplate what to do next, his doorbell rang.

It was Isla. Looking stressed.

68

While Isla was hunting down John, Kaley was at Rachel's front door pressing the bell over and over again. Kaley had heard nothing from Rachel. She didn't even know if she was out of custody. After the fifth bout of bell ringing, a weary-looking Rachel opened the door, still in her nightdress.

Kaley didn't wait to be invited in, barging past Rachel into the main living room. "My God, babe," she exclaimed, "why didn't you call me to let you know you were out?"

Rachel rubbed her face. "Sorry, it was late when they let me out. Like, past 11pm. I just got a cab and came back home."

Kaley gave her a quick hug but fixed her with a fierce, concerned expression. "Now sit down. I'll get us coffee. We need to talk."

A few minutes later, hot steaming cups in their hands, they sat opposite each other on the easy chairs in Rachel's living room. Kaley took a sip and then fixed her gaze on Rachel's face. "I've got some mind-blowing news to tell you, babe."

Rachel looked at her, tired and expressionless.

Kaley ploughed on. "The thing is, I met up with Isla last night…"

"Oh, she shag you as well?"

"What? No! She's been helping you, Rach. Looking into all the things that have been going on."

Rachel yawned. "Sorry, I'm knackered. I'm guessing the little slut has dug up some dirt."

Kaley frowned. "Babe, why are you being so mean to her? She's found something."

Rachel shook her head. "Okay. What?"

Kaley took a second. What had happened to Rachel? She was being rude and dismissive. Whilst Rachel had always been a high-maintenance friend, this was a level of rudeness she'd never seen. She shook it off as just a reaction to spending another day in the cells.

"Um, I'm not sure how to tell you this, but Lucy has a sister. A twin sister."

The reaction was delayed, as Kaley let it sink in. Rachel didn't say a word but looked at Kaley with a deepening frown appearing on her face. "You what?"

"It's true. Isla looked back at birth records to verify that Lucy was indeed born to her parents. When she was scanning the details, she realised that a second child had been born at the same time. Her name's Maya."

Rachel sat up from her slumped position on the sofa, her facial expression changing as she realised the full implications of what Kaley was saying.

"You see," Kaley exclaimed, "it explains everything. She's the one behind this. The person in the house, the one that bashed you over the head and locked you in that bedroom, the one that killed that Walter guy and planted the evidence to incriminate you. It all makes sense now. You were right. She must blame you for Lucy's suicide and is exacting revenge against you."

Rachel rubbed her face. "My God. I can't believe it. I don't understand why Lucy never mentioned she had a twin sister." There was another brief pause as more implications of the news hit her. "But I guess this gets me off. Doesn't it?"

Kaley smiled. Rachel was back. Her adorable, vulnerable friend. She grabbed her hand. "Yes, babe. We need to go to the police and tell them all about this."

For a second, Kaley wasn't sure Rachel had heard her, as she sat back hard in the chair. "Why is John involved?"

"Well, we're not sure, but there is something. He attended the 999 call when the neighbour reported concerns about Lucy the night she died. He also dealt with the body identification. The thing is, babe, he's met her. Maya. She identified the body."

Rachel sat back up. "But… but… that makes no sense. Why wouldn't he have remembered something like that?"

Kaley sighed. "We don't know. Isla's gone round to ask him about it."

Rachel took a sip of the now lukewarm coffee, suddenly gasping as something else apparently dropped into her thoughts.

"So, Maya was behind this mystery game, which…" Rachel's voice suddenly rose a pitch, "means I was right all along! Abigail was part of this. Her stalking me and winning that money was all part of the set-up."

Kaley didn't say anything, but Rachel picked up on her hesitancy. "What is it? What are you not telling me?"

"I'm sorry, babe, but Abigail's dead."

69

John didn't like the accusatory tone that Isla was putting on as she relayed the same story that Kaley was telling Rachel. The news that Lucy had a sister, whom he'd apparently met, had gone some way to resolving the niggle in his head about the whole meeting Lucy and Rachel thing. Despite Isla's disapproving tone, he really didn't remember the incident, but it at least confirmed that he had met Lucy, albeit in the worst way possible. He didn't remember this Maya person, but it did suggest that maybe he hadn't previously met Rachel, his mind addled by everything that had been going on.

As John poured his heart out about how messed up he'd been and how he could barely remember six minutes ago, let alone six months ago, Isla's mood softened. "We need to go and see Yin, John. Surely this news will get the charges dropped?"

John grimaced. "I'm not sure. Yin isn't going to take birth records as evidence that this twin is behind all this. I mean, no one has actually seen this person. He'll want to find her before he believes that she's involved. No, after my interview with him yesterday, I still think we have a long way to go."

John could tell Isla was a bit deflated by his attitude, but he tried to gain back some positivity by agreeing to call his solicitor. A few hours later, John and Rachel were sat in an interview room with their respective legal representatives, Yin and Baxter.

*

Yin's week was not getting any better. The chief super had assigned him the Abigail Simmons case, due to the potential links with the wider investigation of Walter Cribbens' murder. A preliminary review of the crime scene suggested deliberate poisoning. A distinctive smell of almonds was evident around the victim's mouth and in the wine bottle that appeared to be the vehicle for the poisoning. Cyanide.

The card that accompanied the bottle of wine was interesting. Who was *R*? He knew there was one obvious suspect. But therein lay the problem. Was it too obvious?

But for now, he was sat in an interview room with both his key suspects at the requests of their solicitors. Rachel Keen's solicitor took the lead and outlined the discovery of Maya Beaufort. Yin flashed an annoyed look at Baxter at the revelation, concerned that his supposed team of detectives had failed to find this information. After listening to the theories about how Maya had to be behind this, Yin allowed the group to run out of steam before giving his considered response.

"Thank you for bringing this information to me. It may indeed have a significant bearing on the case and my team need some time to investigate this development. However, until I can find some credible evidence that this person is involved, your bail conditions remain in place."

Rachel was the first to react, pulling out a crumpled piece of paper from her pocket. "Here's the evidence," she screeched as she once again showed Yin the note that said, *Do you really think you've solved the Oxford Mystery?*

"I told you before, Miss Keen, this is not evidence. You could have quite easily printed this off on your own computer and brought it to me to deflect your guilt."

Rachel's solicitor tried to stop her, but she was steaming with anger. "How do you explain Abigail's death then? Are you going to try and pin that on me as well?"

Yin's frown lines seem to deepen. "That investigation has only just started. We will be in touch with your solicitor if we need to speak to you formally about the circumstances behind Miss Simmons' death."

Rachel sat back in her chair. "You are unbelievable," she muttered under her breath.

The interview was terminated, with everyone going their separate ways. As soon as Yin walked out of the interview, he got a message from the chief super.

Within a few minutes he was in her office. "What was that all about?" she said, clearly aware that the two main suspects had been in the station.

Yin sighed. "We've got a development, ma'am. It seems that Miss Keen and Mr Bamford have somehow found that Lucy Beaufort has a twin sister and are now using this as their defence against all their charges."

Her tone was simmering with anger. "Are you trying to tell me that despite having a large detective team on this, not one of them has found this information? And, to make it worse, our prime suspects in a murder case are actually doing your job for you."

Yin didn't know what to say. In a perverse moment, all he could think about was his wife and kid. What would they do if he got sacked, because the way things were going, he was in trouble.

"Well!" she shouted.

"No excuses, ma'am. We've cocked up, but I'm getting the team to focus on finding this twin and the possibility that she is behind the Walter Cribbens' murder. We are also going to treat her as the chief suspect in the Abigail Simmons murder."

The chief super's mood was not softening. "Please tell me you haven't dropped the charges against Miss Keen and Mr Bamford."

"No, ma'am, their bail conditions remain in place."

She stared him down for an uncomfortable minute. "You're dismissed," she eventually said, curtly.

Yin got out of there as quickly as he could, the sound of his boss shouting, "Get me some results," ringing in his ears.

70

Rachel had arranged to meet Kaley in a coffee shop in town after the interview. The sharp hit of caffeine did little to calm her down.

"That cop is a total arsehole. Why can't he see I'm innocent?"

Kaley put on her best sympathetic smile. "He'll get there, babe. What did he say he was going to do about it?"

Rachel let out a huge breath. "He said some bullshit about getting his team to investigate but is refusing to drop our bail conditions."

"What did your solicitor think?"

"She wasn't surprised, but she said she would continue to work on it."

Kaley grabbed Rachel's hand. "That's good, babe. Just be patient."

Rachel rubbed her eyes. "Oh, Kaley, I wish I had your optimism. I mean, how fucked up can this get? Lucy has a twin sister that she never told me about and now the person who I was convinced was stalking me has been found dead."

There was a brief pause before Rachel bolted upright in her chair. "No. No!"

"What?" exclaimed Kaley, unnerved by her friend's reaction.

"This can't be happening. If this Maya person is behind all this, she'll be setting me up for Abigail's murder."

There was silence. Rachel looked at Kaley. The frown lines on her face deepened. "What? Why are you looking at me like that?"

"Murder. You said murder."

Rachel shook her head in disbelief. "Yeah, what of it?"

Kaley shuffled uncomfortably in her chair. "The police never said she been murdered."

Rachel hesitated. "Er… what? I mean, I just assumed she was murdered, if it's connected to all this shit."

Kaley took a sip of coffee without saying anything more.

*

Isla blew out her cheeks as she tapped on the door of DCI Yin's office. She knew she had to fess up to what she had been doing for John and Rachel.

"Come in."

"Ahh, Miss Cowdrey. What can I do for you?"

"Oh gosh, please call me Isla. Sir."

He smiled. "Okay, Isla."

He stared at her expectantly, as she agonised over how to tell him what she'd done. She'd worked with him on a couple of cases, developing the intelligence packages that supported his investigations, always finding him kind and supportive.

"There's something I need to tell you, sir."

"Go on."

"I've been kind of seeing John Bamford for the last few weeks and I've rather got caught up in all this drama."

"Okay. Nothing illegal I hope."

Isla winced, trying to ignore the question. "Look, I'm sorry, but I've been trying to find out information for John and Rachel Keen. You know, to help their defence."

Isla was concerned by Yin's hardening expression.

"The thing is, I was the one that found out about Maya Beaufort. I investigated the birth records for Lucy Beaufort, the woman that Rachel Keen had a relationship with and, according to her, the catalyst for all this. As I was checking the information, I suddenly realised there was a second name recorded at the same time as Lucy's birth. Her twin sister, Maya."

Yin grimaced. "So now Bamford and Keen think they have a cast-iron defence because of this mystery twin. I can't deny, your actions have caused me a whole heap of shit, especially with the chief super."

Isla looked down, scared to catch his eye. "I'm so sorry, sir, that was not my intention, but the thing is, that's not the whole story. Maya Beaufort is a ghost. I can't find any records of her after the age of sixteen. It's like she disappeared off the face of the planet."

Yin leant forward. "You what? Have you any idea what happened to her?"

"Er, no, I haven't had time."

There was an uncomfortable silence. Yin eventually broke the tension.

"Right, Miss Cowdrey." The return to formality was not

lost on Isla. "I'm going to gloss over how you found out this information and put me in the shit. I'm going to give you one chance to redeem yourself. I want you on my team, because quite frankly this bunch of so-called detectives haven't given me anything as significant as this in the whole time we've been investigating Walter Cribbens' murder and now we have another one to investigate."

Isla grimaced. "Thank you, sir. I'd be happy to help."

"Hold on, before you get too grateful, there are conditions."

"Oh, okay."

"You cannot see John Bamford or Rachel Keen. You can't speak to them, call them, message them on social media. Nothing. They are still prime suspects in this murder and your involvement in their defence will give me a major problem. However, the chief super is coming down on me like a tonne of bricks and I need results fast. So, are you in or out?"

Isla knew she had to do the right thing. "I'm in."

71

John watched as the roulette wheel spun. He let out an incredulous laugh as it landed on red and the croupier pushed the pile of winning chips his way. This was pretty much all he had left. Cashing in the last fifty pounds in his bank account to get a train ticket to Reading and buy some chips to gamble with.

Despite his connection with his Gamblers Anonymous sponsor, the demons were nowhere near to being beaten, and he hadn't even considered ringing her as he stood in Oxford Station buying the ticket that would take him back to the place that fuelled his addiction. The noises in his head didn't stop just because he had someone to talk to, someone who knew what he was going through. It was always the same. Whenever his life took a turn for the worse, the darkness descended, his mind shutting out all external influences, luring him back to the thrill of the gamble, urging him on, no rational thoughts allowed.

He idly placed a couple of chips on red, as he reflected on the latest catalyst to his gambling. Isla. She'd messaged him to say it was off. She couldn't see him anymore. No reason. Just a bland message saying it was all over. He had mixed emotions about it. He was struggling to deal with her, but she was the one person on his side. He won again, helping him to forget all about her. Rachel, as well. She was the reason for his final fall into oblivion. If his solicitor couldn't help, he was done. He slugged a neat vodka and placed some more chips on red. He won again.

John's hands began to shake. He'd been here before. A winning streak, which always ended the same way. He'd get more and more bold about his bets. Win after win, tempting him to place more chips on each bet, before the crash. He won again.

He closed his eyes, vaguely aware of the croupier's voice. *Place your bets.* He placed more chips on red. He won again.

He did a mental calculation of what was in front of him. Nearly £500 up. As he was about to bet again, a message pinged on his phone. It was from his sponsor, asking how he was.

He choked back tears. He knew what he had to do.

He walked away.

*

Kaley was pacing around her flat. The latest interaction with Rachel had floored her. Was she reading too much into what she'd said about Abigail? The police had not mentioned murder, so why had Rachel said it? Was it a reasonable assumption by Rachel, given everything that had been going on?

Kaley stared out of the window, the darkness a metaphor for her mood. She tried to calm her concerns.

Rachel had been through a traumatic time. In custody, twice. Accused of all sorts of things, that neither of them could really believe. But therein lay the problem. They had been besties for nearly a year now, but Kaley began to doubt whether she really knew the real Rachel. She had been her emotional crutch the whole time they'd been friends, but as she reflected on recent events, she realised how little Rachel had ever told her about the past. She was vaguely aware of the Lucy relationship and some other failed romances, but it had all been rather superficial. Rachel had always glossed over her past, everything an anecdote of her life.

Kaley's mind replayed the conversations with Isla. Why had Rachel got out of the manor house so quickly? Why hadn't they searched for the person who bashed her over the head, if she was convinced someone was in the house? And then there was the Abigail thing. Kaley had been right. Abigail was just a nice person, yet Rachel was convinced she was a psycho stalker. Was it possible that Rachel had made up the knife incident, staging the scene for some sick, dramatic effect?

Kaley fought back tears. Was this how a true friend should act? Thinking the worst of someone who, despite all the angst that had been flying through her mind in the last few minutes, had been a good mate.

Kaley's gut tightened. She was scared. She couldn't shake the possibility that the police were right. Maybe Rachel was a killer. Maybe she had killed Walter and now poor Abigail.

Kaley screamed. This just couldn't be happening.

Was Maya behind all this, or was her friend a cold-blooded murderer?

72

Isla sat at her desk, stifling a yawn. She'd had a restless night's sleep. Ditching John had been a hard decision, but she knew she had to get on the right side of the law. She'd allowed her infatuation with him to cloud her judgement. The sex had been great, but it wasn't enough. She'd already blurred the lines of legality with the information she'd searched for on behalf of John and Rachel.

She had come to her senses. Yin could have investigated, which almost certainly would have landed her with a misconduct charge. She just couldn't afford to lose her job and thanked her lucky stars that it was only the chief super's stress that had prompted Yin to gloss over her poor decisions.

She finished the last of her herbal tea and opened her computer. She had to develop an intel profile for both cases, quickly and efficiently, if she was to avoid Yin's wrath.

Isla decided to start with Abigail Simmons, the freshness of the case meaning there was very limited information on the file. She reviewed what she'd previously found about Abigail. A stable family background. Both parents living in a very ordinary middle-class area of Southampton, with one younger sibling. Abigail had a good school record, which had undoubtedly helped her get into Oxford. She examined the preliminary statements that had been taken. Her course leader described her as a dedicated, kind student, who was on track for a first. The description at odds with the person that Rachel had described as a lunatic stalker.

Isla reflected on the whole case. Whilst John and Rachel were apparently deep in this thing, the police hadn't secured a complete case against them, which is why no charges had been brought. The links between Rachel, John, Walter and Abigail were unclear. Fundamentally, despite the forensic evidence, there was no logical reason why Rachel or John would kill Walter Cribbens. The links between Rachel and Abigail were stronger, albeit only since the start of the Oxford Mystery game.

The thought of the mystery game prompted her to look back at some information that was on the case file. Isla had forgotten that Abigail had been the apparent winner of the game, but the tech team had noted on the file that the last thing she'd been looking at on her laptop was her bank account. Significantly, the balance did not reflect the fifty thousand pounds that she was supposed to have won. This evidence suggested a strong link between the murders and the mystery game, something else that Rachel seemed sure of. That it was all, somehow, connected.

Isla shook her head. She just couldn't knit it all together. There was a key part of this case that no one was seeing. Could Maya Beaufort be the answer? It was a more logical hypothesis that she was exacting revenge against Rachel and John for their involvement in Lucy's death. But the Walter and Abigail murders still seemed out of kilter, unless Maya was using them to set up Rachel and John.

Isla began to examine Abigail's social media feeds. Despite her apparent dedication to her degree, she was a party animal. She remembered when she did a search on her before, that she was part of several societies, and by the look of the pictures online, most of them involved drinking.

As she looked at a few pictures, zooming in on Abigail's face, the clearer images showed the telltale signs of drug taking. It was all in the eyes. She spent another half an hour poring over the pictures but not much else was forthcoming.

Abigail Simmons had been a young, carefree girl, enjoying her experience at uni, indulging in some vices but nothing that raised a red flag. Isla was convinced that she was not the person that Rachel described.

The thought of Rachel made her change tack. The first discovery was that she was clean. Not known to the police, not even a parking ticket. Employment records were pretty sound, having worked as a theatre nurse for the past five years, preceded by a number of years of training and grafting as a staff nurse. Isla frowned. Initial investigations suggested that Rachel's life was very normal, boring even. Not the profile of a deranged killer. She looked at her credit card spending, banking history and general credit history. There were no red flags.

She switched to Maya Beaufort. Another brick wall. All she found was the same weird history up to the age of sixteen. She searched beyond conventional methods but even in the darkest recesses of the web, Maya Beaufort did not exist.

Her head was pounding. Yin had given her a second chance because she was good at what she did, but if she couldn't find anything useful, he might be less gracious. She stood up, stretching her aching joints, a legacy of too much time sitting at the computer. She went to the kitchen and made herself another herbal tea. Too much coffee was making her wired, and now the heat was on, she needed to calm herself down.

She splashed some water on her face, before resuming her position at the computer. She drew in a deep breath. Something had to give. She started off slowly, idly scrolling through the social media pictures of all her subjects. After twenty minutes, she felt like a voyeur, intruding on the lives of people that seemed so normal.

She cursed loudly. There was no one else in the office to hear her frustrations, which wasn't helping the isolation she was feeling in that moment.

As she glanced at her watch, pondering how long it was to lunch, her enthusiasm for the job sinking rapidly, she suddenly spotted something in one of the social media posts.

One of Abigail's pictures had a group of people bunched together, posing for a group selfie. It wasn't the group that had drawn her interest. In the background, a little bit behind where Abigail was standing, was a woman, seemingly staring at the group. Isla zoomed in, screwing her face up as she examined the slightly grainy image. Was it who it looked like? She zoomed in and out, trying to get a better fix on the image.

She wasn't certain. The shape of the face was similar, the hair a bit different, the nose a different shape, but there was no doubt in her mind who it looked like.

Rachel.

73

Rachel stared at the crumpled note.

> *Rachel and Kaley, Isla and John, what a bunch of busy bodies, you've become*
>
> *Abigail too, another meddling kid, she had to die for what she did*
>
> *Walter was just a pathetic drunk, no one worried when he did a bunk*
>
> *So now it's time for my retribution, face the truth about your contribution*
>
> *To Lucy's death, which I will never forgive, I really don't think you deserve to live.*
>
> *MB*

*

John had slept twelve hours straight. For the first time in as long as he could remember, the noises in his head had not won out. He'd walked away. The message from his sponsor had been exactly what he needed. For once his mind was relaxed and the exhaustion of the last few weeks had allowed him a deep, satisfying sleep.

As he sipped a glass of orange juice, he eyed the handwritten envelope with curiosity. He tore open the end and pulled out a single piece of paper. He read it, making his blood run cold.

*

Kaley sat in the staffroom, heating up the sausage roll she bought from Greggs on the way into work. A moment of weakness, spurred on by the turmoil in her head. She would normally eat a healthy salad or similar for lunch, but the lure of meaty baked goods was what she needed right now as she wrestled with her conscience. Was she being a shit friend or was Rachel really involved in all this horror?

The microwave pinged and she devoured the sausage roll in seconds, revelling in the taste and naughtiness of the experience. She washed it down with a cup of tea before reaching into her bag for the post, which she'd grabbed as she left the house.

A credit card bill, a piece of junk mail about new windows and a handwritten envelope. She opened it. As she read the words, the sausage roll threatened to reappear.

*

Isla was frantically searching through Abigail's social media posts, trying to find further images of the face that could be Rachel. In the short time she'd known Rachel, she hadn't been able to get a fix on her. She was emotional, ready to fly off the handle at any time, but then Isla supposed she would be too if she'd been accused of murder. That said, there was a darkness to her, not only exhibited by her moods but in the selfish way she made everything about her. Isla had to admit that she hadn't found anything to date that would profile her as a killer, but then murderers didn't always come in a neat consistent package. Isla knew the Maya Beaufort angle made more sense, and she decided to focus more on the whole Beaufort family story after she'd had some lunch.

She was just about to leave the office when an email pinged into her inbox.

The title goaded her… *Do you think you've solved the Oxford Mystery?*

She opened the message, stifling a scream as she read the words.

*

Messages started to ping between the four of them. Kaley had started it off, messaging Isla, needing someone to calm her terror. It didn't work when Isla told her she'd received the same message. Kaley messaged Rachel. Isla broke the rules by messaging John.

They'd all received the horrifying message.

A plan was hatched. They all agreed to meet at Rachel's flat later that evening.

It was time to solve the Oxford Mystery.

74

The mood was tense. Wine was poured and the foursome sat in Rachel's living room, nervous and twitchy. John especially didn't want to be there. He'd vowed never again to be in the same room as Rachel, and Isla's sudden rejection had hurt more than he cared to admit. But the revelation of walking away from the casino had given him a fresh perspective, and he didn't like being threatened. He spoke first.

"Okay then, we're all here. What are we going to do about this?"

Kaley fought back tears. "How can you be so calm about this? This fucking psycho is threatening our lives and you're treating this like some everyday task that needs sorting out."

John shook his head. "Jesus Christ. I don't know why I came. You three are all the same. Bloody emotional women with no sense of purpose."

Rachel intervened. "Oh, fuck off, John. You ain't no Mr Big Boots police officer anymore. Maybe you should look at yourself before throwing insults at the rest of us."

John huffed incredulously. "I know I'm a complete failure at life, Rachel. At least I don't try and hide it, like you do."

"You what?"

"I might be a shit police officer, but I'm trained to spot liars, and since I've met you, I don't believe a word that comes out of your mouth."

Isla cut across the argument. "Look, come on. There's no point in us fighting each other. This note threatens us all, which means someone has been watching us."

"Why do you say that?" said Kaley, a distinct wobble in her voice.

"The note is signed MB. It must be Maya Beaufort. This seems to confirm what I found about Lucy Beaufort's twin sister. She's wreaking revenge for Lucy's death as Rachel suspected. The fact she knows about the four of us means she's been close to us quite recently, because I haven't been involved before."

Isla noticed a sense of satisfaction on Rachel's face, as Kaley spoke. "I thought you said this Maya person is a ghost?"

"She is. There are no records of her existing in adult life, which means she's changed her identity."

Kaley looked at John. "Isla said you've met this person. When she identified Lucy's body."

John was stewing but gave a response through gritted teeth. "I don't remember."

The room fell silent. Rachel stood up, grabbing the now empty wine bottle. "This isn't getting us anywhere. I'm going to give this letter to my solicitor as further evidence of my innocence. This is effectively a confession, and if the police do their job and find this woman, we can all walk away from this."

John and Kaley looked ready to bolt, but Isla couldn't let the nagging doubt in her mind go, without asking Rachel some questions. "Rachel, can I just clarify something? Did you know Abigail before you started playing the mystery game?"

Rachel stopped in the doorway. "What an odd question. No, until I met her that day by Carfax, I'd never seen her before."

Isla shrugged. "Okay, but I'm still perplexed as to why you were so keen to get out of the manor house that day. If you were so sure that someone was in there, why didn't we go and look for them?"

"Are you for real? I'd been bashed over the head and locked up in that room for God knows how long. Did you really think I wanted to spend another second in that hellhole?"

Accusing, frightened stares were once again exchanged between the group. There was no trust. No camaraderie. "Get out of my flat. All of you!" said Rachel, her anger simmering.

The three of them left, stopping on the street outside Rachel's flat.

"What's wrong with her?" exclaimed Kaley. "That's not my friend up there. She's changed. There's something going on."

Isla chewed her lip. "I don't know, Kaley, but I definitely think Rachel is hiding something. I was doing a trawl of Abigail's social media posts, and I found a picture that I'm sure was Rachel, standing behind her at a party."

Kaley frowned. "Oh, could it have just been a coincidence? I mean, you don't necessarily know everyone when you attend a party."

"That's true but, like John, I'm not sure that Rachel is telling us the whole truth about this situation. Walking away from that manor house was strange. She was so determined to find this person that she went there on her own. It was only John and I following her that saved her that day, yet when we escaped from that room, she suddenly wanted to bolt. It doesn't make sense."

There was an uncomfortable pause. Isla cut across it. "I'm going to take this note to Yin. He needs to see it."

John recoiled. "Yin?"

Isla immediately regretted mentioning his name. She knew she had to come clean. "Yes, John, I shouldn't be here. Yin's asked me to be on his investigation team. I admitted I was the one who found that information for you and Rachel about Maya Beaufort. It's the reason I can't see you anymore."

John could barely contain his rage. "Unbelievable. So, you're telling me that you're now working for the prosecution? Trying to prove the case against me?"

Isla felt sick. "No, John. I'm just trying to find the truth."

John stormed off, shouting back at Isla, "You wouldn't know the truth if it bit you on the arse."

Isla and Kaley were left standing on the street. "Do you want a drink?" said Kaley. "I need to calm my nerves."

"What a great idea."

They walked into Headington and ordered some shots in the first pub they came to. "You think she's guilty, don't you?" said Kaley as they allowed the sharpness of the spirits to calm their angst.

"I don't know. The Maya Beaufort thing makes more sense than Rachel being a killer, but John's right, she is lying about something."

Kaley fought back tears. "If you'd asked me a month ago whether I thought Rachel was capable of this, I would have laughed you out of the room, but the longer this goes on, the more confused I'm getting. She's always been a good mate, but I have to admit that she has been hard work. I always seem to be the shoulder to cry on. It never seems to be the other way."

They sunk the rest of the shots and immediately ordered some more. As they sat, drowning their sorrows, Isla fixed Kaley with a determined stare.

"Leave it to me. I'm going to find the truth, and that's a promise."

75

Despite the copious amounts of alcohol, Kaley was still twitchy about the whole situation, so Isla walked her back to her flat. Isla got a bus into town, getting off just outside the town hall, a ten-minute walk from her house at the top end of Abingdon Road.

As she got off the bus, she found herself staring at every face that went by, jumping at every noise. The squeak of the bus's brakes, the squawk of a crow, a sudden shout from the other side of the road. She'd never seen herself as the brave one, the shoulder to cry on, the rock. Despite Kaley's obvious distress that evening, it seemed like that was the role she had been playing for Rachel.

She pulled her cardigan around her chest, a chill going through her body despite the warmth of the late evening. At first, she couldn't reconcile how she was feeling. She had been strong for Kaley. It seemed like the right thing to do but, now she was on her own, walking down the relatively quiet street, she was shaking.

She pushed on, trying not to catch the eye of the odd person that walked by. She caught herself in a sob. It was like some post-traumatic stress. She'd been so focused on solving the mystery and helping Kaley that she hadn't realised how scared she was.

She picked up the pace. Her brain wouldn't let it go. Fear was competing with confusion about the case. Were they persecuting an innocent woman? Was Rachel really being set up by this mystery Maya person? Isla hated herself for feeling bad about Rachel. On the one hand she seemed like just another vulnerable, paranoid thirty-something, just trying to cope with all that life threw at her. But John didn't trust her and, she had to admit, she trusted his instincts, despite all his own baggage.

As she reached the top end of Abingdon Road, she stifled a scream as she heard the snap of a twig. She spun round. There was no one there. She scanned a full three hundred and sixty degrees, her eyes trying to pierce the darker recesses that were not bathed by the glow of the street lights. She listened. Nothing.

She started to stride with even more purpose, desperate to get to the safety of her house, to shake off what she knew were irrational fears but… there it was. The note had threatened them all. Were her fears really that irrational? Whoever this was had been close to them. Recently. It was possible that they were out to get every one of them. Walter and Abigail had been murdered. Why wouldn't she be next? She put her hand to her mouth, trying to stifle the terror.

The shaking got worse. Three minutes away.

As she got nearer to her house, the skies darkened, the moon suddenly shrouded by cloud. Isla looked up to the sky, shaking her head. Even the weather was conspiring against her.

Her heartbeat began to slow as she saw the outline of her house. A quick glance behind her. No bogeyman. She got to her gate, fiddling in her bag for her door keys.

Panic set in as she scrambled through the items in her bag. Where were they? Just as she felt the cold, jagged edge of one of her keys, a hand touched her shoulder.

She screamed and swung her arm around in a vain attempt to take out her attacker. Her wild, manic eyes tried to adjust to the figure that was silhouetted in the street light.

"Hey, hey," said the voice. "It's me."

Isla now had the keys gripped in her hand, the point of one of them nudging out between her fingers, ready to strike. A technique she'd been taught in a personal safety talk they'd had at work.

When she realised who it was, she relaxed her hand. "Fucking hell, John. You scared me to death. What the hell are you doing, stalking me like that?"

John held his hands up in mock surrender. "Look, I'm sorry. I was out for a walk, trying to clear my head, when I saw you walking down St Aldates. With everything going on, I just wanted to make sure you were okay."

Isla frowned. "Eh? Earlier I was the queen bitch, so what's changed?"

"I'm sorry about that. I know you have to do your job, and it makes sense that Yin would get you on his team. You are the best at what you do."

Isla knew she shouldn't, but she invited John inside. She shook off his protests. What Yin didn't know wouldn't hurt him. She grabbed a bottle of wine and poured them both a glass.

As John took a sip, he gazed at her. "Just find the truth, Isla. For me. You know I'm innocent."

All of Isla's rational thoughts left her. She put her glass down and stripped off her top.

It had the desired effect.

76

Isla sat in the morning briefing, trying to avoid eye contact with Yin. Despite the warmth and excitement of her encounter with John the previous evening, she felt guilty for betraying her promise to him.

Thankfully, Yin's attention was elsewhere. The chief super was in the room and about to address the briefing. Never a good sign. No DCI wanted a senior officer encroaching on their patch. It was tantamount to a public bottom-smacking. Isla felt sorry for him, but she couldn't help feeling that it was getting her off the hook as she was a terrible liar and wasn't sure she would survive his scrutiny if he suspected what she'd done.

Isla shook it off, as the chief super began to speak. "Right," she said, in full command voice, "I'm not happy with the progress we've made on the investigations into the murders of Walter Cribbens and Abigail Simmons. The press are all over us about the fact that we made two arrests but have been unable to progress to formal charges. It's making us look incompetent, and the chief constable is not happy, which means I'm not happy and nor should anyone else be in this room."

The chief super paused for a reaction, continuing as everyone seemed to be listening.

"I've reviewed the case against Rachel Keen and, need I remind you, one of our own officers in John Bamford. Whilst I can see that we have solid forensic evidence against Miss Keen, the rest of the case has more holes in it than a block of Swiss cheese. If they are not our perps, I want us to find this missing twin sister. We can't get this wrong, so I need you all to double your efforts and get some results. Fast!"

The chief super eyeballed everyone in the room, making sure her message had got through. Isla nodded, not wishing to stir the wrath of a clearly angry senior officer.

Once the chief super left, Yin addressed the briefing, tasking out jobs that split between finding Maya Beaufort and cementing the case against John and Rachel. Isla knew they were clutching at straws. They'd hit a brick wall. The more solid parts of the case against Rachel and John would not hold up when there was so much doubt about the other areas, which were circumstantial at best and, in some cases, non-existent. Isla desperately wanted to believe that Rachel and John were innocent. She was convinced that the Beaufort family was the link between all the characters in this mystery.

The thought galvanised her and, as she got back to her desk, she began to ponder the point. If Lucy Beaufort's death was the key, then the links between Rachel and Lucy were not in doubt. John had found her body, but Isla was still struggling to see why this apparent twin could blame him for anything. Which left Abigail and Walter.

Isla remembered that Rachel had said Lucy's behaviour changed in the last months of their relationship, eventually leading to their split. She could tell from the pictures that Abigail was definitely a recreational drug user. Was it possible that Lucy had somehow got involved with Abigail's party crowd?

She looked back at the file on Walter. He lived alone, did a boring job and spent most of his nights in the local pub. She searched for Walter's social media accounts. He only did Instagram. A quick scan through the posts showed every picture in the pub, Walter always holding a pint, sometimes as selfies and others with various grinning, inebriated friends. As Isla scrolled further back, she froze on one picture. She zoomed in.

"Huh!" she exclaimed as she stared at the same face that she was sure was in the background of one of Abigail's pictures. Once again, the hair was different and there was something about the shape of the face that made her doubt herself, but she was sure it was another picture of Rachel.

Isla sat back in her chair, staring at the screen, trying to reconcile what she was seeing. After a moment she realised this was the breakthrough Yin was looking for. Based on the date stamps, the two pictures confirmed that Rachel knew Walter and Abigail before the mystery game started, if indeed that was her in the pictures.

She felt sick. She'd intended to do more digging into Maya Beaufort but had inadvertently just made the case against Rachel much stronger.

She had no choice. She downloaded the two images and sent them to Yin.

77

Kaley wasn't sure a day off was what she needed in that moment. She was still spooked by the message as she sank two glasses of orange juice, the dryness of her mouth and the thumping headache a symptom of the previous night's binging. She thought about a piece of toast, but her stomach lurched. She clicked the kettle on. Coffee was a better option.

As she sipped at the hot liquid, the smell soothing her soul as well as her headache, she realised there were several messages on her phone. A couple were inane posts that her friends had put on Facebook and Instagram, but one was on Messenger, with a preview line that made her go cold.

Her hand began to shake as she navigated to the message. *It's time to end the Oxford Mystery*, it said. A video file was attached. The terror from the previous day came flooding back, as she fought back tears. Her finger hovered over the play button.

She put the phone down. She couldn't do it. If it was a message from the sick psycho that was suddenly terrorising their lives, she didn't want to be drawn further into the nightmare. She stared at the screen. It began to fade as the screen saver was about to come on. She quickly jabbed at the screen. The screen brightened up, the play button seeming somehow larger, taunting her.

An uncontrollable sob. Fear consuming her. She picked up the phone, going back to the main menu screen. She called Rachel. The call connected but it rang out, going to voicemail. The sound of her friend's voice shocked her more than she cared to admit. She couldn't be a killer. Could she?

She sipped the dregs of the now cool coffee. There was only one other person she could call. Isla. After a short conversation, Isla promised to come straight to Kaley's house. Kaley busied herself, jumping in the shower, cleaning her teeth, brushing her hair. Anything to look a bit more human.

About forty minutes after the call, Isla was in her living room. Kaley showed her the message. "I just couldn't do it. I don't want to see what this sicko has posted now. I'm so scared."

Isla glanced at Kaley, concern etched over her face. "Look, before we watch this, there's something I need to tell you. I've just come from work, and I've found something."

Kaley winced. "Oh God, Isla, I'm sorry. I didn't even think about you being in work. I've got a day off and just couldn't cope with this on my own."

"Don't worry about it. I've just sent what I've found to the DCI. It will keep them off my back for a while."

Kaley shuffled uncomfortably in her chair. "Do I want to know?"

Isla's expression was still serious, which didn't brighten Kaley's mood. "The thing is, I think I've found pictures of Rachel, with Abigail and Walter."

There was a pause before the implications hit Kaley. "Oh no. Isn't that what the police were looking for? Links between Rachel and those two?"

"Yes, I'm afraid so. Whilst we know that Abigail and Rachel met during the mystery game, these pictures are way before that. Almost a year ago."

"And you're sure they are Rachel?"

"Er, well, not 100%. I'm sure both pictures are the same person, but I have to admit there are some differences between the Rachel we know and the pictures. The hair is different and her face… I don't know… it just looks fatter somehow, and the nose is different."

"So, it might not be her!"

There was an awkward pause before Isla picked up Kaley's phone.

"Are we going to watch this then?"

78

As John took a walk along the towpath, the noises in his head were quiet. He couldn't reconcile it. He felt at peace. His life was a mess, but to walk away from a gambling binge for the first time ever was a revelation. Within the next few months, he could be out of a job or, worse, a copper in prison. But making such a significant step in his recovery from addiction was pushing all other stresses to the side.

The brief isolation of being on the towpath, the tweet of birdsong, the rustle of leaves on the trees as the gentle breeze cooled the warm day, were sensations he couldn't remember enjoying. He instinctively glanced over his shoulder as he heard footsteps. The note had threatened them all, but he was weirdly apathetic about it. A determined jogger pounded past him. He let out an ironic laugh.

He was annoyed with himself when he allowed the beep of his phone to interrupt this brief oasis in his tragic life. He glanced at the preview message, frowning at the mention of the Oxford Mystery. He wished he'd never started the stupid game. It had been the final nail in his coffin. Greed and desperation had driven him to follow like a sheep, caught up in the furore and excitement of winning the money. And then there was Rachel. A complete car crash.

He stopped, opening the message, curiosity getting the better of him. It was a video file. He clicked on the play button, his eyes widening as he watched the footage.

*

Kaley was in such a state that Isla decided she had no choice but to take on the driving responsibilities. They sped towards the Green Road Roundabout, haunted by the images they'd just seen on the video. Kaley was scrunched up in the passenger seat, her arms around her belly.

The game had just got horribly real. The video showed Rachel bound and gagged. Alive, struggling against her constraints, her eyes filled with terror. A robotic voice narrated the scene, ending with an invitation to come to the manor house if they wanted to save her.

It was horrifying. Everything they had suspected Rachel of doing had been blown away in one video message. There was now no doubt that Maya Beaufort was behind this and somehow had kidnapped Rachel, taking her back to where poor Walter had been killed.

Isla followed the sat nav, not speaking to Kaley for fear of making her more hysterical. They just had to get to the manor house and confront whatever was going on. Isla's head was spinning. There had always been doubt about Rachel's guilt, but the evidence had slowly been stacking up against her. But was that the point? Was Maya manipulating the whole situation, slowly feeding the police more and more evidence to convict her? The images of Rachel with Abigail and Walter played on Isla's mind. There was something about those pictures that were off. She just couldn't work out what it was.

She drove as fast as she dared. Twenty minutes later they turned into the long driveway that led to the manor house. Isla noticed Kaley glance at her, tears streaming down her face. She drove on, the tree-lined drive making it feel somehow darker and imposing, despite the bright summer's day. It only took a few minutes before they crunched onto the gravel that surrounded the house.

Kaley bolted up. Another car was parked outside. "Who's that?" she said. Isla parked a little bit away, getting out of the car slowly and carefully, in a vain attempt to mask their arrival. As they began to walk towards the car, they both let out an involuntary scream as the car door opened. Shock turned to relief as they realised it was John.

"What are you doing here?" said Isla.

"I could ask you the same thing," he replied.

Isla opened her phone and shoved the video in his face. "Huh, I got it to."

They looked at each other, their gaze instinctively moving to the front door of the manor house.

Was this it? Would they really solve the Oxford Mystery?

79

Isla gently coaxed Kaley towards the front door as John strode purposefully towards it, seemingly unfazed by the danger that might be on the other side. By the time Isla and Kaley reached the marbled hallway, John was already walking down the corridor towards the main living area.

They followed, Kaley flinching as she heard distant moans. They quickened their pace, trying to catch up with John, eyes darting left and right, looking for threats. None were evident as they emerged into the grand expanse of the living room.

In the middle of the room, Rachel was gagged and tied to a chair. John was already in the process of freeing her. Kaley rushed to help, fighting back tears as she tore at the constraints. "My God, babe. What happened?"

Rachel took a second to recover from the unpleasant sensation of having the gag in her mouth. "Someone attacked me outside my flat."

"Did you see them? Was it this Maya person?"

Rachel rubbed her wrists and slowly stood up to stretch her body. "I don't know. Whoever it was attacked me from behind and injected me with something. The next thing I know I'm here, bound and gagged."

Kaley was jumpy, instinctively twitching her head at every sound, scanning for danger. "Where are you?" she screamed at no one in particular.

Isla came over. "Haven't you seen anyone since you got here?"

Rachel rubbed her eyes. "No. Since I came to, I've not seen anyone."

As this was going on, John had moved over to the far right-hand side of the room, feeling along the wall panels. Isla decided to distract herself from the Rachel and Kaley's hysteria show by focusing on his actions. "What are you doing?"

John continued, pushing at each panel. "Don't you remember? When we were in here before, we came out from those secret passages somewhere around here."

The group moved over to where he was, just as a piece of the wall moved slightly. The rest watched as John pushed hard against it. Whilst a defined crack appeared, showing the outline of a door, it wouldn't move. "Shit, it must be locked from the inside," he said.

The other three looked at him, expectantly. "What?" he said. "Aren't we going to try and find this psycho?"

Kaley shot a look at Isla and then at Rachel. Her nerves were shredded and there was no rational thought likely to emerge from her in the state she was in. Rachel still seemed zoned out, groggy from whatever she'd been injected with.

Isla had been watching the scene quietly and calmly, trying to push away the fear response deep in her gut. "John's right. There's a reason this psycho has drawn us here. If she's not going to show her face, we should flush her out."

"I can't be on my own," exclaimed Kaley, "I'm completely freaking out here."

Isla frowned. "Look, whilst not wanting to invoke my inner Scooby Doo, I think we should probably split up, as this is a big place to search. Let's do two pairs and open up a call on our phones so we can give each other a running commentary on what we are finding. I'll search with Rachel and Kaley can go with John."

The group said nothing. "Well?" she said. John was the first to react. "Yeah, fuck it. Let's smoke her out. We'll search upstairs. You do downstairs."

Kaley and Rachel eventually shook themselves out of their malaise and followed John and Isla as they walked out of the living room. John and Isla connected a phone call, putting their phones on speaker so everyone could hear what was going on. As they got back to the front door, John and Kaley began to ascend the wide carpeted staircase. Isla went for the door straight in front of them, which opened with a creak, leading into another corridor.

Isla and Rachel followed the corridor, which opened out into a large kitchen. A central island dominated the room with cupboards, storage and ovens around the edges. They searched, but there was nothing that helped them confirm whether Maya Beaufort was behind all this. Rachel was walking slightly ahead. The niggle in Isla's head was still there. Something wasn't right about this situation. She was giving John a running commentary and he was reciprocating with the odd comment about each bedroom being clear, but she wasn't really concentrating on what he was saying, distracted by Rachel.

Isla couldn't help feeling that Rachel's body language

was strange. She was ambling around the kitchen like she was looking at a show home, the complete antithesis to the tension that Isla felt throughout her body. When Rachel lingered near the knives, Isla froze in fear, convinced that something bad was going to happen.

The moment passed and Rachel navigated to the other door out of the kitchen, which opened out into a small corridor, with doors on both sides. They went left, into the main laundry room. Isla began to form a mental picture of the layout of the house, as there was a door at the back of the room leading outside. Once again, the room looked like it hadn't been used for a long time, as dust coated most surfaces. They came back out, and Rachel immediately went for the opposite door, which opened into a dimly lit passage. Rachel turned and looked at Isla. "I think we've found the underground tunnels."

Isla relayed the news to John, who repeated the same feedback that they'd found nothing. Isla's niggles continued as Rachel strode forwards, heading downwards as the passage appeared to be going under the main house. After about fifty yards, two doors appeared on the right. Rachel opened the first one, which revealed a small library, the second into a drawing room. Rachel didn't go into either, turning right, exploring deeper into the passageway. Isla barely had time to react as Rachel ploughed on.

The corridor carried on for a while, before they came to a junction, a stone wall in front of them, which Isla surmised was the perimeter wall at the other end of the house. To the left was a staircase and the right followed on the same level. Rachel went right, eventually coming to a bolted door. She undid it and emerged back into the main living room.

As Isla and Rachel stood in the room where not fifteen minutes ago Rachel had been bound and gagged, part of Isla's niggle resolved itself. Rachel had apparently gone from the terror of being abducted to someone without a care in the world. Isla gasped at the realisation. The pictures she'd found came sharply into focus.

Rachel wasn't scared because she knew there was no one else in the house.

80

John and Kaley had searched most of the upper floors. There was a long main corridor that had bedroom after bedroom. They were all beautiful rooms with sweeping views of the surrounding countryside. Each room was lavished with luxury. Large beds, some four-posters, with beautiful bed linen and drapes. Some had standalone baths in the main room. All had expensive curtains and various antiques scattered around. Large TVs were on the walls. The bedroom where they'd found Rachel was as they'd left it, the bedclothes still crumpled where she'd lain.

They got back to the staircase and went through the door that was ahead of them. It opened out to another corridor, much shorter but with rooms on either side. These rooms were much more basic. After looking at a couple of them, John turned to Kaley. "I reckon these were designed for the servants."

Kaley grunted as she continued to walk around with her arms tightly crossed against her stomach, desperate for the ordeal to end.

They reached the end of the corridor. A door was in front

of them. John pulled at it and it opened out into a darker passageway. John looked in, realising that it led to a set of stairs that would take you to the ground floor. He turned to Kaley. "I think this is part of the secret passageways. There're stairs leading down. Come on."

He started to move but stopped as he realised Kaley wasn't following him. He shouted. No response. He cursed under his breath. She was stood in the corridor, hunched up and crying. Why had Isla paired him with the hysterical one? It was the last thing he needed. He sighed and reconciled himself to the fact that this would all be over soon. He put his arm around her shoulder and coaxed her towards the door. She responded, robotically, like a dog on a lead.

John went first, glancing back regularly to check Kaley was following. Isla's voice came over the speaker phone. They were back in the main living space. As they got to the bottom of the stairs, the dimly lit passageway went straight on and right. John instinctively went straight on. He was sure this was the way they came when they were escaping the room after they'd found Rachel.

Sure enough, he came to a door, which was now ajar. He pushed at it, feeling Kaley's breath on his neck as she closed in on him, clearly wanting to get out of the dark, spooky passage. As they emerged, they heard footsteps. Isla and Rachel were walking back into the room. "We found nothing," said Isla.

They all watched as Rachel went over to the lavish drinks cabinet that still had several decanters with liquid in. Rachel grabbed a glass, taking the stopper off one of them and sniffing at the contents. She noticed the others watching her. She shrugged. "Smells alright to me, and if you lot are feeling the same as me, I need something to calm my nerves."

Kaley rushed over and grabbed a glass, her hand shaking so much she could barely contain the small amount of alcohol that Rachel poured in.

John looked at Isla, who was watching the scene, biting her lip. In the short time that John had known Isla, the lip biting was one of the more adorable things about her and he caught himself in a brief feeling of nostalgia, thinking back to when it had been all about the sex and not about murders and mystery. She hadn't noticed his scrutiny, so he nudged her. "What's up? You look like there's something on your mind."

Isla glanced at John. "This is all a charade," she whispered.

Despite trying to keep the volume low, they both noticed Rachel shooting them an accusing look. "You gossiping about me?" she shouted.

Isla and John closed the gap. "Not at all," said Isla. "We were just debating why we hadn't found anyone here."

Rachel shrugged. "What can I say? As I said, I never saw anyone once I woke up here."

Isla couldn't hold back any longer. "Who tied you up, Rachel?" she said.

Rachel's face wrinkled in confusion. "What do you mean? I told you. I woke up here, bound and gagged. I never saw who attacked me."

This was it. Isla had worked it out, and she couldn't hold it in any longer.

"That simply isn't true, is it, Rachel? Or should I call you Maya?"

81

Yin's head was pounding. The combination of pressure being applied by the chief super and his wife getting increasingly annoyed at his erratic hours and lack of time at home, meant sleep had been at a premium. Caffeine wasn't helping.

The case files of Walter Cribbens and Abigail Simmons were on his desk. He needed to do a full review of what the team had found so far. Forensics in the Abigail Simmons case had confirmed cyanide in the wine bottle that had been delivered to her house, but no further evidence on, or in, the bottle. The file on Walter Cribbens hadn't changed much in a week. The forensic evidence on the murder weapon and scarf found at the scene were confirmed as belonging to Rachel Keen but everything else was still shaky. They had her leaving the hospital at the right time to give her opportunity to get to the house and do the deed, but her alibi of being at the optician's had not been conclusively proved. The problem was that if the defence called the receptionist to give evidence, any competent defence brief could easily prove reasonable doubt. The case against John Bamford was even worse.

The team were poring over records trying to find Maya Beaufort. Although she appeared to have disappeared off the planet at age sixteen, the fact remained that her presence as an aggrieved twin sister made more sense than Rachel and John killing random strangers.

But therein lied the latest twist in this frustrating drama. Isla had sent him some pictures which, for the first time in this case, appeared to show a connection between Rachel, Abigail and Walter before the mystery game kicked off. Isla was right that the pictures were not of great quality and there was some doubt as to whether it was actually Rachel Keen, but Yin had sent them straight to the tech team to enhance them for facial rec purposes.

He idly read the background information on Walter and Abigail. There was no obvious reason why they were killed. The picture of John and his statement was next on the pile. There was no doubt he'd made many mistakes in his life, fuelled by a gambling addiction that he'd hidden well from his colleagues until recent events. The problem was, Yin just couldn't see John as someone who would be an accessory to murder. It was curious that he'd been involved in responding to the 999 call when Lucy Beaufort's body had been found, but no one had been able to establish whether this was relevant to the case. He huffed. Maybe Maya Beaufort could answer that question, if they could ever find her.

He was about to refill his coffee cup when Baxter and the lead tech came rushing into his office, excited looks on their faces. "I hope your expressions mean you've got something for me?"

"Yes, sir!" said the tech.

Yin sat back down, and the tech opened his laptop, wasting no time in explaining what they found. "Right, sir, we've had a breakthrough. We enhanced the pictures that Isla gave us to get fairly decent images that we could put through the facial recognition system."

Yin stared at the images. "So, they are Rachel Keen?"

The tech put on a more serious expression. "Well, no. The percentages at the bottom of each image reflect the match against facial recognition with Miss Keen's custody photo. You see, 85% and 88% respectively."

Yin pulled a confused expression. "I don't understand. We'd normally be pretty happy with a match like that."

"I agree, sir" said the tech, "but look at this." He switched to another window. This time there was a similar but slightly different picture alongside the ones they'd put through facial recognition. The percentage matches were 97% and 95%.

Yin was getting annoyed. "Why are you showing me more pictures of Rachel Keen?"

The tech ploughed on. "That's not Rachel Keen. These are pictures of Lucy Beaufort."

The room fell silent as Yin stared at the images, flashing looks at the tech and then Baxter, who had a distinctly sheepish look on his face. It took him a few minutes, but he eventually fixed Baxter with a fierce expression.

"Sergeant, are you trying to tell me that this is the first time we've reviewed a picture of Lucy Beaufort?"

"Er, yes, sir. Sorry, sir."

Yin's voice rose a notch. "Because from what I'm seeing here, Lucy Beaufort and Rachel Keen are bloody well related. In fact, they look fucking identical."

"Yes, sir," replied Baxter, trying to ride the bollocking.

Yin stood up, putting both hands over his face. "Holy fucking shit. This is why Maya Beaufort is a ghost."

Baxter gave a nervous nod.

Yin shook his head. "Now we've got her."

82

John and Isla took evasive action as the glass Rachel had been holding flew in their direction, eventually smashing against the base of a lamp on one of the numerous occasional tables dotted around the room. Kaley had watched the action open-mouthed as she tried to process what Isla had just said.

The distraction of the glass being thrown had been enough for Rachel to reach into a drawer in the cocktail cabinet. She was now pointing a gun at them.

"Well ain't we a clever little bitch?" Rachel said to Isla.

"Babe!" exclaimed Kaley. "What's going on?"

Rachel gestured for them to gather on the sofas in the middle of the room, standing far enough away to keep them in range.

Isla sneered with a bravado that she wasn't feeling inside. "I'm sorry to say, Kaley, but we were right all along. Rachel is a fraud and a liar. She's Maya Beaufort and has been engineering this whole charade."

Kaley was distraught. John seemed to have a satisfied expression on his face, despite the danger.

Rachel smirked. "Took you all long enough. I mean, I hear they might be nominating me for an Oscar."

Isla knew it was a cliché but sensed that Rachel wanted her moment in the sun. If they could keep her talking, they might be able to find a way out of this mess. She cursed her stupidity at leaving work without telling anyone where she was going, the need to help Kaley consuming all her rational thoughts at the time. "Come on then, *Maya*," Isla said, a sarcastic edge to saying her real name, "you've obviously got something to say to us all, so why don't you get on with it."

Isla could tell Rachel didn't like the challenge, her expression growing dark, her grip on the gun a little tighter. "Do you always leech onto other people, Isla? I wasn't really planning for an interloper, but I guess you'll have to be dealt with like all the others."

"Babe!" screeched Kaley.

Rachel fired a shot at Kaley's feet, garnering screams from the group. "Shut up. Shut up, you stupid little bitch."

Kaley buried her face in a cushion, crying uncontrollably. The others tensed up, now in no doubt that all their suspicions about Rachel were being horribly confirmed as she appeared to be revelling in her endgame.

They waited. Rachel took in a deep breath. "Anyhow, now that you know who I really am, it won't come as any surprise when I tell you that this whole sorry mess is about revenge. The people that killed my poor, pathetic sister have to pay for what they've done."

For the first time, John engaged. "We didn't kill her. She committed suicide."

Rachel rocked her head from side to side. "Um. No. That's not how it was."

John shot a confused look at Isla, who continued with the tactic of keeping Rachel talking. "How was it then? I guess we are going to have to put up with your self-obsessed ramblings, so why don't you just tell us?" Isla retorted.

Rachel drew up a chair, making sure the gun was still pointing in their direction. She began to speak. "You see, I was the black sheep of the family. My father barely acknowledged my existence, always favouring Lucy. By the age of sixteen, I was so sick of it that I left the family home. I delved into the dark world of fake identities and became Rachel Keen, getting my nose fixed and changing my hairstyle, anything to get away from the hell of living in this house. I didn't see my father or sister for years until my mother died. At the funeral, they barely acknowledged my existence. I'd given up on them until my father died. Suddenly Lucy needed me. She found me, apologised for everything and begged me to be back in her life. But she was weak."

Isla nodded. "I'm guessing this is where Abigail and Walter came in. She started taking drugs at Abigail's parties and went drinking with Walter."

Rachel shot Isla a disapproving look. "God, you really are a know-it-all. I might just have to shoot you first, so I don't have to listen to any more of your sanctimonious judgements."

The comment was met with another squeal from Kaley, as Isla tried to front it out with a stern expression that masked the terror she was feeling. "Why did you blame them? She was a grown woman," said Isla.

"She was weak and pathetic. Her whole life she relied on our father. When he died her world fell apart. I thought I could finally be there for her. Be a friend. Be a sister, but no. She was out of control, and they drew her into their vices."

"But Abigail was a nice person. She was just enjoying life at uni. How could you do that to her?"

Rachel let out a laugh, laced with pure evil. "Ahh, I have to say that was one of the better parts of this plan. I'd been keeping an eye on her for days before the mystery game started, getting used to her routines and the places she went. I made sure she was around the centre of Oxford when the mystery game launched so we could have that chance meeting. She didn't even have the barest sense of recognition as to who I was. It just cemented my hatred for her even more. The irony was, she wasn't stalking me. I was stalking her."

"So, you were behind the mystery game?" said Isla.

"Yes," Rachel smirked, "a nice little touch, don't you think? It's amazing what these cyber nerds will do for a bit of cash. Same with my little assistant who tied me up today and locked the door in that bedroom when you thought you were saving me the other day. Money talks in the criminal world."

As Isla and John listened to Rachel's rantings, they hadn't noticed that Kaley had stopped crying and was now staring at Rachel. "The knife in your drawer," Kaley said, her voice still uncertain, "that was all a lie. My God, Rachel, you had me convinced that Abigail was a nutter when all the time, the person that purported to be my bestie was abusing my friendship in the most horrific way."

Rachel crinkled up her nose. "Oh, boo hoo. Poor little Kaley. Don't you realise what a complete bore you are? This mother hen crap is *so* wearing. Why don't you get a life instead of latching onto other people's?"

Kaley was fighting the urge to sob her heart out. The betrayal she was feeling was competing with the realisation that the person she thought was her best friend was on the verge of killing them all. From somewhere she found some courage. "I… I can't believe this. How could you do this to me? How could you be so cold? I've been there for you every time you've needed a shoulder to cry on. I've been your friend. How, Rachel? How could you deceive me like that?"

Rachel said nothing but her knuckles were getting whiter as the grip on the gun grew tighter.

Kaley flashed a panicked look at Isla, who picked up on the signals.

They had to keep her talking.

83

Yin called a rapid operational briefing with as many of the team as he could find. An urgent call over the radio had resulted in eight officers being present in the briefing room, all seemingly curious as to why the DCI was suddenly jumping up and down like an excitable puppy.

After all the agonising over Rachel Keen's case, he couldn't believe they'd made a breakthrough. She was a liar. A psychopath. She'd sat in front of him on so many occasions protesting her innocence, playing the victim, whilst all the while she was a calculating murderer. He'd dealt with many murder cases. More often they were domestic situations that had gone horribly wrong, mostly fuelled by the fine line between love and hatred, or the scourge of mental illness. It was rare to find a psychopathic serial killer on your patch.

He called the room to order. "Right, we have just been presented with evidence that confirms Rachel Keen as our chief suspect in the murders of Walter Cribbens and Abigail Simmons. We now have clear evidence that Rachel Keen is in fact Maya Beaufort, the twin sister of Lucy Beaufort.

This fact gives her clear motives for these murders on the assumption that she is seeking retribution for her sister's suicide. We have been able to establish a link between Lucy Beaufort, Walter Cribbens and Abigail through pictures on social media, suggesting that she knew them, thus resulting in Maya blaming them for her sister's death. Whilst that may not sound rational to you and I, we're dealing with a cold, calculating killer. We need to find and rearrest Rachel Keen, aka Maya Beaufort, as a top priority."

Yin stopped to make sure the team had taken it all in. The concentrated looks on the collective faces told him all he needed to know. He pushed on.

"We are going to run a live job with the assistance of the control room. We are going to deploy to three locations. Rachel Keen's home in Headington and the manor house where Walter Cribbens was found, which also happens to be the Beaufort family home. I also want to find John Bamford. As you know, he is up for a conspiracy to murder charge alongside Rachel Keen, but I am now worried that he is an innocent victim of Miss Keen's murderous plans. Rather than being our second perp, his life may be in danger. We need to find him, so I want one unit deployed to his house. If you need backup, contact the control room inspector."

As the teams that were deployed to Rachel and John's houses left the room, Yin looked at Baxter. "Where is Miss Cowdrey? She's the one that set us on this path, yet she seems to have disappeared. Do you know where she is?"

"No, sir. Sorry. One of the station duty officers said they saw her leave the station late morning, but no one has seen her since."

Yin frowned. "Well, we haven't got time to look for errant intel analysts. Hopefully she'll turn up when she's ready."

Yin and Baxter walked out to the back yard to pick up a vehicle. They were joined by one of the detective team and Yin decided they would go to the manor house.

They were fifteen minutes into their journey when two radio calls came through in quick succession. The teams deployed to Rachel's and John's houses had found nothing. They were not at home.

Yin checked in with the control room. They'd tasked out a job to check if there had been any ANPR hits on John's or Rachel's cars that day. Nothing had been found.

Yin cursed. What was Rachel Keen up to? Was she wallowing in her success? Thinking that she'd beaten them. He worried what her endgame was. He couldn't help feeling that John was in danger. There'd been mention of him attending the scene when Lucy Beaufort's neighbour had called expressing concern about her welfare. From what he remembered, the report said she was DOA. He was struggling to see why Rachel might be blaming him for Lucy's death, but as the thoughts raced through his brain, a horrific explanation flashed in his mind. John was gambling all his money away. Was it possible that she had paid him to help her?

Baxter was driving, using the blues and twos when traffic got in their way. Yin watched as the countryside flashed by. The sat nav said they would be at the manor house in seventeen minutes.

His heart was racing, his gut tight with stress.

He knew this might be another dead end but, for some

reason, he had a horrible feeling they were heading to the right place.

He kept glancing at the time.

He hoped they weren't going to be too late.

84

"So, what about Walter?" said Isla. "Why did he deserve your retribution?"

Rachel was still waving the gun around but did at least seem content to talk. "Huh, what a waste of space he was. God knows why Lucy latched onto him. A drunk. Pure and simple. I locked him up and watched him suffer as the withdrawal symptoms kicked in. He was pathetic. Thought I was Lucy so kept trying to suck up to me, going on about how we were great mates. It was nauseating but so satisfying when I finally plunged that spear through his heart."

Isla didn't have a plan. She hoped that Yin and the team had come to the same realisation that she had about Rachel's real identity and were somehow on the lookout for them. In the meantime, all she had was questions that she hoped Rachel was happy to answer. She carried on. "That always bothered me. Why did you implicate yourself with the forensics on Walter's body? The fingerprints. The scarf."

Rachel smirked. "I wanted the police to think it was me, but then as the finer details of the case emerged, I knew the evidence against me would not stack up. I was confident that if it ever got to court, I would be acquitted. It was a gamble, but then you know all about that, don't you, John?"

The sudden focus on John was not lost on the group. Isla flashed a concerned expression his way, but he seemed unfazed by it all.

"I don't know what you mean," he replied.

Rachel's sudden rage made them all tense up. She let out a wail of frustration.

"Oh, John, you don't know how long I've waited for this moment. Even now, you act like you have nothing to be sorry for, nothing to be ashamed of."

"I don't," he retorted.

Isla and Kaley tensed up further as they watched the interaction between the other two. Rachel looked like she was ready to combust.

"How could you do it? That's what I want to know."

"Do what?"

Rachel gripped the gun tighter, cocking it so it was ready to fire. "Really?" shouted Rachel "That's your line? Deny everything?"

John shrugged. "Oh, for fuck's sake, Rachel, just get to the point."

They all twitched as Rachel stood up and walked towards John, the gun pointed straight at him.

"The fact that you need me to spell it out is just going to make the moment I pull this trigger so much more satisfying. You are the reason we are here. The catalyst for all this. You absolute heartless bastard."

Despite the horror of the situation, John was remarkably calm, staring Rachel down.

"I've no idea what you are talking about," he said. "Either tell me or shoot me. I don't care, either way."

The gun began to shake in Rachel's hand. John's apparent ambivalence to death confused her. She needed the satisfaction of watching him squirm, to see him suffer just an ounce of what she'd been through. She gripped the gun tighter, thrusting it towards his face. "You fucking bastard. Is this really how you want to play this?"

Tension hung in the air. Rachel took a moment to compose herself, letting out a deep breath before she continued. "Okay, for the benefit of the room, let me tell you why you are sat here today. How about we start with the fact that Lucy was alive when you entered her house."

Gasps from Isla and Kaley, but John continued to stare, stony-faced, at Rachel. "But of course, that's not what your report says, is it, John?"

Rachel let out a pained laugh as she watched John's face. "How interesting. I can see you are wondering how I knew that. The thing is, I couldn't let it go. I couldn't believe that my sister was dead. I found your partner, the one who was with you when you responded to the 999 call. I could tell she was carrying a heavy burden about that night and was relieved when she was able to tell me what happened. She was the first one to inspect the body. She told me there was a faint pulse. You told her to call an ambulance but when she came back in the room, you were over Lucy's body, shaking your head. She tried to check her pulse again, to satisfy herself that Lucy was dead, but she said you pushed her away. Told her that you were going to report it as a dead-on-arrival case. She was distraught but as her senior, she felt she had to do what you said. You let her die, John. She could have been saved."

The room was a powder keg.

"Is that true, John?" asked Isla.

He didn't answer.

"You see, Isla," said Rachel, "he's not the fucking hero you think he is. Just another poor excuse for a human being, who couldn't care less about anything or anyone."

"That's not true," said John, finally re-engaging in the conversation.

Rachel screamed, thrusting the tip of the gun against his head. "My God, you absolute piece of shit. You know what I've said is true and even now you show no remorse."

John glanced up at Rachel like he didn't care.

Rachel still had the gun to John's head, her voice beginning to tremble. "The thing is, Isla, that's not all. When his partner told me about the situation, I began to research his background. I became obsessed. I wanted to know everything about his life. Where he went, what he did, who he cared about. Anything that I could use to get back at him. But all I found was a pathetic man with a gambling problem, who was estranged from his parents."

John shrugged. "Guilty as charged."

Rachel's face was turning redder with rage. "Oh, but that wasn't all, John. I dug deeper and eventually I found something. A fact that blew my world away. A fact that I eventually realised was the real reason you let Lucy die."

Isla and Kaley were transfixed. For the first time, John looked worried.

Rachel's rage had peaked as she screamed out the revelation. "Johnny boy here is the bastard son of my philandering father. He's my fucking half-brother!"

85

They were six minutes away.

Baxter had turned the blues and twos off at Yin's request. The country roads were empty of traffic and a backup unit he'd requested from the control room had arrived at the perimeter of the manor house. Yin's greatest fears were realised. Whilst the unit had held back on the end of the approach road to the manor house, they were close enough to report that two cars were parked outside. A quick check had confirmed them as belonging to John Bamford and Isla Cowdrey.

Yin's mind was racing. Why was Isla at the manor house? She'd been the one to find a breakthrough in the case and then disappeared from the station, apparently to join John in some wild adventure. He cursed at her stupidity. He'd been very clear that she was to have nothing to do with John or Rachel Keen.

The thought of Rachel Keen made him wince. Was she in the house? Had she somehow lured Isla, and maybe John, to some sick conclusion of the game she'd been playing?

He glanced at the sat nav. Five minutes.

*

For a second, the shock on John's face railroaded Rachel. She let it go, her rage simmering.

"I asked myself over and over," said Rachel, "how you could let anyone die like that, especially your sister. But then I realised. Your gambling addiction is so bad that you saw it as a way out of your problems. You must have found out who your father was and, when you realised it was Lucy dying in front of you, the prospect of all that money must have overwhelmed you. You were the heir to our family's fortune. That was until I turned up. Must have been quite a shock to find you had another sister that was going to scupper your plans."

Rachel's rant hung in the air. John sat there, open-mouthed in shock. He looked at Isla and Kaley, shaking his head. "This is all lies," he said. "I never knew who my real father was. When my mother told me she'd had an affair and that the man she married was not my father, it sent me on my spiral into gambling addiction. I never met Lucy before that night, and I didn't know she was my sister."

John reeled as Rachel struck him in the side of the face with the gun, an action framed by screams from Kaley and Isla.

"You absolute bastard," screamed Rachel. "How can you sit there and lie like that? I've waited so long for this moment. To feel your fear, to watch you squirm as the truth is told. Everything I've done was about this moment. Reeling you in with the promise of fifty thousand pounds, watching your life spiral further into oblivion. Oh, it was great to watch and even better when you had to play Mr Police Officer to my oh-so-pathetic victim."

John felt his face, blood appearing on his fingers as he pulled them away. "Well, here we are," he said, "I guess you think you've got it all worked out, but there is one problem: you're avenging a death that had nothing to do with me. She committed suicide, plain and simple. You can blame me if it makes you feel better, but I didn't kill her, and I definitely did not know that she was my sister, so your moment in the sun is a bit fucked up."

Rachel struck him again. "You will not ruin this moment with your lies!" she bellowed.

There was a stand-off, which was eventually broken by Rachel pulling the gun away from John's head. "Huh," she said, looking around at the splendour of the room, "it's rather fitting that you should be sat here, lying. It's what my father used to do with my mother. He bleated like you when I killed him. Denied everything as the poison I put in his drink began to take effect. Even with his last breath he couldn't be honest. I thought it would be my way of getting Lucy back, but you all put paid to that. So, have a good look, Johnny boy, at what you could have won, because the last thing you are going to see is my face as I blow your brains out, you pathetic piece of shit."

Rachel had overplayed her hand. The revelation that she'd killed her father galvanised John, confirming to everyone that she was a psychopathic killer. The next thing she knew she was flying backwards as John launched himself out of the chair, pushing all his weight against her. Kaley and Isla screamed. Rachel landed unceremoniously on the floor, as John loomed over her. She still had the gun in her hand, which she tried to aim at John as he threw himself down on her.

John was on top of Rachel, who was clawing at him with her spare hand, like a deranged wildcat. She landed some blows, scratching at his head and face. His reaction to the painful attack allowed Rachel to shove him to the left but the advantage was only momentary as he recovered his position, trying to pin her down.

"Stop it! Stop it!" shouted Kaley. Her pleas were ignored.

Rachel had somehow managed to grip her hand around John's throat, forcing his head backwards as she pushed with all her strength. The gun was still in her other hand, but John's body weight had trapped it between them. John hit at Rachel's arm with his spare hand, but he couldn't stop the pressure on his throat.

John changed tack, easing the pressure on Rachel's body, allowing himself to roll away from her, freeing his throat from her grip and pulling Rachel on top of him. She wasn't ready for the surprise move and had no answer to the momentum swing.

There was a struggle. They were both trying to grab at the gun.

Suddenly, the sound of a gunshot filled the room.

86

Yin's car sped onto the gravelled area surrounding the house, pulling alongside the backup team that had waited patiently outside.

As Yin bolted out of the car, the officer in the other car shouted, "Gunfire, sir."

"Are you sure?" Yin said.

"It certainly sounded like it."

Yin ignored the protests of Baxter as he went for the door, the suggestion of waiting for armed officers lost in the wind. He turned right as he entered the house, the sound of voices, distressed and fearful, drawing him in.

He ran down the corridor to be greeted by a scene it took a moment to take in. Isla was hugging a sobbing woman he didn't recognise. John was sat on the floor with a gun in his hand. Rachel Keen was lying on the floor next to him with blood seeping from a gunshot wound.

"Put the gun down, John. Now!"

John glanced round at Yin, dropping the gun immediately. Baxter was just behind Yin. "Cuff him."

Baxter dragged John up and cuffed him behind his

back. Yin got on the radio to request an ambulance, though a quick feel of Rachel Keen's neck told him it was a fruitless exercise.

John was dumped in a chair, Baxter standing guard as Yin encouraged Isla and the girl to sit down. The officers in the other car were attending to Rachel but a shake of the sergeant's head told Yin what he needed to know.

"What happened here?" he said, glancing first at John and then at Isla.

Isla took the lead.

"Sir, that's not Rachel Keen. Her real name is Maya Beaufort. She's the twin sister of Lucy Beaufort."

"I know," said Yin. "The facial rec came back based on those pictures you found. As soon as I saw a recent picture of Lucy Beaufort, I realised what was going on. I'm just mad that no one thought to get a picture of her before now. It could have saved us a whole heap of shit."

Isla wasn't sure whether the barb from Yin was aimed at her, but the look on Baxter's face told her he'd already taken some heat about the situation.

Isla carried on. "I'm sorry, sir, but we were lured here under false pretences. We were all sent a video of Rachel bound and gagged in this place, telling us we had to get here to finally solve the Oxford Mystery. Kaley here was distraught, and I just left work to help her, without thinking of telling you where I was going. I'm so grateful you worked out where we might be."

Yin looked back at John. "Why did you shoot her, John?"

Isla went to speak, but Yin cut across her. "John?"

"She was going to kill me."

"Huh," replied Yin, "so you are trying to tell me that you're not her partner in crime? That the conspiracy to murder charges against you are just a huge mistake?"

John sneered at Yin. "I don't care what you believe. That girl is a total psycho who engineered this whole sick charade to get back at the people she blamed for her sister's death. She also admitted to killing her father."

Yin frowned. "That always bothered me, John. Why does she blame you?"

The furtive glance between John and Isla was not lost on Yin.

John sighed. "She claims that her sister was alive when I attended the scene."

Yin recoiled. "Really? That's not what your report says."

"Because it isn't true. She was DOA."

A slight gasp from Isla drew Yin's attention. "Something to say, Miss Cowdrey?"

She hesitated. "Er, no, sir."

Yin stared at them in turn, convinced they were lying to him. He changed tack. "So, John, explain to me what happened here."

"I told you, she was going to kill me. She was doing this big speech about why she was seeking revenge against the people that had led to her sister's suicide, admitting that Walter and Abigail were part of that story. As I said, she wrongly accused me of not saving her sister when I attended the scene. She had the gun to my head, and I was convinced she was about to pull the trigger. I lunged at her. We fought on the floor and in the melee the gun went off."

Yin immediately flashed a look at Kaley. "I don't know you, young lady, but as you seem to be less invested in this drama, I'm asking you if John's account of what happened here is correct."

For a moment, Kaley was like a rabbit in headlights, but Yin's unwavering stare forced her to utter a meek *Yes.*

He glared at Isla. "Miss Cowdrey?"

There was a brief hesitation, which concerned Yin, but eventually Isla spoke. "Yes, sir. It was self-defence. Rachel, or Maya, whichever, was getting more and more agitated as she told us the story. Whilst she was mainly focused on John's apparent guilt, I was convinced she was going to kill us too. He did what he had to do."

Yin searched their faces, the glances between John and Isla adding to his doubts about their story. He stood up.

"Whatever the truth here, I need to take you all back to the police station to get your official statements. Maybe it will give you time to consider whether everything you've told me is the truth."

87

ONE WEEK LATER

Isla and John sat in a pub, on their third round of drinks.

"What happened with Yin?" probed Isla.

John shrugged. "I gave him my statement and walked away. I decided to resign. There's no way back for me now."

"What did he say?"

"Not much. I think he knows they've got to drop the charges against me with the evidence they have about Rachel being Maya Beaufort and the fact that three of us heard her confess to murder."

Isla sighed. "God, poor Kaley, it's going to take her a long time to get over this."

"Uh huh," replied John, "I'm sorry that happened to her, but to be honest, I'm thinking about number one. My solicitor is confident I'll be free soon and I'm going to leave the country and start a new life somewhere else."

Isla took a large slug of the wine she was drinking. She leant forward, fixing John with a concerned gaze. "I need to know, John."

"What?" replied John, annoyance in his tone.

"Was Rachel right? Was Lucy alive when you got there?"

John finished his pint, creating a deliberate diversion from having to answer the question.

"John! Come on."

He let out a deep sigh. "Yes, okay, she was alive when we first got there, but I wasn't in dereliction of my duty. The special constable that was with me did get a faint pulse but, by the time she'd called the ambulance, Lucy had passed away."

Isla's expression told John she wasn't satisfied. "What?" he shouted.

"The thing is," replied Isla, "did you know she was your half-sister when you attended the scene?"

"What makes you say that?"

"Just answer the question."

"No! Until Rachel, Maya, whoever, mentioned that I was their half-brother, I had no idea. I admit that I knew my biological father was not the man who raised me, but I swear I didn't know anything else."

"Look, John, I want to believe you, but why did Rachel go to such elaborate lengths to seek revenge on you, with all that Oxford Mystery stuff, if she wasn't certain you'd done what she accused you of?"

John looked at Isla, tears welling up. "What can I say? You saw how unhinged she was."

"Yes, I suppose, but can't you see it from her perspective? If she thought you had deliberately let your sister die, I can kind of understand why she was so bitter."

John shook his head. "My God, Isla. Are you for real? Are you trying to justify murder? Are you trying to say that someone who invents a bloody mystery game, to ultimately lure someone to their death, is a sane individual?"

"Of course not, but it just seems odd that she got you so wrong, and you must admit, you've landed on your feet. You're a very rich man."

"Oh, fuck you, Isla. I don't care what you think."

An uncomfortable silence followed. Isla just couldn't help feeling that something was off. She knew why she was feeling this way. In the midst of the final melee, when Rachel and John were wrestling on the floor, she saw something that unnerved her. As she tried to intervene, just before the gun went off, she caught an expression on John's face that was out of place with what was going on. It was a brief moment, when his face changed from the screwed-up expression of someone fighting hard, to a sudden look of calm, followed by… there was no other word for it… a look of triumph. She hadn't been able to shake the image, trying to remember exactly what was going on. But every time she thought about it, she kept coming back to the same conclusion.

She was sure that, in that moment, John had got control of the gun. Isla couldn't help but feel that he made a conscious decision. That the gun did not go off by accident. She hated herself for thinking it, but she was convinced that John had suddenly realised what it would mean if he shot Maya.

She just didn't believe his version of events, leading to only one conclusion.

John was a murderer.

88

ONE YEAR LATER

The casino's other games fell silent. John eyed the massive pile of chips in front of him. It was the biggest score he'd ever had. 250K or thereabouts.

Place your bets.

John put it all on black.

The ball bounced around the roulette wheel.

A massive roar from the crowd. A couple of guys slapped him on the back. A busty blonde draped herself all over him. He took a shot of vodka.

Black.

500K. John's head was reeling. The alcohol giving him Dutch courage.

"Come on, baby," the blonde whispered in his ear.

A bead of sweat splashed on one of the chips. *Red or black? Black or red?*

He placed it all on red.

Silence.

The ball clattered to a halt. Black.

The crowd took a moment to react. Gasps. Shouts of *no.* The blonde walked away. A sympathetic pat on the shoulder.

John shrugged and smiled as he got up from the table. He reached into his pocket and flicked a 5K chip to the croupier.

He glanced over at the vista on the west side of the casino, with sweeping views of Anzio's coast.

"Seems like we are having a good night, sir."

John smiled at his casino manager. "Yeah, I think the house is definitely winning tonight."

"No luck then, sir?"

"I was close, Marco. I made the mistake of swapping colours."

"Sorry to hear that, but I think this will please you."

John took the iPad from Marco and examined the casino's dashboard. "Very good. Make sure our high rollers are well looked after."

"Of course, sir. You have a reservation in the restaurant, sir. I'll let the chef know you're on your way."

"Just have him send something to the villa, please, Marco."

"As you wish, sir."

As he walked out of the casino, John smiled as the punters continued to bet, lining his pockets further. The head valet moved quickly towards him as he emerged from the front of the building. "Which car would you like, sir?"

John patted the valet on the shoulder. "The Ferrari please, Gianluca – no – the 911, please."

*

There was no plan. The accusations, while Maya pointed the gun at his head, were a nightmare. John could see Isla believed what Maya was saying, the same sense of betrayal evident on her face that he'd experienced when he found out about his father.

As the gun pressed harder into his head, he knew he had no choice. It was her or him. Despite the gun, Maya was revelling in what she thought was her moment of retribution. She'd become complacent and let her guard down. It was all John needed.

He often thought about that last fight. The moment that changed his life.

He had to stop pretending. When he rolled over onto his back, he'd managed to grab the gun from Maya's hand. He was strong enough to push her off and apprehend her for Yin to make the arrest. But that wasn't how it was.

Everything around him had suddenly become a blur. All he could think about was what would happen if he pulled the trigger. Maya would be gone, and he would be the only one left to inherit the money.

He had the chance, and he took it.

The Beaufort family solicitor had been a piece of cake. The police scrutiny didn't seem to bother him. The solicitor was pleased that he could finally settle the estate, undoubtedly relieved that he wasn't going to be left with a massive problem to sort out. When Yin confirmed that all charges had been dropped, John felt like this was the first thing that had gone right in his life.

So here he was. A rich man. Inheriting a multimillion-pound fortune. John was still an addict, but the ultimate irony of owning a casino seemed like a neat conclusion to his otherwise worthless life. Like the fox getting the key to the henhouse. He still gambled, but now he could lose as much as he wanted because the punters in his casino were ploughing unlimited funds into his lifestyle. Every hour of every day.

He'd been duped into chasing fifty thousand pounds by playing the Oxford Mystery, but this was a different level. Anger gripped him. The betrayal by his parents, the dark descent into gambling and his real father not the faintest bit interested in his existence. He deserved a break in life.

The one thing he regretted was lying to Isla. She'd worked out what he did, but he couldn't admit it. He couldn't run the risk of her blabbing to Yin. She was the briefest moment of joy in his life, but it had to end.

He took the biggest gamble of his life and got away with it.

ACKNOWLEDGEMENTS

As always, a big thank you to my alpha readers, Hannah Wade, Jacky Wade, Karen Warner and Anthony Cooper for their continued dedication in reading my first draft and telling me what needs to be improved!

Also, to my friend, fellow author and go to editorial guru, Tony Guntrip, who always does such a comprehensive job in making the final story so much better.

Much gratitude to my growing readership for your kind comments about my writing and for buying each new book that comes out. There are so many hurdles for independent authors that getting positive feedback from you makes it all worthwhile.

Whilst my books can be purchased in so many places now, I want to highlight how grateful I am for the support of local independent bookshops in Oxfordshire who do so much to promote independent author's work. Particular thanks to Mostly Books in Abingdon, Wallingford Bookshop, Madhatter Bookshop in Burford and Bell Bookshop in Henley-onThames.

Finally, a big shout out to all the other people that make writing so enjoyable and encourage people of all ages to read books. These include the members of my author group

– Oxford Independent Authors (OXIA), all the brilliant staff that work in the library system and all the dedicated staff at my publisher, The Book Guild.

See you in 2026 for Book 8 – The Book Club Murders.

Much love,
Colin xx